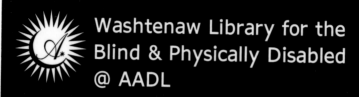 **Washtenaw Library for the Blind & Physically Disabled @ AADL**

If you are only able to read large print, you may qualify for WLBPD @ AADL services, including receiving audio and large print books by mail at no charge.

For more information:

Email • wlbpd@aadl.org
Phone • (734) 327-4224
Website • wlbpd.aadl.org

THE COLD HARD FAX

*Also by Leslie O'Kane
in Large Print:*

The Fax of Life
Play Dead

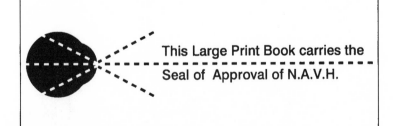

This Large Print Book carries the
Seal of Approval of N.A.V.H.

THE COLD HARD FAX

Leslie O'Kane

Thorndike Press • Thorndike, Maine

Published in 2000 by arrangement with The Ballantine Publishing Group, a division of Random House, Inc.

Thorndike Press Large Print Mystery Series.

The tree indicium is a trademark of Thorndike Press.

The text of this Large Print edition is unabridged.
Other aspects of the book may vary from the original edition.

Set in 16 pt. Plantin by Minnie B. Raven.

Printed in the United States on permanent paper.

Library of Congress Cataloging-in-Publication Data

O'Kane, Leslie.
    The cold hard fax / Leslie O'Kane.
        p. cm.
    ISBN 0-7862-2833-4 (lg. print : hc : alk. paper)
    1. Masters, Molly (Fictitious character) — Fiction.
2. Women cartoonists — Fiction. 3. Albany (N.Y.) —
Fiction. 4. Large type books. I. Title.
PS3565.K335 C6 2000
    813'.54—dc21   00-056816

This book is dedicated to Francine Mathews, who encouraged and inspired me to aim higher, and to Dr. Carol Foster, without whom I might still be going in circles.

Chapter 1

Enjoy Your New Home

The car was approaching my house. Though my back was turned to the road, the sound of that particular automobile had become all too familiar. Bits of gravel crunched between asphalt and whitewall tires as the baby-blue Buick puttered past my property at five miles an hour. The piercing eyes of its overweight, polyester-clad driver would be surveying my home and gardens like a lioness on the prowl.

I held my breath and didn't move, hoping against all odds and logic that she wouldn't see me kneeling by the garden at the side of my house. Or would mistake me for a lifelike lawn ornament. Or, just this once, might see fit to leave me alone.

No such luck. The engine stopped. A moment later, a car door opened, then slammed shut, and I heard the deep, almost masculine voice of Helen Raleigh call, "Oh, um, excuse me? Molly Masters?"

She always addressed me by both my first and last name. Next she would introduce her own full name, as if it were possible for me to forget the former owner of my house. Then she would tell me she "just happened to be driving by." This despite the fact we lived on a cul-de-sac.

"Molly Masters? It's Helen Raleigh."

Helen had driven past my house at least once a day since we bought this property three months ago. She always stopped every time she spotted me. I had dubbed these encounters My Visits From Hell . . . N.

Gripping my little dented spade, I grimaced and rose. If only I had a can of roach repellent in my hand.

She strode across the lawn toward me. In upstate New York's saunalike June afternoons, it was a mystery to me how she could tolerate full-length slacks and long-sleeve outfits, yet I never saw her wear anything else.

During one of her numerous attempts at prying for personal information, she had let on that she was forty-five. This made her just nine years older than I, but she seemed to be from a different generation — in a different galaxy. In her garish pantsuit, splashes of yellow, red, and green in posie-like shapes spattered across her wide body. It looked as though she were wearing the seat cushions from patio furniture. Yet, as

8

always, my eyes were drawn to the world's least flattering hairdo. Dyed jet black and curled under, it reached only midpoint to her ears. The dark, bristly hair along the nape of her neck had been trimmed close to the scalp.

She neared. Waves of sickeningly sweet perfume emanated from her body. She flashed a nervous smile and said, "I just happened to be driving by, and I . . ." She froze, staring at the grass. She bent down and yanked up some green, leafy plant. "This is a weed, you know." Her lips curled distastefully as she held it out to show me. It was less than two inches tall, even if you counted the threadlike roots.

"Well, Helen, even though I'm not a botanist, I can tell that isn't a blade of grass. However, it is approximately the same shade of green, and it blended into my lawn quite nicely. That's my entire criterion for whether or not a vegetative substance gets to stay put."

Her eyes widened and her thick, bloodred lips parted in a small gasp at my lackadaisical attitude. Annoyed, I decided I might as well try to egg her into a full faint. "Now dandelions, for example, get yanked. No matter how often Jim mows, those pesky dandelions keep popping up their heads. I suspect they give one another high fives when our backs are turned."

Helen stared at me, her sharp features blank. Beads of perspiration dotted her forehead and her cheeks were flushed. Uh-oh. Maybe she really *was* going to faint. She was something on the order of five-ten and two hundred pounds. If she passed out, my thin, five-six frame was not going to be able to support her, let alone steer her into shade. I considered suggesting she get out of the direct sun, but was afraid she'd take that as an invitation to plant *herself* inside my home.

She tightened her fist and stashed the tiny weed in her pocket. No doubt she intended to have it analyzed to determine if we'd been fertilizing the grounds properly. "You shouldn't have *any* dandelions. But don't worry. I scheduled a lawn service."

"You *what?*"

"It's the same company that I used for the past two seasons, and they're first-rate. They should be here in a few days."

"You had no right to do that! This isn't your yard!"

"I realize that." She scanned the side yard as we spoke.

I gripped my spade with both fists as if it were a samurai sword. So help me, if she pulled one more thing out of my yard, I'd whack her knuckles.

"This is a full acre of land," she went on. "*Somebody* has to take diligent care of it. I hope I didn't cross the fine line between being helpful and imposing."

Fine line? More like the Grand Canyon, in this case.

"*Nobody* schedules lawn services for someone else's property just to 'be helpful.' " My voice was nearly a shout. "You're obsessed with this place. You've got to stop this!"

I took a deep breath and exhaled slowly. Everything would be all right. I would cancel the lawn service. I would try to locate a friend or two of Helen's in the neighborhood and ask them to please convince her to seek therapy. Immediately.

"You've got to let go of this place." As I spoke, she knelt and used my watering can to rinse off her hands. "By the way, there was concentrated fertilizer in that water. If it's half as effective as the label claims, wash thoroughly the moment you get home. Otherwise your hands'll turn green." I had to get her to leave. Soon. She had moved into a condo a few miles from here, at the center of Carlton, our small suburb of Albany.

Helen ignored me and stared at the upturned soil. "You're planting something? Did I forget to tell you that this is the perennial garden?"

"No, you didn't forget. But you see, this *used* to be the perennial garden when it was your house. It's *my* garden now, so I'm dumping in bulbs and seeds all willy-nilly. I like to be surprised by what grows."

Wide-eyed, she searched my face. "I do hope you understand how much work I put into this property. I bought this place with the proceeds from my divorce. It was the first thing I ever owned on my own. I simply can't stand to see it go to ruin, just like my marriage did."

"I do understand, but it's not 'going to ruin.' Furthermore, *you* need to understand that this property doesn't belong to you anymore. So even if I did opt to allow it to 'go to ruin,' that would be my right."

She brushed past me to the spigot and, without asking permission, turned on my hose, rinsed off her hands, then focused the spray onto my newly turned soil. "This will encourage the roots to grow deep," she said.

"Hmm. Well, that'll be a trick, since I deliberately planted the bulbs upside down. I'm helping my daughter with an experiment for next year's science fair." None of that was true, but I was now determined to make this visit as unpleasant for her as it was for me.

She bent down and pointed. "Is that a pumpkin plant?"

"Yes, my son is —"

"You can't put a pumpkin plant this close to flower bulbs!" She straightened, clicked her tongue, and frowned as she scanned my handiwork.

"Why not? Do flowers and pumpkins belong to hostile political parties?"

"You know, Mrs. Masters, I would prefer you not dig up this flower bed. I spent months putting it in." She made a parting-of-the-seas motion with her arms. "This area is xeroscaped, height- and color-coordinated to perfection. The front garden could use some work, but this side garden is my pride and joy."

"And I'm sure *your* 'pride and joy' will look very nice alongside the tennis court we're putting in."

Her jaw dropped. "You never said anything about putting in a tennis court! I forbid you to do that!"

With effort, I stopped myself from shouting: *Are you nuts, lady?* In fact, we couldn't afford said court — I'd told her that just to annoy her — but that was beside the point. "Listen carefully to me. This is *my* property

13

now. If my husband and I decide to reland-scape, we will do so."

She twisted the nozzle shut with so much force I half expected her to wrench off its head. She dropped the hose, leveled a finger at me, and shouted, "I had higher bids on this house than yours! I allowed you to buy it because you told me you weren't into gardening!"

That was true. My husband's "temporary" assignment in Albany was well into its second year. We'd been living in a small, rented house, when my mother called and told us about this place, a few blocks from theirs, listed at almost fifty thousand less than market price. But I was reluctant to buy, believing that would make my plan of someday returning to my beloved home in Boulder all the more remote. So when we met Helen Raleigh at the Open House and she went on ad infinitum about the property's "flora" — not to mention the grassa in the lawna — I admitted we weren't into gardening. Then we bid below her asking price. To my complete surprise, she accepted it.

She spun on one heel of her canary-yellow pumps and marched back across my lawn. "I'm talking to Sheila Lillydale right away," Helen called over her shoulder. "She's a lawyer. I'll sue you for breach of promise."

14

I watched for a moment to see if she was just going to move her car to the other side of the cul-de-sac where the Lillydales lived, but she drove off and turned toward downtown.

Was there such a thing as "breach of promise" regarding real estate transactions? In any case, it was unfortunate she would bother Sheila Lillydale, of all people. Sheila had a feisty energy that I appreciated. But I had yet to decide if she was merely hard to get to know, or just plain didn't like me. On the other hand, my daughter had a crush on the Lillydales' son, who was indeed very good-looking — for a nine-year-old. He was growing into the image of his dark, broad-shouldered dad.

I glanced at my watch. It was not quite two o'clock. That gave me just over an hour until my children would be home from elementary school.

Somehow my momentum for gardening had been lost. It took the last few drops of my gardening enthusiasm and acumen just to turn off the spigot and return the spade and watering can to the garage.

This truly was a nice house, though not the Taj Mahal its former owner seemed to believe it was. The siding was colonial gray with maroon trim, tastefully accentuated in the front with red brick. The gardens, while difficult to maintain, were lovely. Again, though, we weren't talking "O Garden, My Garden!" here. No one, other than Ms. Raleigh herself, had ever given this particular acre of grass, maple trees, and a few flower clusters much more than a passing glance.

The temperature descended into heavenly cool air as I stepped down into my basement office. This was the location of my business, Friendly Fax, for which I designed faxable humorous greeting cards. My earnings were enough to fund a family vacation to Hawaii last summer. After having paid for construction of the office, this year we'd be lucky to afford two weeks in Poughkeepsie.

My office entrance featured oak and glass French doors. Two window wells afforded me small, semicircular views of the sky. A built-in, walnut-stained pine desk ran the entire length of that wall. I had a major and minor light table in the back corners of the room. Having two permanent drawing surfaces gave me the luxury to move to a second drawing when one I was currently working on wasn't going well. Plus, the floor was linoleum and my office chair had wheels on it, so I could propel myself from one table to the next with one good shove — which entertained me when neither drawing was working.

I got right to work at my major table on a cartoon about dealing with difficult former home owners. My real-life experiences give me much of the material for my greeting cards. My reasoning is, since you can't rid your life of unpleasant experiences, you might as well find a way to laugh about — and profit from — them.

In my cartoon, a couple, carrying boxes as they enter a gate, are staring in horror at a rowdy group having a party at the far side of a swimming pool. One of the partiers calls to the couple, "Didn't the former owners tell you? We own half of your pool. But don't mind us. Enjoy your new home."

As I worked, I pondered once again why Helen had sold the house in the first place. She'd explained to us that she was forced to sell because the mortgage payments were too high for her income. Yet it seemed to me that the extensive surveillance operation she ran on our house was what prevented her from earning full-time wages.

I finished the cartoon and now tried to decide what to do with it. I had already fulfilled this month's quota for my main customer, an office products chain. They used my cartoons to demonstrate their fax machines. I decided I'd let them have my cartoon pro bono; I gleaned many new customers from my exposure at their stores. Besides, it was unlikely a prospective customer would contact me any time soon to request a personalized card about obnoxious former home owners.

I tried to fax the cartoon to them, but cursed as my machine beeped, then printed the error message: Check Condition of Remote Fax. Ever since we'd moved to this house, I'd been getting tons of error messages, and my machine had developed a penchant for blaming others. According to it, there was something wrong with everyone else's fax machine in the country. More likely the problem was with our line.

I grabbed the phone. This would be a good time to catch my best friend, Lauren, at home. She had agreed to help me test my machine the next time I had a problem. Better yet, Tommy Newton would not be there. Having had more than my fill of bickering with Helen Raleigh, I wasn't up to my usual verbal sparring with Tommy.

Though Tommy, Lauren, and I had been in the same classes during our school years, our relationships had grown increasingly complex over the last two years. Tommy was a police sergeant. Lately he was all but living with my best friend, right next door to my parents. Somehow, the proximity and peculiar combination of authority figures made me feel as though I needed to use a secret language and hand signals to converse with Lauren.

The line crackled as she answered. "Jeez, Molly. What's the matter with your phone? I could probably hear you better if you just shouted out your window."

I smiled. I could picture Lauren standing by her phone, most likely in her kitchen. She had straight, shoulder-length brown hair, a round face, with an absolutely stunning smile. "Probably so, but I wanted to try faxing you something while we're both on our other lines."

"Oh, sure thing. Got any new cartoons you can send me?"

"Actually, I'm working on one about —" A loud bang from outside startled me. "Did you hear that? It sounded like a gunshot."

"A car must've just —"

I leapt out of my chair in alarm as a dark, furry shape fell onto the clear plastic cover of my office window well. Had someone just shot a cat?

Then I screamed so loud my ears rang. Just outside the basement window, Helen Raleigh collapsed in front of my eyes. Her head was twisted to the side, her face inches from her hideous black wig.

Chapter 2

Not a Pretty Picture

I swept up the dangling phone, shouted, "Call nine-one-one," at Lauren, then tore out the door.

I charged down the front porch steps, then glanced around for a neighbor to yell "Help!" at, but no one was nearby.

Should I pound on Simon Smith's door? He was an elderly, retired man who never seemed to leave home. No. Helen needed immediate assistance.

I darted around the bushes that lined our front walkway. Please, God. Let Helen simply have fainted. Let her have seen I'd uprooted some favorite plant and promptly gone into a swoon. I raced around the corner of our house, calling, "Helen?"

She was still lying facedown atop my clear window-well cover. Her polyester pantsuit was drenched with blood. Her wig was laying in front of her. Beneath the wig, her hair had been short, almost a brush cut. I knelt beside her, grabbed her motionless arm, and said into her ear, "Helen, can you hear me?"

My thoughts were jumbled. I battled a desire to scream like a helpless, hysterical female until the cavalry arrived. But with the thought that she might still be alive and need mouth-to-mouth resuscitation, I rolled her over. Her eyes were glassy and open.

"Helen?" I fluttered my hand directly in front of her eyes, but she didn't blink. Get a grip, I chastised myself. That's not how you're supposed to tell if someone's dead. I'd seen enough television shows to know I should feel for the carotid artery. In a hurry and lacking any medical training, I ignored the tremor in my hands and placed both of my palms to cover the entire surface of her neck. Nothing. No pulse.

I stumbled to my feet, vaguely aware of dirt chunks sticking to my bare knees. Helen Raleigh had been shot to death, just moments ago, in my yard. Here I was, standing, perhaps on the exact spot where she'd been at the time. Maybe the gunman was aiming at me right now.

"Molly?"

I jumped, even though I'd recognized the voice.

Before I could warn her, Lauren Wilkins ran to my side. Panting, she said, "The police are on their —" She gasped, then averted her gaze.

"It's Helen. Helen Raleigh. She was over here, talking to me, just a half hour ago."

A dark sheet of plastic near Helen's feet caught my eye. A garbage bag. Next to the bag was a sizable hole in my garden that Helen must have been digging. She'd brought a large shovel and a garbage bag to my home. Apparently, she had been trying to dig up something, right below the spot where I'd planted tulip bulbs, and had planned to haul whatever it was away in the bag.

A distant police-car siren grew louder. I grabbed my pounding head. "What the hell is happening? What was Helen doing? Digging up buried treasure?"

"Come on, Molly," Lauren told me gently, putting her arm around my shoulders. "Let's go out front and meet the police."

"Is Tommy coming?"

"Probably. But they'll send the nearest cruiser first."

Despite the muggy heat, I shivered uncontrollably. A cruiser, in the metallic blue of New York State police vehicles, pulled into the cul-de-sac and parked behind Helen's Buick. The elderly officer who'd been driving stood beside the car, leaving his door open, and called to us over the car

22

roof, "Lauren, what's the situation?"

"There's been a shooting," Lauren said, nodding in recognition of the officer.

"The woman who used to own my property was shot," I interjected. "Her body is over there, by the side of the house."

A young, possibly postpubescent, officer in the passenger side remained seated and promptly began to use police-speak into his radio. His elderly partner asked us whether the shooter was still in the vicinity. When I answered, "I sure hope not," he slid back into the car and, rather rudely, yanked the radio handset away from his young partner.

In the meantime, my knees feeling a bit wobbly, I plopped down onto the grass. Lauren sat down beside me. Suddenly it seemed too hot to think, or to do anything other than breathe. I leaned back against the rough bark of the maple tree that shaded much of my front lawn. Why was Helen's hair so short? Why did she always wear such an ugly wig? "If you had some sort of . . . hairless condition and had to wear a wig all the time, wouldn't you get one that was flattering? Why buy one that's too short? Do they price wigs according to hair length?"

"What are you talking about, Molly?"

"Nothing. Just rambling incoherently. I'm not used to having someone get shot to death a few feet away from me." I closed my eyes, but was unable to shake the grotesque image. All that blood.

"Do you think she was here to collect the plants you'd removed?"

I shook my head. "That hole was too deep for that."

Lauren said nothing. I glanced over at her. She was chewing on her lip, a thoughtful expression on her face. "Did you ever meet her ex-husband?"

"No."

"Let's hope he didn't come with the property . . . six-feet down."

I felt a wave of nausea at that thought. Could I have been standing atop Mr. Raleigh's grave while I gardened? Surely not. "Somehow I can't see her trying to unearth an entire body with me still in the house. That's too irrational, even for Helen."

The young officer emerged from his vehicle to keep watch over us, while his partner, using darting and crouching SWAT-team maneuvers, dashed to where Helen's body lay. "Look at Officer Greg go," Lauren whispered to me. She giggled. The sight of the elderly, portly police officer trying to sprint across the yard was slightly comical, and Lauren, to her considerable embarrassment, was prone to nervous giggles. I had to be careful not to catch them from her. That was all Sergeant Newton would need. A dead body in my yard, and Lauren and me laughing. "What do you suppose Officer Greg'd do if I suddenly shouted, 'Look out!'?"

"I don't know," I whispered back, "but I wouldn't want to be sitting next to you when you did it."

Lauren elbowed me and put a hand over her mouth in an attempt to muffle her giggles. The baby-faced officer gave us a long look. "Um, you're Lauren Wilkins, right? We met at the station house picnic last month. I should be getting your statements now." He shifted his gaze to me. His soft cheeks were bright pink. He looked so young and inexperienced, I was surprised he'd been on the force a whole month ago. "Plus, you two shouldn't be together."

"Pardon?" No one had suggested that the two of us shouldn't sit together since our school days.

He shot a desperate look at his partner in the distance, then turned back toward me. "Er, let's go back inside your house, Miss . . ."

"Masters."

As we got to our feet, the older officer, who had holstered his gun and was now at

Helen's body, called to his partner, "I'm going to secure the area." He pivoted and scanned the woods behind our house. Our home was at the very end of the cul-de-sac, and our property line backed against a densely wooded park. "I gotta warn you, Dave," he called over his shoulder, "it's not a pretty picture."

I winced, and Lauren let out another shrill giggle. Our baby-faced officer raised an eyebrow at her. She combed her hair back from her eyes, gasped for air, and said, "Sorry, Dave. You see, Molly creates cartoons for greeting cards, and she happened to do one the other day where this well-dressed couple is at an art gallery. They're standing in front of this one painting of all these ugly, ghoulish faces, and the man looks at the woman and says, 'That is not a pretty picture.' "

The officer, whose name, I'd gathered, was Dave, colored even further.

Lauren finally gained control of herself. She cleared her throat and said, "You had to be there. I mean, you have to see the cartoon yourself to get the joke." Then she leaned toward me till our shoulders were touching and muttered, "Well, *I* thought your cartoon was amusing."

"Let's go inside," Officer Dave said. "I'll

get each of your statements and —"

He broke off at the sound of a siren. Sergeant Tommy Newton drove up. The moment he stepped out of the car and whipped his mirrored shades off, his eyes were locked on Lauren's. He'd gotten a haircut since the last time I'd seen him. His red hair was almost as short as Helen's, sans wig. The blue fabric of his uniform was now taut with the extra weight he'd recently put on. This was probably due in no small part to Lauren's hobby: baking.

Lauren took a small step toward him. She seemed to be yearning to rush into his arms, but restrained herself, knowing this wasn't the time or place.

"I haven't taken their statements yet, Sergeant," our young watchman said. "I've been with them the whole time and they haven't been discussing the case. Greg's checking the woods."

"Lauren has nothing to do with this," I told Tommy. "I just happened to be —"

"Molly had just called me," Lauren interrupted, still gazing into Tommy's eyes. "We'd chatted for maybe half a minute, when I heard a bang in the distance, and Molly said, 'Did you hear that?' and I started to say it was probably a car engine backfiring. Then Molly screamed, and I

27

knew something horrid had happened. She told me to call nine-one-one. I did, then I ran over here to see if Molly needed help."

"Okay. The paramedics'll be here any minute." Tommy's voice and behavior toward Lauren were so gentle it made me feel as if I were intruding on a private moment. "Maybe I should walk you home."

"No, I'm fine. The bus will be here soon, and I need to take the kids over to my house."

No sooner had she said this than we could hear the air brakes and creaks of the bus nearing the entrance to my street.

"Oh, shoot," Lauren muttered. "Now I won't have time to get Rachel off a stop early. I left the front door open, though, so she'll be fine for a couple of minutes." Rachel, who, like my daughter Karen, was nine, would be home alone until Lauren could get back. Lauren's husband had died a couple of years ago. Her daughter Rachel and my Karen were best friends.

"Okay, then. Gotta go," Tommy said. He headed toward Officer Greg at the side of the house. The young officer glanced at him questioningly, then apparently decided he should stay with me.

An instant later, Karen and Nathan came tearing down the sidewalk toward us. Seeing them so soon after my confrontation with mortality, I felt such a surge of love and protectiveness my body ached.

Though Karen was giving it her best effort, Nathan was faster. For the last six months or so, it was as if someone had been stretching Nathan on a rack. He ate all the time, but seemed to gain no weight, only height. He was now considerably taller than Karen, who was two years his elder. A band of brown freckles ran across Nathan's nose from one cheek to the other. His sandy brown hair was naturally curly, which he detested, so he insisted on keeping it short.

Karen spotted the officer and Lauren standing beside me, eyed the police cars, and slowed, her smile fading. She had her eight front permanent teeth, oversized for her dainty features. Her wispy, light brown hair was cut to her jawline. Her eyes were so dark they were almost black. Though petite, she had a wonderful gift for always looking a person straight in the eye.

"Something happened!" Nathan shouted with glee as he spotted the police vehicles. He grinned back at Karen triumphantly when he reached me first.

Karen paid him no mind. Her eyes were riveted to mine. "What's wrong, Mom?"

"Don't worry. I'm fine. So's Daddy." I

held out my arms for a hug. Karen and Nathan merely gave me their backpacks. Mom, the hat tree.

"What are they doing in our yard?" Nathan asked, pointing at Tommy and the elderly policeman. "Can I go watch?"

"No, I want you both to go to Lauren's house."

"So," Lauren said, forcing a smile. "Karen, Nathan, we're going to bake some cookies at my house."

"Can I bring Spots?" Nathan asked.

Lauren immediately shook her head. "Our cat Missy wouldn't get along with him." Spots was Nathan's guinea pig, who had gotten the name not because of his color, but because he had a weak bladder.

"Then *Karen* doesn't get to bring Tiger," he asserted.

Tiger was Karen's guinea pig. We had purchased the two pets for the children's birthdays this past spring. At the time, we'd been unaware of my mother's birthday present to Karen: six frog eggs, now well on their way to full froghood.

An ambulance pulled up beside Tommy's cruiser. The children's eyes widened.

"I need you to go with Lauren right away."

"Why?" Karen asked again. "What happened?"

The paramedics got out, but remained near their vehicle and watched the officers. Tommy held up his index finger, and one of them headed toward Helen's body while the other remained by the ambulance.

I chucked the backpacks behind me and knelt to eye-level with my children. "Remember the former owner of our house?"

"You mean that lady you hate?" Nathan asked.

"I didn't hate her. I just wasn't terribly fond of her."

The baby-faced officer a few feet away raised an eyebrow and began scribbling in his notepad.

"You said she drove you crazy," Karen correctly recited to me.

"Yes. She did. And now, well, she's had an accident and she died. So I need to talk to the officers. I'll explain more later. Just go over to Rachel's house for now and I'll —"

"Can I tell Grandma and Grandpa about this?"

I had to fight back a shiver of dread at that thought. My father was out of town, which left Mom with nothing to obsess about except me and my family. A murder in her daughter's yard wouldn't go over particularly well. "I'd rather you didn't. Besides, Grandpa's on his fishing trip. He won't be back for a week."

I gave the kids good-bye hugs. Lauren grabbed each child gently by the hand, and they headed in the direction of her home. Tommy approached. He spoke quietly to the officer who'd been keeping watch over me all of this time. That officer moved off toward his partner, and Tommy strode up to me on my front walkway. He gave me a small smile and shook his head to acknowledge what a sad ordeal all of this was. "So. Molly. Did you get a good look at the victim?"

"I rolled her over. I know I probably shouldn't have, but I hoped she might still be alive and in need of mouth-to-mouth."

"Notice anything unusual?"

"You mean aside from the bizarre short haircut and the fact that she was dead?"

He nodded.

"No, that was about it. Why?"

"Mind comin' with me for a second look?"

I shuddered at that thought, but he had piqued my curiosity too much for me to refuse. We walked side by side to the scene, ducking under the police tape.

I took a deep breath, then stared. Helen Raleigh's ample bosom had relocated itself. I leaned closer. "She's got a receding hairline." This was not unlike passing a particularly gruesome traffic accident. As much as I didn't want to look, it was all but impossible not to. "She has male-pattern baldness."

"You sure this is the Helen Raleigh who used to own your house?" Tommy asked solemnly. "Not some man dressed up to look like her?"

I studied the face. Those were the same deep-set eyes, sharp nose, full red-painted lips I'd seen so many times. A quarter-inch-round, black "beauty mark" was on her chin, right where it had always been. The mole, unlike her breasts, hadn't shifted one iota.

"That's . . . that's her," I stammered. "I mean, that's him. That's Helen."

Chapter 3

Which of These Women Is Dead?

"You're absolutely certain this was the person who's been claiming to be Helen Raleigh all along?" Tommy asked me again.

"Yes, I'm certain."

The gory scene made me dizzy. I took a deep breath of the steamy air and looked away, pretending to be interested in watching the policemen tromp into the woods behind me. The yellow plastic police-scene tape covered a huge distance, from the corners of my house clear back to the trees. The gunshot must have come from those dense woods. "Maybe you can get the killer's blood type by checking for squished mosquitoes."

"Squished mosquitoes?" Tommy repeated.

"The woods back there are teeming with mosquitoes. Anyone staying there for any length of time would probably have had to swat a few."

He rocked on his heels, looking thought-

34

ful. "So we put out a search team to comb a square mile or two of woods, then we autopsy any dead bugs they find." He chuckled and ran his fingers through his red hair. "And here I was, wasting my men's time talking to your neighbors about whether they'd heard or seen anything. Sure 'preciate your suggestion on how to run this here investigation. Gotta admit, that's one I wouldn't have come up with on my own."

To my considerable annoyance — since Tommy had never stepped foot in the South — he was using his patented good-ol'-boy sergeant's drawl. "It was just a thought," I said under my breath. "You don't have to be sarcastic."

"We're shorthanded today so I'm working a double shift. It's been a long day."

I glanced at him, surprised. His mumblings had been as close to an apology as I'd ever heard from him. We rounded the bushes that lined my front walk. Mr. Helen Raleigh could have told me precisely what those bushes were, but all I knew about them was that, at the moment, they were in my way.

My mind raced to put this assortment of incongruous facts in order. "So," I murmured, more to myself than to Tommy. "The 'woman' who'd sold me the house was a man. He had lived in drag in this house for two and a half years. He was a gardening fanatic, but apparently only because there was something important buried in my yard. He tried to dig up that something *after* selling me this house, then was shot in the process."

The screen door creaked as I opened it. Tommy held it for me and asked, "Back when you were first buyin' this place, did you have any indications that Helen Raleigh was a man?"

"No, though in retrospect, Helen had a man's sense of interior decorating. Cinderblock bookshelves, mattresses on the floor, that sort of thing. When we first looked at the place, I'd wondered why someone so meticulous about the gardens had such cheap furniture."

"That hole. In your garden. Did the victim dig that?" Tommy hesitated in the doorway as he awaited my answer.

"Yes, she . . . I mean *he* brought the garbage bag here, too. And he seemed inordinately upset that I'd been planting bulbs. He told me not to dig up the gardens, and that he'd do it himself if I insisted on planting anything new."

"We're going to have to dig deeper and see if we can locate what . . . Helen was looking for."

"Molly?" a very familiar voice warbled from down the street. I winced and stepped back onto the small cement front porch.

My mother stood on the sidewalk where it intersected with my front walk. From her vantage point, she would be able to see some of the goings-on in the side yard, perhaps even Helen's body. She brought a trembling hand to her lips as she eyed the commotion. As if mesmerized she said, "I heard all of the sirens, and I just knew something had to have happened at your house."

The thought pattern was Mom's personality in a nutshell: *Sirens? Must be my daughter!* Admittedly, though, having The World's Most Pessimistic Mother only bothered me when she happened to be right.

"Hello, Mrs. Peterson," said Tommy, who strode toward her, perhaps, I hoped, to convince her to go back home. I followed.

My mother was a thin, remarkably tall woman — nearly six feet. She kept her hair in a short, efficient hairdo that hadn't changed in the last forty years, though its salt-and-pepper hue had gradually become mostly salt. With sojourns to their condo in Florida every winter, she maintained a perfect tan, which had somehow not destroyed her skin or her perfect health. The instant Tommy was within reach, she grabbed his elbow. "Tom, is anyone in my immediate family dead? Or seriously injured?"

"No."

"Thank God."

She turned her panicked eyes onto me. I managed a small smile and said, "I imagine you'd like to know what's going on."

"Not if you think it's none of my business," she replied with a martyrlike droop to her voice.

"Of course it's your business, Mom. I just —"

"The coroner's on his way," some male voice called from the crowd at the side of my house.

"Coroner? Oh, my God!" She stepped back for a better vantage point. "Is that a dead body in your yard? It's not Jim, is it?"

"Of course not! Jeez, Mom! I'd hardly be standing here if that were my husband!"

Mom pursed her lips and shot me a look that said, "There's no need to shout."

If this were anyone else, I wouldn't have lost my temper so quickly. Nonetheless, part of me wanted to reproach her for having asked me such an inane question. The dutiful daughter part of me, however, managed to say in a softer tone of voice, "It's Helen Raleigh."

"The crazy lady who used to own your house?"

"Yes. More or less."

Tommy raised his eyebrows in a signal that meant not to divulge any information that might compromise his investigation. I raised my eyebrows, to signal *him* that he didn't stand a chance of keeping something like this quiet. Medical and police personnel already knew that, within our little town of Carlton, a man had been shot to death while posing as a woman. No chance of *that* becoming a conversational topic of any interest.

"Can I help you pack?" Mom asked.

"Pack?"

"You're not thinking of staying here, are you?"

"Well, actually —"

"You, Jim, and my grandchildren are moving back home until things settle down."

An officer called out from his squad car, "Do you think we'll need a bulldozer, Sergeant, or just some men with shovels?"

"Shovels," Tommy answered.

Mom gaped at me.

"It's a long story," I said.

"So, *do* you need help packing?"

"Let me call Jim. I'll leave the decision up to him."

" 'Fore I let you do that," Tommy said, again raising his eyebrows at me, "I need to get your complete statement." He gave my mother a pat on the back. "Sorry, Mrs. Peterson. This will take a few minutes."

Promising to call her later, I convinced Mom to go home, then allowed Tommy to usher me inside my house. The elderly responding officer asked Tommy about the need to test my hands for gunpowder residue, but Tommy told him I wasn't a suspect. A shred of good news, at last.

Tommy and I took seats in my living room. After I'd related the pertinent events of the day, he asked me to recall every conversation I'd had with Helen Raleigh in the last three months as best I could, just in case something proved helpful. That didn't take terribly long, since the bulk of all of our conversations had concerned the upkeep of our home and gardens.

"Do you think there's any possibility he's actually *Mr.* Raleigh, Helen's husband?" I asked. "Perhaps he'd killed her and buried her in the garden, and was living a double life as both himself and his wife, so that nobody would suspect she was even dead?"

Tommy furrowed his lightly freckled brow and considered the question. "Uh . . . I guess that's . . . Look, Moll. Just leave the questions to me, so we can move this along, all right?" He paused, then asked, "You did say Helen claimed to have bought this place with the proceeds from the divorce, right?"

"Right. And we never discussed Mr. Raleigh at all."

"Helen ever give you any indication where he was from? Part of the country? Cities relatives lived in, anything like that?"

"No. I just never wanted to encourage her . . . him to stay and chat by asking questions about her life." *His* life, I mentally corrected. It was hard to keep the gender straight in my mind. All of our previous encounters now had to be reclassified to make sense of the notion that all that time, Helen had been a man. I'd only known Helen for three months. I could only imagine how this would strike the people in the immediate neighborhood, who'd known . . . him for almost three years.

"Helen ever talk about having any children?"

"No, and having children would've been physically impossible for him, considering."

He glared, and I raised a hand in apology at my flippant remark. "No, I never asked about children. I'd gotten the impression somehow sh-he was childless."

"Uh-huh." Tommy merely stared at me,

41

as if waiting for me suddenly to remember the one clue to Helen Raleigh's past that I'd forgotten. But there was nothing. All I knew was that Helen was supposedly forty-five.

At my suggestion, I rummaged through the oak rolltop desk in the living room and located our packet of papers from the closing on the house. We looked at them together, and Tommy commented that everything had been signed simply as Helen Raleigh. "Which tells us what?" I asked. "That *Raleigh* is our boy Helen's *maiden* name?"

Tommy fought back a smile, but made no comment. He refolded the documents. "Can I take these as possible evidence? I'll get 'em back to you soon."

I had no reason to object, and Tommy zipped them back into their plastic pouch.

"Should I move my family in with my mom for a few days, Tommy? Would it be safer?"

"Wouldn't hurt," he said. "May as well warn you. It's possible this was an accidental shooting."

"*What?*"

He flipped through his notepad as he spoke. "Your neighbor," he paused and referred to his notes, "Simon Smith, has reported seeing hunters in the area behind

42

your homes. Park's off-limits to hunting, of course, but there are deer in the area. Shell casing we found out back was from a hunter's rifle."

"That's the stupidest thing I've ever heard in my life!" I retorted. Even as I spoke, I knew how desperately I did not want to accept that we may have bought a home where my children could be in the line of fire of some renegade hunter. "Helen was wearing an outfit that was so bright she would've glowed in the dark. You're suggesting a hunter could've mistaken her for a deer? Wearing Day-Glo clothing?"

He shrugged.

"How long ago did Simon report seeing these 'hunters'?"

"Couple days back. Sent someone out to check on it, but —"

"You mean Saturday?"

He nodded, so I continued, feeling a surge of relief, "Tommy, your sons were crossing my property that day with a pellet gun on their way to the park."

Tommy paled a little.

"As a matter of fact," I continued, "I stopped them and lectured them. I told them that if they were thinking of shooting in the park to think again, because it wasn't permitted and I wouldn't hesitate to call you."

"This happened on Saturday?" he asked solemnly.

I nodded, seeing in his eyes an angry glint that meant his sons were in trouble with Dad. "You need to know about Simon Smith. This is a man who spends almost all of his time peering through his windows with binoculars.

"As a matter of fact," I continued, suddenly remembering, "we almost didn't buy this place because of him. When we first came to see the house, Jim spotted Simon looking at us through binoculars. We asked Helen about it. She told us Simon was retired from the CIA, and that he was always keeping an eye on the neighborhood. It made me so hesitant, though, that before we bought, I asked another neighbor, Joanne Abbott on the other side of Simon's house, about him. She also said he was retired from the CIA. She said that he was harmless and kept to himself, and that he was so effective as a one-man Neighborhood Watch team that not one neighbor had had any break-ins or criminal mischief complaints since he'd moved in."

Tommy rose and stretched. "Y'all have got some interesting neighbors, Moll."

"Oh, you think *your* street's better? Wait till you get to know my parents."

Tommy smiled broadly, but not just because he knew I was kidding about my parents. We both realized this was the first time I'd acknowledged the full extent of his relationship, and future, with my best friend. It struck me then that some of the intricacies of dating hadn't changed from high school, when friends' bad approval rating of a prospective date could doom the relationship. Even as an adult, Tommy still hoped for my blessings as he courted Lauren.

Tommy gave my shoulder a friendly squeeze, then promptly slipped back into his policeman's persona as easily as if he were donning his cap. "Gotta help my men knock on some doors. See if we can find a witness." He paused at my doorway. "Don't tell anyone about Helen Raleigh being a man. We need to keep that under wraps, so to speak, for a few days. Least till we learn Helen's real name."

As soon as Tommy was out of sight, I called Jim at work, pulling him out of a meeting. "Helen Raleigh was shot to death in our yard," I greeted him.

"What?"

"Our former house owner was shot to death. And it turns out that Helen's a man, wearing women's clothing." Oops. Ah, well. Surely Tommy didn't expect me to keep secrets from my *husband.*

After a moment of silence, Jim said, "Could you run that by me again?"

"I was in my office and heard a bang. I rushed outside, and there was Helen. He must have buried something in our yard, because he'd been digging a hole. So now the police are going to have to dig up the yard and find out what it was."

Again there was a long silence. "Could you start over? Where was . . . Why . . ." He sighed. Right about now, poor Jim would be massaging his temples with his free hand. "My secretary pulls me out of a meeting and I think, 'Uh-oh. Bet the car's broken down or one of the kids is sick.' But no. You tell me that the woman who used to own our house is a man and is now dead, and the police are digging up the yard."

"Did anyone overhear you just now? Because I promised Tommy I wouldn't tell anyone about Helen being a man in disguise. I'm sure he didn't mean you, though. There has to be some sort of spousal indemnity clause, since spouses can't be forced to testify against each other in criminal cases."

Jim said nothing. There was no noise in the background. That probably meant no one was nearby. "Could we . . ." Jim paused, then said irritably, "Start from some point that makes sense. When I left for work this morning, what happened next?"

The correct answer was: I cleaned up the breakfast dishes. This was an opportunity for me to suggest that instead of soaking his cereal bowl in the sink as he had every morning for the past thirteen years, he put it in the dishwasher. But Jim sounded a little edgy. He would probably not appreciate receiving constructive criticism at this particular moment.

I launched into a full description, starting with my first encounter with Helen this afternoon. Jim made me repeat nearly every sentence three times. Finally, he decided to leave work early and come home, and that we should spend a couple of nights at my parents' house.

That accomplished, I went outside to see if the police had dug up a buried treasure. A tow truck was just pulling away from the curb with Helen's car.

Though our cul-de-sac consisted of just four other houses — one of which was currently unoccupied as its owners vacationed overseas — the sidewalk was now filled with gawkers. Most of them had the same, semiembarrassed posture — arms crossed, staring at my house as if their vigilance had been, against their will, mandated by a

47

higher authority. At least this made the officers' jobs easier. They didn't have to knock on doors, since residents were standing in front of them.

I made a quick scan of the neighboring homes. Surprisingly, Simon Smith, the crotchety retiree who lived next door, was nowhere to be seen. It would kill him to learn that the one time he wasn't peering with binoculars was the one time something worth watching had happened.

Stan and Joanne Abbott, who lived on the other side of Simon's house, were outside. I'd never known Stan to return home from work this early, but then again, I didn't know him well enough to be familiar with his daily patterns. Joanne, on the other hand, was gradually becoming a friend.

Stan immediately waved and called to me, "Molly, what's going on?"

Nothing like a corpse in your yard and a batch of policemen with shovels to turn your standoffish neighbors into your very best friends. Actually, though, Helen's body had apparently been removed while I was inside on the phone. The policemen were now purposefully digging away at my empty yard.

"I'll tell you later," I called back, "when I know more." Too bad I had to honor my

48

promise to Sergeant Newton not to mention the only part that might have been fun to discuss.

Sheila Lillydale pulled into her driveway and wasted no time before she walked across the asphalt toward me. A startlingly pretty, petite woman, she was smartly dressed in a light blue cotton skirt suit. It brought out the color in her eyes. Her dark brown hair was fastened into a bun. This must be her official attire for court appearances. Her lips were pursed and her high forehead was knitted. She greeted me with "Do you need representation?"

"Uh, no. I certainly can't think of any reason to hire a lawyer. After all, I didn't kill . . . her."

"Kill?" she repeated. "Someone's been murdered?"

"The former owner. Helen Raleigh."

"Helen? Helen's been killed? Oh, my God! What happened?"

She looked deeply upset. Helen must have been a friend, though, on the surface, the two women had nothing in common. Not even gender.

"I don't know. I was gardening, and Helen came over and —"

"Gardening? Could you be more specific?"

More specific? Had she forgotten we weren't in a courthouse? "I was . . . planting bulbs. Tulips. Red tulips, to be precise. Along the west side of my house, the garden that faces Simon Smith's property. Then —"

"You were planting tulips in the middle of June?"

"Yes," I answered pointedly, not appreciating her insinuation that I was a gardening ignoramus — which was true, but ill-mannered. "Why? Are you supposed to plant them only in months that contain the letter 'r'?"

"Just go on, please." Her pretty features remained strained.

"So, as I was saying, Helen Raleigh stopped by and said —"

"What time was this?"

"Eight minutes before two P.M. Then —"

The baby-faced police officer did a double take at the sight of Sheila and me talking and raced over to us. He said to Sheila, "Excuse me, ma'am. We need you to clear the area. There's —"

"I'm Ms. Masters's lawyer."

"That's news to me," I responded. "I don't need a lawyer. I haven't done anything illegal in years."

"Of course you haven't," Sheila said. "If only guilty people needed lawyers, our workload would be cut by a good third."

"Just a third? You have a high opinion of your clients."

"We're all guilty of something at one time or another. Of bad judgment, if nothing else. Molly, I'm serious. You may need me to protect your rights. Did you know that some men are digging up your yard as we speak?"

"Well, sure. But —"

"And did you think your property wasn't going to sustain damage as a result? Or that you weren't deserving of restitution?"

"Um . . ." My head was in a whirl and I was not enjoying any of my current exchange with Ms. Lillydale. Time to change subjects. "How's Ben doing these days? Is he glad third grade's almost over?"

She shot me a queer look and handed me her business card. "We'll talk later." She walked briskly back toward her house. Her attitude annoyed me. I felt like calling back at her, "Even though you're a lawyer and someone's been killed in my yard, we're still mothers." *My* priorities, at least, were solidly in the right place.

My husband drove up a minute later. He was dressed casually in gray Dockers and a blue-collared T-shirt. He had a mustache and gorgeous dark brown eyes. His brown hair was now all but plastered to his forehead. He steadfastly refused to turn on the air conditioner in the car, willing to sweat to save a few pennies on gasoline.

We went inside and, after assessing each other's emotional state, which was more one of disbelief than anything else, we began to pack. I told him, "You know what strikes me as the most strange in all of this? Why, if *Helen* had buried something important in the garden, wouldn't he have dug it up before selling? And why would he now have tried to recover it in broad daylight, when he knew I was home?"

"If this is a contest, I think the fact that he went around posing as a woman for more than two years is a lot stranger."

I called Lauren to check on the kids, and she told me my mother had already collected them with the explanation that we would be "moving in" with her for a few days. I tried to decide if this was worth getting miffed at, and decided it wasn't. After loading a pair of suitcases and Spot's and Tiger's cages, I grabbed my cut-glass punch bowl, which now housed Karen's six would-be frogs, and gingerly scooted onto the passenger seat of Jim's Jeep Cherokee. This had been the first time I'd actually found a use for the enormous punch bowl — a wedding present from my aunt Louise.

Jim had to drive so slowly to avoid my getting a lap full of pollywogs that a strolling basset hound could have passed us, but we arrived in time for dinner. By then I felt seasick from staring at bobbing frog-faces.

The children were delighted at the arrival of their pets, and I went off to help in the kitchen. Mom was nothing if not regimented. Every day since I could remember, at five P.M. sharp, Mom started to make dinner, which was on the table promptly at six-thirty. Tonight, we had pot roast, potatoes, and green beans — Mom's version of light summer fare. It was lucky we were so high-strung. By all rights, my sister, parents, and I should have weighed two hundred pounds each.

Tonight's dinner conversation centered on soothing our children's — and my mother's — fears. Neither Karen nor Nathan seemed to truly grasp the magnitude of what had occurred. Though we monitored their television viewing fairly closely, they had probably become so inured to murder that it wasn't real to them.

Perhaps, too, my apathy that an acquaintance had been murdered had a lot to do with their reaction. I tried to muster some sadness, but failed. According to all of the data currently at my disposal, Mr. Helen had been a miserable, unpleasant, and, probably, crazy person.

Nathan said it was too bad they weren't doing show-and-tell during this last week in school, as "I could tell my class about the lady getting killed in my yard." Then Karen argued that it wasn't *Nathan's* yard, because it was closer to *her* bedroom window. At which point, Mother suggested a game of Old Maid, and that brought an end to the discussion.

While cleaning up after dinner, a silly idea for a card occurred to me. Later, I sat on the winged-back chair in the living room and worked on the cartoon in my sketch pad while Jim sat on the antique gold jacquard couch across from me and read the sports section. The caption across the top of my drawing read:

At first glance, the women in the four drawings below look identical, but one of them is slightly dead. Can you find the dead woman?

The drawing showed three smiling women with identical beehive hairdos and polka-dot dresses. All you could see of the fourth woman, shown from ant's-eye view, were the soles of her shoes and her polka-dot dress as she lay on the floor.

Nathan came skipping down the stairs. He took the last three stairs in one hop, landing on his feet with a thud on the hardwood floor near me. He was wearing his "Born to Be Wild" T-shirt and his plain white underwear.

"Where are your pajamas?"

"You forgot to pack them. That's okay. I'll just sleep like this."

"No, no," I said, hoping I didn't sound too eager, which would alert Jim to my ulterior motive: This was a fine excuse to check on the scene at our house. "I'll get them for you." I tossed my sketchbook onto the coffee table.

Jim lowered the sports section and peered at me.

I smiled. "We forgot Nathan's pajamas, blast it all. I think I'll just wander on over to the house and get them."

"Could you water Peter while you're there?" Nathan asked.

Uh-oh. The pumpkin plant. It was just a few feet from the hole Mr. Helen had dug. "Peter?" I repeated lamely, filling with dread.

"My pumpkin plant. I named him Peter."

For the last two months, Nathan had kept a two-liter soda bottle filled with water near the back door as a reminder and dutifully watered his beloved pumpkin plant. "Peter" had likely fallen prey to a policeman's shovel, but maybe I could find "him" and get him replanted. I gave Nathan's narrow shoulders a reassuring hug. "I'm not sure what condition Peter is in. I'll go see."

"What?" Nathan cried, backing away to stare into my eyes in horror.

"I'll have to check the —"

"What?" he cried again. When a conversation wasn't going well for him, Nathan had a frustrating tendency to yell "What?" louder and louder, as if raising his voice would change your answer.

"Nathan," Jim said firmly, "your mom said she'd check on your pumpkin. We'll let you know if it's all right."

Nathan, who tended to obey his purposeful dad better than he did his sometimes waffling mom, spun on his heel and dashed back upstairs without a word.

"I'll come with you," Jim said to me. While rising, he picked up my drawing pad and stared at my newest creation of the dead-woman guessing game. His brow was furrowed. Finally, he shut the sketchbook, gave me a wan smile, and said nothing. Jim has never shared my perverse sense of humor, but then, he's an electrical engineer by occupation, and he considers The Three Stooges hilarious.

We located my mother, who was in the den watching television with Karen, asked her to keep an eye on the children for a few minutes, then left.

The evening air was still hot and muggy. This was one of the many things I missed about Colorado. There, it cools down in summer evenings. In upstate New York, the heat continues to radiate, as if the fact that the earth has rotated 180 degrees from the sun has no bearing whatsoever on temperature. Jim took my hand as we walked the three blocks to our home. Though romantic, that left us with only one free hand apiece to ward off mosquitoes.

We could see under police floodlights that no one was digging when we reached home. Their work-stoppage was no doubt influenced by the fact that there was very little ground left to dig. It looked as if they were installing an Olympic-size swimming pool; the site of the diving competition would be where Helen had first broken ground. Piles of dirt covered most of what remained of our lawn.

From the three uniformed policemen still in the vicinity, I recognized Tommy. He nodded in greeting. I responded with,

"Good grief! Are you removing the topsoil from our entire yard?"

"Had a little trouble locating anything."

"Look at all these holes and dirt piles! You've killed Peter!"

"Peter?"

"Our son's pumpkin plant," Jim explained.

"Y'all name your vegetables?" Tommy snorted.

"Not as a rule," I snapped, making a visual search in the fading hope that I could replant it. "Our son named it. He loved that plant. Besides, pumpkins are fruits, not vegetables. They grow on vines, so they're considered berries."

"No way," Tommy said. He called out into the darkness, "Hey, Greg. Is a pumpkin a fruit or a vegetable?"

"Vegetable," came the disembodied answer.

"They're right," Jim told me. "It's a vegetable."

I clicked my tongue. "We're standing here, where someone's been *murdered,* arguing about whether a pumpkin's a fruit or a vegetable."

"You brought it up," Jim and Tommy said in unison.

My husband. Benedict Arnold. I turned my attention to Tommy. "Did you find what

Helen had been looking for?"

"Finally. But since it was several feet from where Helen'd been diggin', we had to check the whole area for anything else."

"What was it?"

"Not what you were expecting."

Just what did he think I was expecting? Then I remembered: the real Helen Raleigh's body. "It wasn't a body?"

" 'Fraid that's confidential."

"Oh, come on, Tommy. This is our property. Don't we have a right to know what you're removing from our own yard?"

"Prob'ly so." He pushed his cap back on his forehead, paused, and gave me a long look. Finally, he said, "It was a dog."

"A dog? You mean a bow-wow, 'Here, doggy' type of dog?"

"Yeah. There's some other kinda dog I don't know about?"

"And that was all there was?"

" 'Fraid so."

"No diamond-studded collar, or packets of heroin in the doggie's stomach?"

" 'Fraid not."

Jim squatted down and looked at a wooden stake by one of the deeper, wider holes. "Was this where they dug up the dog?" he asked.

"Yep."

"That's exactly where Peter used to be," I said, as I made sure by lining myself up with the back corner of the house. I peered into the hole, curious to see if the police had drawn chalk lines around the dog's body. They hadn't. "What kind of a dog was it?"

"A toy poodle." He jammed his hands into his pockets. "Could be that your friend Helen was simply an eccentric who'd returned to fetch a beloved pet's remains."

I sighed and glanced up at Simon Smith's window. The curtains were parted, and two dark circles of binocular lenses were plainly visible. I waved.

Chapter 4

Damn. Elevator Music.

Nathan paused from eating his cereal the next morning, looked up at me, and said, "Gravity is kind of bad and kind of good. It's good because without gravity you'd just float around, but it's bad because if you fall off a big building, you get killed. But I guess having gravity is the best choice. Until you fall off a building."

Having explained the pros and cons of gravity to me, he then continued eating as if he'd never spoken. In the meantime, Karen, seated across the kitchen table from him, entertained herself by adding columns of three-digit numbers.

My mother was reading the newspaper while fortifying herself with the necessary caffeine. I toyed with the idea of asking her whether my sister and I were like this as children — apt to discuss gravity out of the blue and to do arithmetic for amusement. But I held my tongue. Mom never spoke of her own volition prior to her second cup of coffee. And if you forced her to speak, she never said anything you wanted to hear.

A few minutes later the children left for school, and Mom was back to her friendly, if jittery, self. To my good fortune, Nathan hadn't asked about his pumpkin, so I was holding on to the hope that I could find a Peter imposter at the local nursery today. Jim had gone into work early this morning, having instructed Karen and Nathan to get off at "Grandma's stop" after school.

If we decided to stay here for a few days, I needed to order call-forwarding and hook up my fax machine at my parents' house. That would allow me to shed some guilty feelings for my most recent dealings with Ma Bell. Last week, some phone salesperson urging me to "Take advantage of this opportunity to order call-waiting!" had caught me at a bad time. I despise call-waiting. I interrupted the salesman and said, "Hang on a minute. I have someone more important than you on my other line." Then I hung up on him.

This being Tuesday at 8:45 A.M., my mom made her grocery list and clipped coupons. She was always at the store by 9:00 A.M. on Tuesday. She asked if I needed any groceries, which I probably did but said no. While she backed down the driveway, I located my drawing pad and the keys to her and my front doors. In exactly two hours, she would be home to put away groceries before she started to make lunch. That gave me plenty of time to decide whether or not I felt safe enough in my home to allow my family to return to it tomorrow. Maybe even enough time to purchase a new Peter.

The short walk home left me overheated. The sun was downright brutal, even this early in the day. It was cranking up to be a real scorcher. And I'd forgotten to put sunblock on the kids. Just what every mother needs: one more reason to feel guilty.

Not wanting to see just how decimated my side yard looked in natural sunlight, I went straight to the door and headed directly to my office. To my utter delight, there was a message on my recorder from a woman who was seeking to publicize a county fair. She had seen my work at an office products' store and wanted to know if I could work up a humorous single-panel cartoon about horses or fair entries she could incorporate into her advertisements.

I grabbed my sketch pad to work up some roughs. Perhaps it was a result of all the craziness of late, but all I could come up with were absolutely absurd ideas. My favorite was almost embarrassingly bizarre. It showed a horse and a bow-legged cowboy about to step into an elevator. In the elevator, a man dressed in a tuxedo with tails plays a grand piano. A thought bubble shared by both the horse and the cowboy reads: Damn. Elevator music.

After completing a rough of the drawing, I called the prospective client and described the cartoon. Though she said my drawing "wasn't exactly what she had in mind" — no surprise there — she chuckled at the concept and asked to see it. I used my standard procedure of placing an X cut from black construction paper on the drawing before faxing it. That way my cartoon couldn't be pirated. Within minutes, she sent me a return fax that said she "loved it," but would have to discuss this with her committee chairperson, and she'd get back to me in a week or so.

The doorbell rang. It was Joanne Abbott. Joanne had green eyes, a prominent chin, and a large Roman nose that gave her an almost regal appearance. Last spring, she had spearheaded a campaign in our subdivision to pass a school referendum, though she and her husband Stan were childless. Based on my resulting admiration, I had decided she was a good person before we'd even met. Yet, with her being childless and occupied in her own pursuits, we'd had all too few occasions to strike up conversations.

I swung open the door and greeted her warmly. She was holding a loaf of bread in a disposable aluminum baking pan. She smiled somewhat sheepishly, then handed me the bread.

"Here, Molly. Stan and I got to talking last night, and we realized we never did give you a formal welcome to the neighborhood. So I brought you a banana bread. It's frozen, but it defrosts almost as good as new. Better late than never, I hope."

A welcome was, indeed, always "better late than never." But judging by the grayish, shriveled appearance, "never" might have been the better choice for the banana bread.

"Thank you. Would you like to come in?" As if I didn't know she had really come over because she was dying to pump me for information. If I were in her position, I'd want to know all about it, too, but I would've simply asked, not come bearing gifts of old banana bread. Then again, I'm baking impaired.

She adjusted the pleats on her gingham jumper as she took a seat on my living room couch. Wearing denim shorts and a T-shirt myself, I curled my legs under me and took a much less ladylike seat on the recliner across from her.

I offered her something to drink or a slice of banana bread. She declined, then said, "So. Quite the brouhaha yesterday, wasn't it?"

"Yes, it was." For some reason, I love the sound of the word, and so I smiled despite the serious nature of what that "brouhaha" really entailed. But I quickly sobered as the image of Mr. Helen's body popped unbidden into my thoughts. "I hope I never go through anything like that again."

"In the paper, it said they were withholding identification of . . . the body, until relatives were notified." As she spoke, she gently ran her fingertips along her neck in an unconscious gesture. "It was Helen Raleigh, though, wasn't it?"

"I'm afraid so. Were you and Helen close?"

"No, I barely knew her. Nobody knew her. She was a complete recluse." She smirked. "Some of the neighbors used to say that she was always out working on the yard, because she had so much more in common with plant life than human life."

"Who exactly used to say that?"

"Oh, I don't remember. It was just a joke that made the rounds at one of the cocktail parties. You know how those things are."

"Cocktail parties?"

"Every four months, three of us families rotate a get-together." She paused and reddened. "Weren't you invited to the Lillydales' last month?"

I shook my head, feeling awkward and a little hurt.

"I'm so embarrassed. I just assumed you . . . were shy and didn't want to come." She cleared her throat. "I'm sure it was just an oversight. Sheila would never have *deliberately* not invited you."

"These things happen," I murmured, though all of this gave credence to my suspicion that Sheila didn't like me. Ah well. It had been my experience that nothing worsened a person's opinion of me faster than my deliberately trying to correct an unfavorable first impression. "Who was the third host?"

"The Cummings, next door to you. They're in Europe for another two weeks."

"Yes, they told me." At least *somebody* in this immediate neighborhood had acknowledged my presence — though in their case, it had been along the lines of, "Oh, hi. You're our new neighbors. We're leaving for four months. See you when we get back." Having grown up in this town and then having lived for seventeen years in Colorado, I knew this cautiousness toward "strangers" was endemic to Carlton, and I tried not to take it personally.

"Does Simon Smith go to your parties?" I asked, hoping to get a feel for the interpersonal relationships of my fellow cul-de-sackers.

"No, though we always invited him. We wouldn't want to make him feel unwanted. Same thing with Helen. Every time, we'd extend her an invitation. Every time, she'd politely decline."

"Did she say why?"

"She always said, 'Thank you so much, but I'm afraid I have other plans that evening.' Not that she ever actually went anyplace or entertained." Joanne smiled and said in conspiritorial tones, "The neighborhood rumor was that she and Simon were romantically involved and didn't want anyone else to know."

Helen of wig and falsies fame involved with the spy next door? I had to stifle a smile. "Somehow I doubt that."

"Why?"

I was not at liberty to answer "Because Simon and Helen were both men." Besides, they could have been gay men. "Because they were both single. They'd have had no reason to keep a love relationship secret. And I thought you just said Helen was a complete recluse."

"True, but so was Simon. They were a great match. And Simon likes to keep everything secret."

"So did you ever see the two of them together? Acting interested in each other?"

Joanne paused and looked thoughtful. "No, we never saw her even speak to him the whole time she lived here."

"*We?*"

"The Lillydales, the Cummings, or Stan and me."

Hmm. The three families were tight enough to gossip about their neighbors. Simon Smith and Helen had been invited to their parties, but not my husband or me. Strange. The problem couldn't rest with my husband; Jim is one of the most likable people you'd care to meet. Was I using the wrong brand of toothpaste or something?

"So," Joanne said, leaning forward in her chair, "is it true that you found the body?"

"Yes."

"How dreadful."

"Yes, it was."

She stared at me expectantly, but, to my disappointment, this conversation had somewhat cooled my desire to become friends with Joanne. I reminded myself that this was the childless woman who fought for school budgets — the person whom, sight unseen, I'd described as "my hero."

After waiting unsuccessfully for me to chatter, she asked, "Why were the police digging up your yard?"

"They were looking for something, but I'm not at liberty to say what they found."

"Of course."

She was still watching me, as if she expected me to whisper my answer. Time for some subterfuge to glean information from *her*. "I noticed the baseboards aren't scratched at all in this house. Helen's dog must have been very well behaved. Did she take it to obedience school?"

Joanne tilted back her head and peered down her sizable nose at me. "She didn't have a dog."

"I thought she said something about her pet. Was it a cat?"

"No, she never owned any pets, as far as I knew."

"Maybe she was talking about one she owned before she bought the place."

"That must be it." Joanne held my gaze for a long moment, then smiled. "I suppose I should be going. You're going to the home-owners' meeting this week, aren't you?"

"I wouldn't miss it. You know how volatile the issue of mailboxes is. Near and dear to everyone's hearts." Our home-owners' association was trying to pass an ordinance that would ban "unsightly metal mailboxes." However, Simon Smith's goose with the opening chest and another neighbor's green frog with the flopping lower lip were wooden, and therefore deemed "sightly."

I escorted Joanne out, then scanned the mess that was once my garden. How could we even begin to reassemble this mud hole into a yard? Maybe I should have hired Sheila Lillydale to protect my property after all. Not one to choke while swallowing pride, I decided to give her a call and see what she had to say about this now.

As I returned to the front door, an elderly voice called out, "Made a damned mess of your property, huh?" The voice had all of the endearing qualities of a rusty hinge.

I turned, surprised to see Simon Smith peering at me over his cedar privacy fence. His sharp features and bony body befitted his screechy voice. He was not six feet, let alone eight feet tall, so he had to have been standing on a stepladder.

"You can say that again," I murmured.

"What they find?"

"A dog," I answered without thinking, then winced and realized I had just "compromised the investigation."

"A dog? Dead, I presume?"

71

That question didn't warrant an answer, so applying the "in for a penny, in for a pound" adage, I said, "It was a toy poodle."

Simon snorted, shook his head, and said, "Helen didn't have a pet dog. Poodle or otherwise."

"Really? Are you sure?"

"Sure as shootin'. She was allergic to the damned things."

"Did you ever see Helen digging in this yard?" It was strange to have to crane my neck to speak to a neighbor, but I didn't want to stop his momentum by suggesting he round the fence. This was the longest conversation by far the two of us had shared, and I was curious to know more about him. "By digging, I don't mean just planting flowers, but something else."

"Something else? No, no. Never saw her do any heavy-duty digging." He cackled. "Heard about how she was digging in your yard when she got shot, though. She was probably just planting a tree, or something."

"What makes you think that? Did she ever tell you she wanted to plant a tree in my yard?"

He guffawed and shook his head. "She told me you was damned useless when it came to gardening."

Having heard enough of Helen's and Simon's speech patterns to differentiate between them, the "damned" part had come from Simon, not the late Helen. I gritted my teeth, but turned my grimace into a reasonable facsimile of a smile. The point, I reminded myself, was not that I was forced to bemoan the fact that plants died en masse in my presence, but that Simon's information contradicted the image of Helen as a "complete recluse." "Yes, well, she was certainly more than willing to compensate for my shortcomings in that area."

"Yep. Could've had yourself a free gardener, if you'd have just let her. That's all she wanted."

"It sounds as though you knew Helen pretty well."

"Yep. One damned fine lady, that gal."

"If you ever feel like talking to someone about her, I'd love to listen."

"Come on over right now. I'll brew us up some coffee and tell you all about her."

This was the first friendly invitation I'd received from any of my immediate neighbors, and I never would have expected it to come from Simon Smith. Something was up.

He was already standing by his front door awaiting me when I headed up his front walkway. To my surprise, he was even shorter than I'd thought he was — only my height, though his narrow shoulders were so stooped a good chiropractor might have adjusted him to five-eight or five-nine. He struck me as the sort of geeky person everyone made fun of in high school and who wound up volunteering in the audiovisual department.

Simon's house had a musty smell. Framed circuit boards, spray-painted gold or silver, hung where you'd normally expect to see pictures. The kitchen clock was merely hands mounted atop what looked like the inside of a radio. While Simon brewed the coffee, I stood in the kitchen doorway, watching the clock on his food-splattered wall, surprised that its second hand could clear all of those resistors and capacitors. An infinitesimal benefit of being married to an electrical engineer was that it gave me the vocabulary to call small electronic components something other than "doohickies."

Exactly three and half minutes later, he poured us coffee and handed me a plain blue mug with a chip on the rim. Then he steered me to his living room. The furniture was old and well-worn, except for the coffee table. He had made the frame of the table out of four-by-fours, and the surface area out of a dozen circuit boards soldered together. I blew on the surface of my coffee, but it needed to cool a bit — a lot, actually, because on a hot morning like this, coffee had no appeal beyond its social function. I was afraid I'd electrocute myself if I set my cup down on the circuitry.

Simon noticed my hesitation and flicked a wrist at me. "Go ahead. It's a table, ain't it? Put your cup down."

I promptly set my cup down and gave him a smile. "You must have a hard time dusting this coffee table, with all of its solder joints."

"Nope. Just haul it out back 'n' hose it down. Comes out looking brand-new. Made it myself. Tried to patent it, but some genius at the patent office said, 'This ain't only unoriginal, but ugly.' Ha! Damn thing would sell like hotcakes to computer nerds. And I got a set of coasters to go with it." He pulled out a stack of small circuit boards and tossed them on top of the table.

I picked up the nearest board and examined it. "Where do you get these?"

"I got a standing order for bulk rejects from an electronic-assembly plant. Also get 'em at junk yards." He patted the table lovingly. "This is one-hundred percent garbage." He narrowed his eyes at me. "So. How well did you get to know Helen when you was buying the place?"

That was not a typical question when making small talk. After all, buyers and sellers don't get to know one another during run-of-the-mill real-estate transactions. Simon, like Joanne, wanted to pump me for information, which, as I'd suspected, had motivated the sudden invitation for coffee. "Not at all."

"And why is that? Ain't you a friendly sort?"

"Sure, I am. She and I didn't seem . . . we didn't share many interests. You say she *didn't* have a poodle?" I asked abruptly, trying to change subjects.

"Nope."

"How do you suppose the dog's body could have gotten there, then? Could the pet have belonged to the people who owned this house before Helen?"

"You mean, the original owners? Not likely. They owned a big German shepherd. Would have eaten a poodle for breakfast."

Which could explain how the dog died. I kept the thought to myself, though. "Were you here yesterday afternoon when all the excitement was going on?"

"Nope. Damnedest thing. Got a call from some damn idiot claiming to be my cousin George from Philadelphia. Said he was at the train station in Albany and had to catch

76

the next train out, but wanted to see me to discuss something important. So I headed clear out there, and George wasn't there. Whole damn thing was a hoax."

"Did you tell the police about this?"

He nodded emphatically. "Sure did. Nothing they could do about it, though. Probably some damned kids, playing a joke."

"But it had to be someone who knew you had a cousin George in Philadelphia. Right?"

He sighed. "That wouldn't be so hard. See, I don't *have* a cousin George in Philadelphia. That's why the whole phone call episode had me so damned confused." He shrugged and eyed me sheepishly. "Sounds stupid, I know, but when you're as old as me and you've got the last name of Smith, you start to forget who in tarnation you're related to."

I chuckled in spite of myself. "I got the impression that Helen was what you might call a recluse."

"Oh, she was friendly. She just liked to keep to herself, that's all. I was damned sorry when she moved out of the neighborhood."

"What were her hobbies?"

"Chess. She'd come over here, and we'd

play sometimes. I made a chess board. Was going to give it to her this Christmas. Would you like to see it?"

Naturally, I said yes, and he brought out a large board from the closet. It was wrapped in royal-blue velveteen, and he uncovered it as if he were uncovering a rare, fragile piece of artwork. Not surprisingly, the board had been made out of dark and light circuit boards, inlaid on a plywood base. Frankly, it was "damned" ugly, but I complimented him anyway.

"Do you make these things at home?"

He wiggled his thumb in the direction of the stairs. "Got a workshop upstairs."

"Can I see it?"

"No, no," he blurted. He gave me a nervous smile. "Nobody's allowed in my workshop but me. Man's got to have his space."

Hmm. Simon was habitually nosy and had lived next to Helen for more than two years. If anyone could have discovered Helen's true gender, this was the person. To test his reaction, I said, "There was a rumor that you and Helen were sweethearts."

He straightened that stooped backbone of his more than I would have thought possible. "No! That's a damned lie! Who told you that?"

"I . . . don't recall."

"Joanne Abbott, wasn't it? I saw her going into your house, with one of those banana breads she bakes whenever she wants something from someone. Want my advice? Don't eat the damned thing. Tastes like wet sawdust." He snatched my untouched coffee cup up from the table. "Thanks for dropping by. I have —"

The doorbell rang.

"Place is suddenly Grand Central," Simon growled. "Hang on a moment." He shuffled off to answer.

I rose, intending to show myself out, then took one last glance at the coffee table and noticed a red LED — which was a tiny light that looked like a glass bubble — flashing. Perhaps Simon had become hard of hearing and had rigged this to the doorbell as a visual signal. Then again, Simon had said earlier he cleaned this table by "hosing it down." How could that have been true if the table had live circuitry?

Curious as to how such a thing could have been powered, I crouched down and looked underneath the table. A thin black wire ran from the LED down along the inner side of one table leg and disappeared into the nap of the carpeting.

I could hear Simon and another man's voice from the doorway. The doorbell wasn't ringing, yet the light was still flashing. I scanned the baseboards for wire and picked up the trail at the wall across the room that led up the stairway. The workshop! Maybe he had some sort of electronic gizmo in there that fed a signal to this table. But what had tripped it?

I overheard Simon telling his guest to "hang on while I make myself some more coffee." That would keep him occupied for another three and a half minutes. I decided to take a quick peek into the workshop while in the guise of searching for the bathroom.

I snuck upstairs and followed the wire as if it were a trail of bread crumbs. It led to a doorway, open just a crack. I pushed open the door a few inches with my foot. The room had two television monitors, similar to the ones in shopping malls. I stared at them, not believing my eyes.

Both screens were showing my yard from different angles, where a policeman was walking.

Chapter 5

At the End of My Rope

Simon Smith's "workshop" resembled the inside of one of those surveillance vans frequently depicted in cop shows. A tape recorder with a set of large earphones was hooked up to a telephone in the corner. Two television sets with video recorders were displaying my side yard, where the elderly, portly police officer from last night now stood. The flashing light imbedded in the coffee table must have been a signal from a motion detector that went off whenever anyone was in my yard.

In a low-tech surveillance operation of my own, I parted the curtains and noted that this was the window through which Simon Smith had peered at me with binoculars last night. And he'd had two cameras on me at the time. Talk about overkill. It was like a sports fan who brought a battery-operated television to the stadium, to see the same game.

As the disbelief faded, rage seeped into

me. How dare he! What gave this man the right to pry into my life like this?

Affronted and appalled at this egregious violation of my privacy, I marched downstairs and headed toward the voices, which still came from Simon's front room. Apparently, Simon still hadn't brewed his coffee or invited the officer into his living room. En route, I searched for more flashing LEDs. Sure enough, in the kitchen there was one built into what looked like a bizarre pop-art picture composed of recycled electronic parts.

The young officer with the pink cheeks stood in the small foyer. His name, I remembered, was Dave. Unfortunately for me, young Dave would be harder to spur into action at this violation of my rights than Tommy would have been.

Simon cast a nervous glance my way over his narrow, stooped shoulder. "Mrs. Masters was just leaving. As I was telling her and told your . . ." He paused and did a double take at me, no doubt wondering why I *wasn't* leaving. I planted my feet and, arms crossed, glared at him. He blinked a couple of times, then returned his attention to the officer. "Who was that old fellow I was talking to last night?"

"My partner, Officer Greg Hess."

Old fellow? Simon was at least fifteen years older than Officer Hess.

"As I told your partner, I wasn't here when everything was happening. There was nobody in the house. I live alone. My wife divorced me some twenty years ago." With a proud lilt to his voice, he added, "Couldn't take the element of danger in my chosen field." Simon had stepped aside so I could pass, but I had no intention of doing so. I squared my shoulders and maintained my post at the far side of his foyer. Now he cleared his throat and made little jerky motions with his head indicating for me to use the door.

"Could I speak with you in private, Officer?" I asked.

"He's here to speak to *me*. You're not the only person on this street who's important to the police."

"Mrs. Masters, maybe I —"

Hearing the hesitation in the young officer's voice, I blurted, "Ask him why he's got cameras trained on my property!"

Simon's jaw dropped. He put his hands on his hips. "Now, Molly. You had no right to —"

"*I* had no right? It's okay for you to have cameras trained on my house without my knowledge or consent? Yet you think I have no right to peek through an open door after having been invited inside your house?"

"Open door? I . . . I always keep that door closed."

Oh, all right. So I'd pushed it open with my foot. No sense nitpicking.

"Man's got a right to his private space," Simon continued. "And what were you doing going upstairs in the first place?"

"Your coffee table was flashing me and you were busy. For all I knew, that could have signaled someone's heart monitor was on the fritz. So I followed the wire up the stairs."

"You have cameras trained on Mrs. Masters's home?" the officer asked. Thank goodness that the policeman hadn't missed the important thrust of this conversation.

Simon's eyes darted between the startled-looking officer's and mine. "Er, I was just testing the equipment."

"Testing the equipment, my ass!" As soon as the latter phrase left my lips, I started to mentally replay those one or two occasions during the past three months where I'd passed my window in a state of undress. Had I ducked low enough to escape the camera's eye?

Officer Dave spread his hands. "I'm sure you two can work this out yourselves.

Neighbor to neighbor?" He looked at both of us pleadingly. *This* was an officer of the law? He needed some assertiveness training.

"He's got video recorders on both of those cameras. He must have a tape of the shooting. You can arrest him for withholding key evidence."

Simon stomped his foot. His pinched, weathered features were twisted in anger. "I don't *have* any evidence. Helen covered up the lenses yesterday afternoon while I was gone."

"But those cameras are aimed from clear up above the fence," I said. "Did Helen climb onto your *roof?*"

"She, er, used my ladder."

I tried to picture the series of gyrations Mr. Helen must have had to go through yesterday: find and carry Simon's ladder to one corner of the house, tape up one lens, repeat this at the other corner of the house, then come to my yard and start digging. Tommy's theory was that Helen was merely an eccentric and the shooting was accidental. That meant he had to have done all of this just to retrieve a poodle's remains in private. A poodle that wasn't even his pet. That cemented everything for me. This was no accidental shooting. Helen had been murdered.

"I'll need to have that video recording, Mr. Smith," the policeman said.

Simon winced. "My tapes just show her blocking the lenses. That's all I got recorded." When the officer held Simon's gaze, he added, "And you're welcome to it, Officer, sir."

"Don't you think you should get a search warrant and confiscate the equipment, too?" I asked. "He's got all sorts of devices upstairs, including something hooked to a phone." Before the officer could respond, an unsettling thought occurred to me and I whirled toward my neighbor. "You've been tapping my phones, haven't you? That's why I keep getting error messages on my fax and crackling noises on the line!"

"Nope. I'm tapping my own damn phone. Nothing illegal 'bout that."

"I don't believe him. I demand to have this man arrested! He's done all kinds of illegal things to me!"

"Please, Mrs. Masters. Why don't we just all sit down and have a calm discussion about this?"

"I'm as calm as I care to be under the circumstances." I pointed at Simon. "You still haven't explained why you were spying on me!"

"Wasn't spying on you. Not ever."

"Then you were spying on Helen Raleigh. And you left the equipment there after we bought the place."

He pursed his lips and narrowed his eyes at me. With this expression on top of his wiry features, he looked like a rattlesnake set to stick out his forked tongue at me. "I'll go get the damn tapes."

"I'll come with you and give you a hand," Officer Dave said.

Simon shook a knobby finger at me and demanded, "You stay put, young lady." He led the way, mumbling to Dave, "Man's got a right to . . ." His voice trailed off.

As soon as the coast was clear, I returned to the living room and glanced around for something to smash the LED with. There was a sooty poker by the fireplace, but that seemed too extreme, considering a policeman was readily available to arrest me. Instead I reached underneath the coffee table, located the wire, and gave it a good yank. It held firm. A floorboard creaked upstairs. The men were returning. I rose and stuffed my hands in the pockets of my denim shorts.

Officer Dave gave me a sympathetic, though helpless look as he returned carrying two VCR recordings. Simon slunk down the stairs a step behind him. He clicked his tongue and shook his head when he spotted me and realized I hadn't "stayed put."

"Like I said," Simon muttered. "All you can see is Helen covering the cameras. Then a couple of minutes later you hear the gunshot."

He had audio, too! What if he had a high-powered audio recorder aimed at my house? My inane daily conversations with my family might have been recorded and tittered at by this old coot! Every time I'd been a less-than-perfect mother, nagged, or whined, my words might have been permanently recorded for all the ages. The thought made my stomach spin.

"You have motion sensors that are triggered when anyone's moving in our yard. Do you pick up our conversations as well?"

Simon nodded. "Got all your conversation with Helen before the shooting. And you weren't being very nice to her, by the way. Can't hear a damn thing when you're inside your house, though. 'Less a window's open."

"What a relief," I snarled and gave him my most evil glare, but he seemed unaffected. "I insist you stop this invasion of my privacy this instant! I want that equipment dismantled!"

He crossed his arms and set his jaw. He seemed to be proud of his contemptuous behavior.

The officer looked absolutely lost, staring at the tapes in his hands as if searching for the answer to some multiple-choice test of correct police responses. "I'll need to talk to the sergeant about this, Mr. Smith." Though Dave had tried to deepen his voice to affect an authoritative presence, it just didn't match the soft-cheeked face. He made his way back toward the foyer as he spoke, and we followed.

"You do that," Simon answered. "The cameras are aimed at the yard, not at the windows, and they're there just to make sure my fence is secure. I'm not doing a damn thing that's illegal." He lifted his chin as he looked at me. "Not a damn thing."

The officer pushed out the squeaky screen door to the front porch and rapidly descended the steps as if in a great hurry to leave. I lagged behind, but wasn't about to stay alone with Simon.

"We'll see what Sergeant Newton has to say about all of this. He's a close personal friend of mine." I brushed out the door, but turned on the front porch and leveled a finger at him. "Even if this somehow turns out to be legal, which I doubt, spying on your neighbors like this is reprehensible."

He shook his head. "Man's got a right to do what he wants in his own home!"

"So does woman and child, without being spied upon in the process! You should be ashamed of yourself." I marched down the porch steps without waiting to assess Simon's reaction. If he'd been one of my children, he would have had a quivering lip right about now. Too bad guilt trips don't work as well on seventy-year-olds as they do on seven-year-olds.

Halfway between our homes, I scanned his roofline, trying to spot the cameras. Along the underside of his roof at each corner were two domes of glass, not unattractive, which I'd always taken for some sort of overhead light. I'd never seen them illuminate. Now I knew that was because they weren't lights in the first place.

Not only did I stick my tongue out at the nearest dome, but I gave Simon Smith's camera the finger. I also toyed with the idea of throwing a rock. But I have a terrible arm and probably would have missed not just the camera, but the entire house.

Once at home, I chastised myself. Giving one's neighbor the finger is extraordinarily childish. There had to be a more mature way of handling this. I should have mooned him. Maybe I could send him a particularly nasty greeting card. That would surely bring him to his knees.

The nastiest card I'd ever created was for a woman client who felt widowed by her husband's attention to his computer. She had me design a card that showed a woman clinging to a rope by one hand. To the right of the drawing, an arrow indicated "Rope." Then a second arrow indicated "End of Rope." A third arrow pointed to the woman and was labeled "Me." The caption below read, "We need to talk."

I eyed the Smith house through my window before picking up my phone. If he was going to listen in on this particular conversation, all the better. I'd give him an earful. I opened my window to make sure he could hear, then called the station house. Tommy was not in his office, and I got his voice mail. "Sergeant, it's me," I began, wanting to make it clear that Tommy and I were such good friends he would recognize my voice. Not that I would normally address my "good friend" as Sergeant. "I've uncovered a major crime here. In fact, I'm quite certain this phone call is being recorded by the perpetrator, Simon Smith. And I wouldn't be at all surprised if he had a hand in Helen Raleigh's murder. In any case, he is not a nice man. Plus, he's a rotten neighbor. I don't feel safe having my two little children living next door to such a despicable person. Who should be ashamed of himself."

I hung up and was now all the more determined to find Tommy and explain to him in person what was going on before he heard that message and drew incorrect conclusions about my sanity. Last night after we'd fetched Nathan's pajamas and returned to my mother's house, Tommy had remained on my property. That meant he had endured an inordinately long day. Playing a reasonable hunch, I locked up and headed to Lauren's.

Sherwood Forest, the unfortunate name of the subdivision in which we lived, was a truly attractive area that featured exceptionally nice, large, two-story homes and lush, well-manicured lawns — not counting mine. Most houses were colonial style, which was appropriate because some of the old farmhouses immediately outside the division were more than a hundred years old. The heat and humidity, however, only served to blot out my appreciation for the scenery and increase my indignation toward Simon as I walked.

I glanced at my watch as I had to stride

past my parents' house to get to Lauren's. The garage and front door were shut tight. Mom was still at the store, though she'd be returning in half an hour.

Lauren's house was nearly identical to my parents', though it was a mirror image. Only the screen door was shut, but now that Tommy was essentially living there, I rang the doorbell and waited, instead of calling, "Hi, it's me," and letting myself in as I used to.

Lauren was wearing sandals, black culottes, and a silk top the color of Dijon mustard. She grinned at me as she opened the door. "Uh-oh. You look ready to kill somebody. I hope it's an enemy we have in common."

"No, but consider yourself lucky you don't know him. Is Tommy here?"

She led me to her dining room. Tommy was eating an enormous breakfast of bacon, eggs, and fresh-baked muffins. Lauren pulled out a chair for me across from Tommy, handed me a buttered muffin, which had some sort of crunchy sugar-cinnamon globs on top, and left the room. I greeted Tommy, then took a bite. It was delicious. The globs reminded me of a Sara Lee crumb cake — warming those up in the microwave was as close to baking as I ever got myself.

"Simon's got all sorts of surveillance equipment trained on my property," I said after my first swallow.

"Uh-huh. Noticed what looked like cameras when I was checking the scene yesterday afternoon. They were covered up with duct tape, though."

"Yeah, that's true. But they were covered up by the *victim* just prior to getting shot to death. So there goes your theory that she was just digging up her *poodle*."

He munched away at his breakfast, staring into space for a minute. Finally he shrugged. "Prob'ly so, but you never know. Maybe Helen didn't want anyone spying while moving the remains."

"You think Helen wanted a private moment with a dead dog? Give me a break! She didn't even *own* a dog. And so first, Helen had to get Simon out of the house on a wild-goose chase. Then fetch the ladder and climb up it. Then put —"

"Let me ask you this, Moll," he interrupted. "S'pose you were Helen. S'pose you'd known about those cameras and, let's say for the sake of argument, you'd asked him to take them down but he refused. What would you have done?"

I'd probably borrow one of Tommy's sons' pellet guns and shoot out those "damned" cameras myself. This was not a good answer to give to a policeman, however. "I'm not sure."

He leaned back in his chair and eyed me. "Now, I know you pretty well, Moll. I can see you climbing up a ladder or two to cover 'em up. Though you'd probably take a pick ax to 'em instead."

"Maybe so, but —"

"Know what else? Mr. Smith never worked for the CIA. That's just a story he concocted. He's retired from the post office in downtown Boston."

Surprised, I took a moment to let this revelation sink in. "Are you sure?"

Tommy nodded.

Suddenly a sympathetic pang for Simon tugged at me. The man must have been desperately lonely to feel impelled to create a fictional personal history to give new neighbors.

"Got some more news for you," Tommy went on, "but you're probably not gonna like hearing it." Tommy shoveled some dripping eggs-over-easy into his mouth.

I averted my eyes. It's difficult to pay serious attention to someone who's currently dribbling egg yolk.

Through a mouthful of food, he muttered something along the lines of, "Think I got your shooter in custody as of five A.M. this morning."

"You arrested someone already?"

He nodded and, thankfully, wiped his chin. "Got us a pair of hunters. Same kind of rifle as did in our Helen."

"Were they shooting in the vicinity of my house yesterday afternoon?"

He nodded. "They were loaded to the gills. Doin' whiskey shots as well as firin' off the other kind. Havin' themselves a regular twenty-four-hour party back there in them woods. It's likely they were the culprits."

"Can you do a ballistics check on the bullet casing to see if it was fired from one of their guns?"

Lauren, drying her hands on a dish towel, reentered the room. "Hey, Lauren. Hear that? Molly thinks I should test the rifles. Now, why didn't I think of that?"

Lauren, to my immense pleasure, glared at Tommy and said, "You need to get caught up on your sleep and stop sniping at our friends."

I gave Tommy a smug smile, which he pretended not to see.

It suddenly occurred to me that Lauren should be at her office at Carlton High School by now. She worked mornings as secretary for the principal. "Aren't you late for work?"

She grinned. "I called in sick. Cough, cough."

"You're playing hooky?"

She swept up an empty cereal bowl near Tommy and turned on a heel to return to the kitchen. "This is the first day I've missed all year, and it's the last week of school, so I'll be done as of Friday anyway."

I returned my attention to Tommy. "None of this answers why Simon Smith has cameras surveying my yard twenty-four hours a day."

He gave me a one-shoulder shrug. Then he stood up, grabbing his last strips of bacon and two muffins as if he intended to eat those in the car. "Look at it from his view-point. Here's a postman who's got all his gullible neighbors believing he's a retired CIA agent. Guy's obviously off his rocker."

"But, Tommy, why would he zoom in on my house? And the former owner gets killed right under his nose. Doesn't that sound like, at the very least, Mr. Smith might be guilty of considerably more than voy-eurism?"

"Check out the other side of his house sometime, Moll. Look for those dome-type lenses."

"More damn domes," I grumbled to myself. "He's got cameras on the Abbotts' house as well?"

"Uh-huh."

I paused for a moment to digest this news. I wondered if Stan or Joanne were privy to this unsettling information. "But I didn't see any TV sets in his 'workshop' showing anything from that side."

"Probably got those in a room on the other side of his home."

"He's got some sort of audio hookup recording my conversations in my yard, too. Can I get this guy arrested, Tommy? Please say yes. There's no way I'm putting up with this!"

He shrugged. "Looked it up last night after spottin' the cameras. Might make a case for aggravated harassment, so long as those cameras of his have a view inside your windows. Even so, we'd have to show he was usin' the videos for sexual gratification or was able to witness you with, er, exposed body parts."

I grimaced, realizing now the significance of his claiming those cameras *weren't* aimed at my windows. I should have mooned him after all!

"Got a better chance at gettin' him for eavesdropping," Tommy continued. "Depending on what he's doin' with those audio recordings, he could be guilty of a Class Six Felony."

"What do you mean, 'depending on what he's doing' with the tapes?"

"It all hinges on his intent. For it to be a punishable 'eavesdropping' offense, he's got to be sharin' the contents of your private conversations with another person for financial gain, such as to aid or abet a crime, or conspiring to —"

"What if he's just recording us because he's a nosy old coot?"

"Then you're out of luck."

Even if I let my imagination run wild, there was no scenario I could concoct in which Simon was sharing his audio recordings with someone else. *Here's a hundred bucks, Simon. Eavesdrop on the Masterses till you get me that hamburger-and-vegetable-soup recipe of Molly's. The future of Western civilization depends on it!* I let out a sigh of frustration as Tommy rounded the table and walked past me toward the front door. I followed him as we neared the entrance to the kitchen. "Have you discovered Helen's true identity?" I asked.

"Nope. 'Sides, we've got an obligation to notify relatives 'fore we let any names get out."

"Have you even figured out why Helen was disguised as a woman for the entire time he owned the house?"

Lauren dropped a dish. Tommy pivoted and shot me a glare. Then he ran his hand through his red hair. "Helen Raleigh was a *man?*" Lauren cried, rushing into the hallway.

Tommy ignored her, but when she met my eyes I nodded enthusiastically, then asked Tommy, "Has someone come forward to claim the body?"

"No. Ran a fingerprint check through AFIS, but nothing. Still don't know who Helen is."

"But we *do* know somebody who could have been recording Helen's every movement for the last two and a half years," I said. "Under the circumstances, doesn't that sound like you've got good legal cause to confiscate all of that equipment as evidence?"

Tommy grinned broadly and winked at me. "Works for me. 'Course, that's not to say the judge'll agree, but I'll give it my best shot."

Good, I thought, glancing around for any signs of Tommy's sons' pellet gun. Then *I* won't have to give those cameras *my* best shot.

Chapter 6

Check Condition of Remote Facts

If I'd even remotely considered the notion of staying in my house while this shooting was being investigated, Simon Smith had sealed my fate. Call me a worrywart, but there was no way my family could remain in a house where a murder had occurred *and* a neighbor had video cameras and bugging devices trained on us.

Egged on by the knowledge that my mother would return from the store soon and fear for my whereabouts, I jogged home and ordered call-forwarding, which would allow me automatically to receive my business calls and faxes at my parents' number. Let's see how well ol' Simon's cameras could pick up my family's activities when we were living three blocks away.

My fax machine rang as I was in the process of packing up the computer. I awaited the fax eagerly. Maybe they'd already decided to buy my cowboy-in-an-elevator cartoon.

I was surprised when the display panel on my machine showed the fax had been sent by S. Smith. Could Simon have sent me a letter of apology? In defiance of the watched-pot-never-boils philosophy, I stood over my machine as it slowly chugged forth my printout. Curiously, the inch-wide margins were solid black and the message was handwritten. Before the mechanism could fully release the sheet of paper, I tugged it free and read:

My Dear Mrs. Masters,
    You are messing in matters of no concern to you, at a terrible risk to your own and your family's safety. I must urge you to stop this at once. You don't know how dangerous the people involved in this are.
    I wish I could identify myself to you, but I am not in a position to do so. Please, heed my warning.
    LET DEAD DOGS LIE!
                        Sign me:
                        A Concerned Friend

I tsked and rolled my eyes. Simon must have used a magic marker to blacken the borders of his original document in attempt to cover up the margin text where my fax machine had printed the phone number and name of the sender. Unfortunately for him, the sender tag printed above his blacked-out margins. Plus, the transmission log for my machine would have registered this information, even if his black margins had done the trick or I hadn't been physically present to read his name on my display panel.

This seemed too stupid an oversight for someone to make who was supposedly a retired postal clerk posing as a former spy. Maybe he really was a CIA agent after all.

The last line of his fax — Let dead dogs lie — ran through my brain long after I'd set the fax aside. Was that just a takeoff on the cliché about sleeping dogs? Or maybe "lie" meant tell a lie, as in: Let the dead poodle conceal the truth of what was really buried in my yard.

I heard some loud engine noises outside and went out to investigate. Someone was out there with a Bobcat bulldozer pushing the dirt around. I waved at him, trying to get his attention, but he merely waved back. I ran up to him and shouted over the engine noise, "Excuse me. This is my house. What are you doing?"

"The police sent me over here to fill up these holes again, ma'am."

I stepped back and watched as one of my tulip bulbs toppled into a hole. Four feet of dirt was dumped on top of it. That was going to have to be one heck of a long-stemmed flower. Would just the little petals peek out above ground level?

Helen Raleigh, or whoever he really was, would roll over in his grave at the sight of his property in its current condition. Brown dirt was ground into the grass by tracks from the miniature bulldozer. How pathetic. The one time I ever actually tried to install a garden of my own, and it resulted in not only the destruction of my entire yard, but in someone's death. This had to go down in the annals as one of the world's worst gardening debacles.

With the distinct, though predictable, feeling that someone was watching me, I turned and looked up at Simon's white curtains. I caught just a glimpse of my wretched neighbor before he stepped away.

That reminded me. Did Joanne Abbott have any idea she was being watched, too? I edged my way past Simon's property, keeping a watch on the place. Every harmless detail of his property now struck me as a possible bugging device. If that was really a bird feeder hanging from the elm tree out front, why were no birds or squirrels eating from it? He had a lamppost placed a step or two in from the sidewalk. I studied it, prepared to "accidentally" disconnect anything that looked suspicious. Though nothing leapt out at me as out of place, the petunias that hung from a peg a few inches below the bulb were in a "pot" that consisted of nothing more than a wire mesh. Now, if you choose to go through the considerable effort of raising and maintaining flowers, why hang them such that dirt and roots were the most prominent features? He might have wired the pot for sound. I couldn't study them long enough to be certain — if I stayed near for too long, the flowers would detect my aura, curl up, and die.

Just as Tommy Newton had forewarned, there were two more inverted domes on the opposite side of Simon's house, one on each roof corner. Indeed, my property was not the only one Simon Smith was monitoring.

I continued up Joanne's front walkway, but kept an eye on Simon's house. For the first time, I realized how odd it was that only Simon Smith had a cedar privacy fence that enclosed most of his property, boxing it in from one front corner of the house to the next. Everyone else in the neighborhood delineated the property lines of their large, sprawling lawns by an occasional split-rail fence or, more often, hedges or rosebushes.

The Abbotts had a brass knocker with "Stan & Joanne" engraved in a looping scrawl. I loved door knockers — the little vibrations they sent through my fingertips, the resonant, solemn sound they made.

Joanne Abbott came to the door. She was now wearing leather sandals and odd-looking ballooning apricot pants. Only her white T-shirt saved me from assuming she was on her way to the airport to tap a tambourine for Hare Krishna. I must have interrupted her from some sort of exercise routine, for her strong-featured face was damp with perspiration and her green eyes looked glassy.

"Why, Molly," she said with a slow smile, "what a pleasant surprise."

"I hope I'm not interrupting anything."

"Oh, no. I just finished my morning's Tae Kwon Do and was in the process of making myself some orange juice. Would you care for some?"

"Sure. Thanks."

She smiled and led the way through her house. A baby grand piano, its natural wood grain polished to a perfect sheen, graced the living room. It was atop a full-size Oriental rug in rich red and black hues that protected the hardwood floor. In the area of dull but requisite small talk, I asked whether she played the piano. She said no, that her husband, Stan, was the musician in the family.

I glanced into their dining room as we passed and spotted a gorgeous antique hutch filled with what looked at a distance like Waterford crystal. Not a mark or fingerprint anyplace. A pang of nostalgia hit me for those long-gone prechild days when Jim and I could choose furniture based on its appearance, as opposed to its sturdiness or how well stains would blend with the fabric design.

I followed her into the kitchen, where brass pots hung along one wall. This, in my opinion, ventured into the area of ostentatious display. As much as I loved brass — especially door knockers — those pots had obviously never been used even once. This was not unlike suspending a nice couch from the living-room ceiling and sitting on the one the cat used as a scratching post.

To my delight, Joanne had a juice machine. The closest I came to making fresh-squeezed juice was when I squished the container to get the frozen concentrate out. Joanne tossed in the orange slices. A few whirs later, she handed me a glass. It was delicious. Joanne took a long sip, then asked, "Have they notified Helen's relatives yet?"

"No. They can't seem to locate the next of kin." That brought to mind a good question to ask *her*. "You lived near her for a couple of years. Who used to visit her?"

"Nobody. Like I said, she was a recluse, just like Simon Smith." She tilted her glass and began to gulp its contents.

"Speaking of Simon, did you know he has surveillance cameras on your house?"

She shot out a spray of juice.

I winced and felt my cheeks warm with embarrassment. "I guess you didn't. I'm sorry. I should have put that more tactfully."

She thunked down her glass onto the counter. "How do you know he's got cameras on us?"

"He's got video cameras aimed at our house, too. In our case, the recordings are showing on TVs in a room he calls his workshop. The cameras are installed on each corner of the overhang of his roof." I gestured at the window. "I'll show you." She parted the blue-and-white checkered curtains, and I pointed out the lenses.

"This is an outrage! He can't do this!"

"Actually, according to the police sergeant, he can so long as the cameras don't give him a view inside our windows."

"So what are we supposed to do? Just wave and smile at the camera every day?"

"I've asked the police to look into getting a court order to seize the equipment as evidence in Helen Raleigh's shooting. In the meantime, we might want to bring this up for discussion at the home-owners' association meeting tomorrow night."

She smiled. "Bet we can stage a regular protest rally in front of Simon Smith's house. And Sheila Lillydale is a lawyer. We can get her to serve him some legal papers. I can call her right now."

That reminded me of another area in which I wished to compare mental notes. Just as Joanne picked up her handset, I asked, "Have you been getting crackling noises on your phone line, by any chance?"

She dropped the phone and peered down her considerable nose at me. "Yes, as a matter of fact. That's been an ongoing problem for the last few weeks or so. Why?"

"So have I. And Simon Smith has this setup in his workshop that he claims is just a phone tap of his own line."

Her eyes widened in alarm. "You think he's bugging our phones, too?"

She looked so upset at this notion I felt a tinge of guilt for putting my unsubstantiated claim into her head. "I probably shouldn't have said anything. It's just something I'm worried about, but if he is listening in on our phone lines, the police will put a stop to it."

After further discussion and more cajoling on my part, we decided that, since I had additional questions about my current situation, I would call Sheila Lillydale on both Joanne's and my behalf. We exchanged hasty good-byes, and I walked briskly back to my parents' house.

Not surprisingly, my mother was standing just a step away from the front door when I opened it. She had probably been pacing by the door. Since my mother was five inches taller than I, it was difficult not to slip right into the role of subordinate child. She scolded me for not leaving a note to tell her where I was. "I hate to be meddlesome," she went on, "but after all, someone was shot to death some three feet away from you. Any mother would be concerned under the circumstances."

"It was more than three feet. Plus, we were separated by a wall and tons of dirt, since I was in the basement. But you're right. I should have left a note."

Mom pursed her lips. "No. That's okay. You've been on your own for so many years now, you're not used to reporting your whereabouts. I'll just have to tell myself not to worry. Somehow."

I muttered more apologies, but having

known the woman for thirty-six years, I had long since realized that if Mom wants to take the blame for something, sooner or later you had to let her. However, I did appease her by announcing that I had decided to keep the family out of our house until Helen Raleigh's killer was in custody.

Mom naturally assumed that meant we'd move back home and that she should "take the guest room, at least till your father gets home. After all, there's only one of me and there's two of you."

"No, no. Please. I like the guest room. It's right next to the office, where I'll have to put my fax machine anyway."

Mom parted her lips as if to protest, but then smiled. "Whatever makes you happy, dear. Can I do any laundry for you?"

"No, thanks." The rational side of my brain had to assure the emotional side that I was not, God forbid, reentering my childhood. I dashed downstairs.

I grabbed the phone in the room that would once again become my temporary office headquarters. Using the number listed on the business card given to me yesterday, I called Sheila Lillydale. She answered on the first ring, saying melodically, "Sheila Lillydale speaking."

Hmm. Since no receptionist answered,

Sheila's practice must be very small, indeed. I told Sheila I wanted to hire her after all, that my yard was an unmitigated mess, and that Simon Smith had cameras on both my house and the Abbotts' house.

There was a pause. "You're certain about this business about the cameras?"

"Yes. I was in his house earlier this morning and saw the television screens myself. Then I told the police about them, and the officer told me that Mr. Smith wasn't necessarily breaking any laws. But there has to be something we can do to put a stop to this. Oh, and I think he's listening to my phone conversations as well. That's why I'm calling from a different phone now."

Again, there was a pause. "I think, under the circumstances, you and I had better have a face-to-face."

"I can come to your office."

"It's almost lunchtime. Tell you what. Can you meet me at my house in twenty minutes?"

I agreed, wolfed down a turkey sandwich and iced tea that Mom, bless her, had set out for me at my old spot at the cherry wood dining table. I apologized to my mother yet again for eating and running, but assured her that I was simply going to speak to a lawyer down the street and would return in an hour. Just as I strode up Sheila's walkway, she drove in, giving me a friendly wave. I cast a glance behind me at Simon Smith's house, but if he was watching me right now, he was at least doing so subtly. I stared at his wooden mailbox, though. For an instant, it had seemed as though the goose's eyes had followed me. On second glance, they were just painted black circles. Basic paranoia on my part.

Sheila left her car in the driveway and let us in through her front door. Today she was wearing her long, dark brown hair down, instead of in its usual efficient bun, adorned by a pair of shining gold barrettes. I wondered if she consciously chose the bright red skirt suit she wore to make herself stand out in court despite her small stature.

Sheila's house was a nicely decorated trilevel. She led me to an office on the main level, which had a direct view through a bay window to Simon's house across the street. When Sheila sat at her desk, I had no choice but to sit on the stuffed bench seat with my back to the window — where Simon was probably aiming binoculars right about now.

Before we could settle into a discussion of my legal concerns, I said, "I got the impression the other day that you and Helen were close. You must have been really sad when she moved out of the neighborhood."

Her thin eyebrows drew together. "I was shocked at the news. To be honest, though, Helen and I *weren't* close." Her dark eyes met mine. "I was actually relieved when Helen moved."

"Relieved?"

"My husband and she were getting a little too friendly, if you know what I mean."

Under most circumstances, I would know exactly what she meant. But the thought of handsome Roger cheating on his stunning wife with homely, not to mention *male*, Mr. Helen was too bizarre for me to fathom. "Friendly . . . as in romantically?"

"I was afraid the two of them might be having an affair." The expression on her pretty face was inscrutable, and her voice was matter-of-fact, as if she were merely reciting a bit of trivia. "It was a load off my mind when she finally moved. Though she was still in town, at least the two of them were no longer flaunting their affections for each other in front of my face."

This was simply too bizarre. What on earth was going on here? If Mr. Helen's choice of wearing women's clothing had simply been a lifestyle choice, could he have coincidentally found two men on the same cul-de-sac attracted to him? Or, if Roger and Mr. Helen *weren't* having an affair, then what? What was Roger *doing* with Helen to lead his wife to conclude that they were lovers?

To test Sheila's reaction, I said, "I really don't think your husband and my ex-owner Helen Raleigh were having an affair."

"Why? Because she was ugly? Looks aren't everything, you know."

"Yes, I do know. In fact I've known that for a sizable portion of my life." Again, I tried to read her expression, but couldn't. Even her body language told me nothing. Her forearms were resting on the desk. No telltale fidgeting or shaking hands. It occurred to me that, as a lawyer, Sheila was used to keeping tight control on her emotions. "But, beyond that, there's . . . Helen was rumored to have been a recluse. That she avoided everyone in the neighborhood."

"Everyone except Roger," she said quietly.

So, if that were true, Roger Lillydale was the best source of information about Mr. Helen. "Has Roger talked to the police yet? If he knew Helen at all, he might be able to help them locate her missing relatives."

"He's out of town. A business trip. He'll be gone for a couple of weeks."

"Does he even know about Helen's death?"

"Yes, I called him yesterday. He told me he intended to speak to the police about it immediately, since he knew Helen better than anyone in the neighborhood." She tossed her shiny dark hair back from her shoulders with an angry flick of her wrist. This was the closest she'd come to an emotional display — not someone I would want to play cards with. "But enough about Helen and my husband. It's time to get to the reason for your visit. Simon Smith's snooping."

"Try saying that five times fast," I said, trying to lighten the mood.

Sheila merely blinked.

"How would you advise me to handle this? What type of law do you specialize in?"

"Family law. That's somewhat of a euphemism, though. Mostly divorces, actually. The destruction of families is my specialty." For just a moment, pain was written all over her face.

Uh-oh. Her husband's out of town and she grimaces at the mention of divorce. "Yesterday I got the impression you handled murder cases."

"No, that was just to keep the police from trampling all over your rights."

"As well as my lawn."

Sheila straightened and, returning to her officious tone of voice, said, "Here's what I'll do. I'll have a conversation with Mr. Smith. I can threaten to bring him up on charges of both eavesdropping and aggravated harassment. Unless I badly miss my guess, he'll be taking those cameras down before the home-owners' meeting tomorrow night."

"That would be fine with me."

Sheila then told me how much she charged an hour. It was so high I nearly choked and asked her if she'd be willing to accept cartoons as payment. She was not amused, so I told her all I wanted her to do was draw up something that might intimidate Simon, but wouldn't take her more than two hours from start to finish. She agreed, studied me at length, then said, "I must admit that I haven't been particularly friendly to you."

That was a tough one to respond to, because it was unflinchingly correct, yet she awaited my reply as if expecting me to let her off the hook. "That's okay. After all, it's not like you opened fire on my house or put up surveillance gear. My standards for being a good neighbor are lowering by the minute."

She averted her eyes and said wistfully, "This has been a difficult time for me. I've felt so isolated. Roger spends all of his time with his son."

"With *his* son? Are you Ben's stepmother?"

Sheila nodded. "His mother, Roger's first wife, was a horrible woman. She left him years ago. Deserted him and the baby. I'm the only mother Ben has ever known. But still. It's hard to step in, instantly become both a wife and a mother. If I've failed, it isn't for lack of trying." She paused and ran a hand through her hair. "That's what was so difficult about having you move in across the street. You're going for Mom-of-the-Year award. You seem to focus every ounce of yourself into your kids. I just can't do that. And watching you made me feel like the wicked stepmother."

Her words took me by surprise. I hadn't been aware of Sheila observing my behavior around the children and recognizing me as a devoted mom. I wasn't a stepmother myself so I couldn't relate to the complex emotions within that relationship, but she'd said Ben was just a baby when she came on the scene and that his biological mother wasn't around. Was that really so different from adoption? There was an implied lack of bonding between her and nine-year-old Ben that bothered me deeply.

"Now that Roger no longer has Helen in his life," Sheila continued calmly, "he'll probably just find some other woman."

"Sheila, I don't know Roger well at all, but I did get to know Helen somewhat. Well enough at least to be positive that she wouldn't have been having an affair with your husband."

"What makes you say so? Because they were so different?"

"Well, yes, there's that, but . . ." As my attorney, everything I told her was probably privileged information, and she might need to know that Helen Raleigh was a man to best represent my interests. But I wasn't absolutely certain I wanted Sheila to represent me. More to the point, I didn't feel I should be the one to break this news to my neighbors.

Sheila was watching me so intently that I continued, "She just . . . wasn't the sort to have an affair." Sheila's stare made me uncomfortable. What if *she'd* hired Simon to find out if her suspicions about her husband and Helen were correct? Come to think of it, Sheila had a motive for murder. "Did you like Helen?"

"Why do you ask?"

"No reason." I chuckled nervously. "It's not as though you shot Helen in a fit of jealousy, after all."

Sheila stiffened. "I was in court at the time of the shooting. I have at least a hundred witnesses to my whereabouts."

"Of course. I was kidding. But inappropriately, and I'm terribly sorry." I rose. "I hope you and Roger work out your differences."

Our conversation had struck me as so bizarre, I left quickly, wanting to put some distance between us. Why had Sheila shared this private information with me about her troubles with Roger? What had he and Mr. Helen really been up to?

When I returned to my parents' house, my mom was reading in a chair situated suspiciously close to the front door. She gave me a forced smile and asked, "Did everything go okay at the lawyer's?"

I nodded and saw my own reflection in her eyes. However much I might be inclined to worry about *her* as she aged, from her perspective, I was forever her child. And I knew precisely how it felt to be concerned about your child's safety. The words, "You poor old dear," ran through my thoughts — but, fortunately, didn't reach my tongue, for Mom would've belted me on the spot.

"Tell you what, Mom. Let's go get some coffee at the mall."

"Coffee? But . . ." She gazed around her house as if it were filled with ready-made cappuccinos. Finally, she slowly smiled and met my eyes. "What the heck. We'll do something unusual and have coffee out. After all, what could possibly happen?"

Chapter 7

Turning a New Leaf

The Carlton Mall was a massive expanse of parquet floors, accentuated with large, built-in white tile planters that children gravitated toward, to walk along tight-rope style. There were full-grown trees in some of the planters, perhaps the lone survivors of the forest that occupied this piece of land during my childhood.

My mother and I strolled over to the nearest "You Are Here" map to locate The Beanery. I knew it was upstairs, but the place was not close enough to allow us to simply follow our noses. The restaurant was indeed on the second floor, at the precise opposite end of the mall. We decided to check out the current displays in the open space on the first level before going upstairs.

The sales topic du jour was apparently hotel art — paintings you'd normally expect to find in your hotel room, since they were too ugly to tempt anyone to steal them. My mother and I scanned the artwork as we ambled past.

Near a limestone sculpture, which looked like an enormous oval sponge that was being wrung out for all eternity, was a young woman seated on a director's chair next to a portable easel, doing caricatures of passersby. The artist looked to be in her late teens or early twenties. Her hair was in a zillion braids of haphazard lengths, and she wore loose-fitting black shorts and tank top.

My mom looked at the artist and muttered to me, "If a woman doesn't want to wear a bra or shave under her arms, she should at least wear sleeves."

"Is this sage mother-daughter advice? I'd better write it down before I forget."

The artist noticed our glances in her direction and called out to my mom to ask if she'd be interested in having her caricature drawn.

Mom, who rarely even allows her picture to be taken, abruptly said no. The artist then turned her hopeful eyes to me. I smiled but said no. Few things strike me as less tempting to hang on my wall than a drawing that looks like me, only more so. Nonetheless, I stopped to appraise her work, for, as a cartoonist myself, I'm always interested in scouting the competition.

She had a couple of dozen pictures on easels and propped against the cement stand that supported the crescent sculpture. She used a felt-tipped pen and drew with crisp, confident lines. Her work, for the most part, seemed quite good, though that was hard to judge without the subject in front of me. Then one of her pictures caught my eye. It was a drawing of Roger Lillydale mounted on a sheet of red matt board. I picked it up off its stand.

My mother, who had been studiously keeping her back to the cartoonist lest the young woman capture Mom's likeness without her consent, peered over my shoulder. "He's certainly a handsome man."

The artist rose and glanced over my other shoulder. "Yeah, that guy was a difficult subject. He had such well-proportioned features, there wasn't much to exaggerate. I'll sell it to you for half price."

"Did you do this one recently?" I asked, setting it down.

"About half an hour ago. He was just biding his time, sitting on the bench over there. I did it on spec, but he told me he didn't like it."

"Do you know him?" my mother asked me.

I nodded, confused. Half an hour ago? Just an hour or so ago, his wife had claimed he was out of town. Sheila had also said she'd called him, so that pretty much eliminated the possibility of Roger having lied to his wife about his whereabouts. The Lillydales must have separated or something, and Sheila was covering up out of embarrassment. "He's my neighbor. I've been wanting to talk to him."

The artist pointed with her chin toward JCPenney. "I think he went that-a-way."

"Thank you." I grinned at my mom and started off in the direction the artist had indicated. "Come on, Mom. The game's afoot."

"Uh-oh." She followed me in a half-hearted, gluefoot gait. "What game?" With her long legs, she could outstride me whenever she wanted to. She just needed to be encouraged.

"We're going to take a slight detour through the department store."

Mom promptly pulled up short a few feet from the entrance to JCPenney. "Aren't we going to The Beanery for a cup of coffee?"

"We are, afterward. This is important. This man was Helen Raleigh's closest friend in the neighborhood. If I can find him, I might be able to help Tommy Newton learn Helen's . . ." Oops. I'd spoken too quickly and there was no way out of this sentence without divulging some of the information Tommy had asked me not to reveal. "Real identity," I mumbled.

"*Real identity?* You mean, the woman who was killed in your yard wasn't your former home owner?"

"It was the former owner, but her name wasn't really Helen Raleigh. That was a pseudonym."

Mom hadn't moved her feet and was now scanning my face with her lips pursed. Rats. This was like trying to convince my children to taste broiled eggplant. "You've seen Roger's likeness, so you can help me find him. Let's split up, circle the store, and meet back here at the entrance."

"And what do I do if I find him? Latch onto him and drag him to the entrance till you get there?"

"No, just say, 'Hi, there. Aren't you Roger Lillydale? My daughter has something important to speak to you about, and she'll be here momentarily.' "

With a heavy sigh, my mom shuffled off, muttering to herself about how my sister Bethany never requested things like this of her. Which was true, but then, Bethany was an efficiency expert who lived in Chicago. Were she here, she would no doubt suggest that we have Roger paged. That would have been more efficient, but less fun and harder to explain to Roger — if we managed to locate him.

My half of the store yielded no Rogers, and Mom took so long to return to the entrance that I started to get hopeful she had located him. Moments later I spotted her heading in my direction. She gave me a happy little wave. She was carrying a shopping bag. I then realized I'd made the tactical error of assigning the children's section to Mom's half of the store. Indeed, she had bought a wide-brimmed sun hat for Karen and a one-size-fits-all New York Mets cap for Nathan.

I thanked her and assured her the kids would love them, then asked, "No sign of Roger Lillydale?"

"Well, I didn't get much farther than the children's clothing section. I do hope Bethany has a baby soon. They have the most adorable baby items here."

"Let's at least let her find someone she likes to date before we start talking babies." My sister had gone through a painful divorce last year, the first one in our extended family. She had joked recently that her poor choice in husbands had cost our family a shot at a stint on television. Entire Family Without a Single Divorce — Next Week on Oprah!

My mother was so clearly not into the spirit, I decided to give up my Roger search. We went upstairs.

The Beanery was a combination coffee-paraphernalia shop and restaurant. Until recently, the place had been something of a local hangout for teenagers who lingered over solo cups of plain coffee and the fresh-baked muffins. Over the past several months, however, the restaurant had grown more upscale, no doubt in an attempt to discourage the younger crowd. They had doubled their beverage prices and struck the muffins in favor of scones. In fact, they had gone so European that nearly everything on the menu ended in a vowel.

Taking in the delicious aroma, we entered the restaurant and Mom headed toward an empty table at the back. I started to follow, then froze. Roger Lillydale was seated at a booth along the wall. He was alone.

"Roger, what a pleasant surprise," I said as I strolled up to his table. It generally *was* a pleasant experience to see Roger; however, from his hangdog expression as our eyes met, the pleasure was all mine. Why was everyone on my cul-de-sac treating me like an oversized canker sore?

Mom had doubled back. I grabbed her arm, hoping Roger would at least be happy to meet *her*. People generally liked Mom. "This is my mother, Linda Peterson."

He stared at me blankly, then rose a little and gave a weak smile to my mom as he shook her hand. "Hello. Uh, Roger Lillydale. Pleased to meet you, ma'am."

"Call me Linda."

Roger had classic even features, dark eyes, and seemed to have a perpetual five-o'clock shadow, which only served to increase his brooding good looks. His physical appearance hadn't gone unnoticed by my mother. During her greeting, her voice had been a little more enthusiastic and her smile a bit wider than usual. Mom, a habitual matchmaker, was probably thinking about what gorgeous grandchildren he and my pretty younger sister would have were they ever to meet, fall in love, and marry.

His eyes were still so blank when he looked back at me that I finally figured out he didn't recognize me, which was odd considering we'd spoken at least a dozen times in the last few weeks. "Molly Masters. I live across the street from you. Moved into Helen Raleigh's house a couple of months ago."

"Of course." He shook his head good-naturedly. "I'm sorry I didn't recognize you. It's been a . . . tough week at work. Would you care to join me?"

"Thank you." I ignored my mother's clearing of her throat that meant she'd rather we sit elsewhere. "We'd love to." I plopped down across from Roger and slid over so Mom could sit next to me. I felt a tad guilty about bringing her out on a mother-daughter jaunt only to join someone she didn't know, but this wouldn't take long. Roger had his check in front of him and his oversized cup was on its last dregs. He glanced at his watch.

"Were you waiting for someone?" I asked.

He looked up, a startled expression on his face, as if he'd already forgotten that I was sitting at his table. "Oh. No. Not anymore." He smiled wanly at me, then my mother.

The poor guy was really out of it. He was a salesman and normally had the typical outgoing, energetic "buy-from-me!" personality. Now he was all but staring into space and wringing his hands. His usually neat hair was slightly unkempt, his silk tie had a spot that looked suspiciously like ketchup, and, most telling, his brown eyes had lost their sparkle. He appeared to be a man trying to hide his broken heart.

"Did you hear about what happened yesterday?" I asked him.

Roger nodded. "You were home at the time?"

"Yes, I was downstairs, heard the gunshot, and ran out."

"But you didn't see the shooter?"

"No, I didn't see a thing. Did you know Helen fairly well?" In the corner of my eye, I could see my mother trying to signal the waitress across the room.

Roger shrugged. "Not really, but better than most, from what I could tell. Last year, I broke my leg and took nearly a month off work. I'm an insurance salesman and couldn't get around to make my sales calls." He smiled at my mother and said, "As you can imagine, it makes people nervous to have somebody in a cast trying to sell them liability insurance. They're afraid you'll slip off their porch and sue 'em." Mom chuckled politely, and he returned his gaze to me. "Anyway, Helen wasn't working then either and we got to visiting with each other during that period. I felt sorry for her. She was something of a difficult personality to get along with. Always angry. She seemed like such an outcast."

"I don't know why this restaurant is so popular," Mom interjected. "The service is — Oh, look!" Mom cried with delight. "My friend's back from vacation."

Mom waved at her old friend who had just entered the store with another woman I didn't know, roughly my mother's age. The two women came over, and my mom greeted them warmly, then immediately announced, "I'm sure my daughter and this young man would rather be alone with each other than have little old me with them."

At five-feet-eleven, my mother is certainly not "little," doesn't act or look "old," but she does know how to embarrass her daughter. On that note, Mom excused herself, nabbed the waitress as she tried to pass by — who grudgingly took our orders: espresso for my mom and hot tea for me — and moved with her friends to the far corner of the restaurant.

Roger now bore the anxious countenance of a man being hit on by a floozie. "How's your husband?" he asked the instant my mother was out of earshot.

"Jim's fine. So's our marriage. Don't worry. That's just my mother's way. She wanted to talk to her friends and didn't want me to feel bad, since I was the one who invited her out for coffee."

Roger settled back into his seat with a relieved sigh. "Sheila tells me the police were trying to dig up something in your yard and made quite a mess of things. Did they unbury anything, other than the poodle?"

"You *knew* there was a poodle buried in

the yard?" I cried in surprise. "Everyone told me she never owned a dog."

For the first time, Roger laughed — though it was just a sad chuckle. "She didn't own the dog. I just happened to see it barking on her porch one day, trying to get in. So I rang the doorbell. Helen told me it belonged to her brother."

"Helen had a brother?"

"Yeah, though I never met him." He shook his head. "That afternoon, I came over and she was burying the dog. She was in tears. Seems she'd run over the unfortunate thing when she thought it was inside and didn't see it in her driveway."

The waitress arrived with my tea, and Roger declined a refill. After she'd left, I asked, "So you never actually met this brother, but you saw him over there visiting her?"

"No, just his poodle, that one time."

I felt on edge, as if I was right on the verge of getting at some major clue to Helen's identity. But I did my best to hide this behind my motions of squeezing out my tea bag and taking a sip. "Did she show you any pictures of him?"

"Ah, no." Roger's expression implied he thought my question had been absurd.

"Did you see the brother's car, at least? Or

any unfamiliar cars parked by her house in the past three years?"

"No, she never seemed to have any friends over or anything. That's what led me to realize how lonely she was. After her husband left her and everything."

I blew on the surface of my tea and took another sip. "She told you about the circumstances of her divorce?"

"She told me that her husband left her for a younger woman. That's all."

"She never told you where her ex lives, or whether she got alimony payments, or where they used to live?"

"No, she didn't. You seem to have taken quite a personal interest in all of this. Are you a private investigator or something?"

"No, I write greeting cards." I had obviously been coming on a bit strong with the questions about Helen, so I decided to back off for a while. "Faxable greetings, usually, but I freelance as well. I used to work for a company in Boulder, Colorado, till we moved here for my husband's job. You have a lovely home, by the way. I was over there today, talking to your wife."

His features tensed. "Did she tell you that I've left her?"

The question caught me off guard. "No, but she did mention she'd worried about your relationship with Helen."

"Our *relationship?*" He clenched his jaw, his eyes fiery. "In other words, she told you Helen and I had been having an affair?"

I made no answer, but he grunted in disgust. "That's so like her. She's the —" He broke off abruptly, then leaned toward me and said in conspiratorial tones, "I met Sheila when I was still trapped in a lousy marriage. So now, Sheila thinks I'm a proven philanderer — I cheated with her on my first wife, so I must be cheating on her with someone else." He clenched his jaw, then said, "I've started divorce proceedings, but it'll be a good six months till I'm free." He fisted his hands. "Like the song says, I should've married an ugly woman. Both Sheila and my ex are real lookers, and it got me no place. At least my *ex* didn't cheat on me."

I had to struggle to mask my surprise — which was all but impossible since I'd nearly dropped my cup. "Sheila was cheating on you?"

He nodded, his features still contorted in anger. "Next she's going to take me to court and try to get money out of me."

"I'm so sorry. Since she's a lawyer, you're —"

"Not now, she isn't." Roger's voice was

rife with bitterness. "She had her license to practice law revoked last month."

"But . . . she offered to represent me."

"She is not an honest woman. Certainly not a happy one."

My head was spinning as I tried to make sense of all this. "What's going to happen to Ben? Are you taking custody of him?"

"You'd better believe it. Think I'd trust Sheila with my son?" He rose. "I gotta run. Sorry."

I murmured good-bye and a few words of consolation at his marital predicament, then drained the last of my tea and joined my mother, who took my standing up for a sign it was time to hightail it out of there so we'd be home in time for the school bus. So much for unraveling the mire of the Lillydales' relationship. I glanced at my watch and realized we had time to make a quick stop at Kessler's Plants 'n' Flowers, which was just a block away from the mall, to pick up a new pumpkin plant.

When I mentioned our destination in the car, Mom said, "Uh-oh. Wasn't Nathan's pumpkin plant all right?"

"No, we lost Peter. Cut down in his prime by a heartless shovel."

"Speaking of heartless, it's been weeks since you've mentioned that miserable PTA president you used to go to school with. What's she up to?"

"Stephanie and her kids are spending the summer in Nantucket. She left last weekend." That woman had long been the bane of my existence, and I didn't even like to think about her, let alone talk about her, so I changed subjects. "Is a pumpkin a fruit or a vegetable?"

"I'm not sure. We could always call Bethany and ask. Her undergraduate degree was botany, you know."

"Right." I sighed. I was painfully aware that my sister had been a botany major and, like Mom and my son, had an affinity for all things green and leafy. "If we can just buy a pumpkin plant that's roughly similar, maybe I can convince Nathan that Peter just looks different in all that upturned soil."

"You're going to try to trick Nathan into thinking Peter's the same plant?"

I pulled into the parking lot of the nursery. "I realize it's not the noble thing to do, but Nathan is so sensitive and gets so attached to things, he'll accuse me of intentionally murdering Peter."

We got out of the car and I held the door to the shop for her. "Whew. It's like a hothouse in here," I said as a wave of tropical-like air hit me.

Mom ignored this last comment and, as we made our way down the main aisle of ultraexpensive potted plants, said, "Well, it worked with that goldfish of yours."

"You mean my pet goldfish we had for a couple years? You replaced it with an imposter?"

Mom nodded. "It died almost immediately. As did the next three replacements." She chuckled. "Then remember those pet mice your father brought home for you and your sister?"

"Yeah, though we only had them for a week or two. You told us raccoons must've gotten their cage door open, and the mice all escaped."

"It wasn't raccoons. Your father and I let them out. The pair that lived after the shower incident, that is." I raised my eyebrows, and Mother continued, "You used to let them run around in the bathtub, and your father turned on the shower and stepped in without looking."

All the years I'd envisioned my pet mice running happy and free through the woods. Death by shower. "Thanks. You just convinced me. I'm telling Nathan the truth about Peter."

We found a plant that was a reasonable Peter facsimile, and I handed it to a woman at the checkout counter.

"Can I get you anything else?"

"Just some information. Is a pumpkin a fruit or a vegetable?"

"A fruit. Despite its size, it's actually a berry."

"Ha! I was right! Would you be willing to come to my house for dinner tonight? I need you to tell that to my husband."

She laughed and rang up my small purchase, mistakenly assuming I was kidding about the dinner offer.

We still had nearly fifteen minutes until the bus arrived, so my mother insisted we drive straight to my house so she could "plant Nathan's pumpkin properly and give it a fighting chance." Apparently she didn't see my knowledge about the genus of pumpkins as a sign that I was capable of turning over a new leaf, so to speak.

I got her my spade and gardening gloves, and she set to work while I went out to the mailbox. The cliché about turning a new leaf had caught my fancy. As I strolled down the driveway, I envisioned a cartoon depicting a branch of maple leaves with faces. The eyes on the smallest leaf would be crossed, with dizzy whirls surrounding it and its stem twisted in circles. The little leaf says to its fellow leaves, "Maybe it's just because I'm so new, but it's driving me nuts the way people keep turning me over!"

Just as I'd grabbed a handful of letters, I heard a distant noise that sounded like a cork being popped from a champagne bottle. This was instantly followed by the sound of a window shattering in my house. I dropped the mail in alarm. A gunshot from the woods!

"Mom!" I screamed. She was sprawled face first on the ground.

Chapter 8

Ask a Stupid Question . . .

"Mom," I panted as I reached her. "Are you all —"

"Get down!" she hollered, gesturing frantically at me. "Somebody's shooting at us!" She'd lifted herself up a little in the process. She had no immediately visible injuries.

Where had the shots come from? I glanced up at the house to see what had made the sound of breaking glass. Nothing was broken on this side. I peered around the back corner. One pane in an upstairs window in Karen's room had shattered.

"Did you —" I intended to ask Mom if she'd been hit by any falling glass, but a violent rustling in the bushes from the woods caught my attention.

Some high-pitched voice wailed, "Holy shit! You just shot Mrs. Peterson!"

Without thinking, I charged toward those bushes as fast as my thirty-six-year-old, nonaerobically and irregularly exercised legs could go. As I dashed past, I heard what

141

sounded like a creaky gate hinge from Simon Smith's property. A moment later, Simon's screechy voice cried out, "Caught 'em on my camera, Molly! It's those damned kids! Don't let 'em get away!"

That was, of course, my intention, though I certainly wasn't going to waste my breath on Simon. The loose topsoil slowed the onset of my fifty-yard dash across my lawn, but I managed to get into the woods with quite a bit of speed. Briars and bristly weeds tore at my bare legs. I crooked an arm in front of my face to protect it from the thin, whiplike branches and fought my way through the first thicket.

Two boys who looked to be roughly my height had gotten a head start and were picking their way through the underbrush in an attempt to head in the opposite direction from my house. Though they wore backward-facing baseball caps, telltale red hair was visible beneath the bills.

I grabbed hold of a sturdy branch blocking my path and yelled, "Stop right there, you Newtons! I'm calling your dad unless you can convince me not to!"

The lead runner stopped, glanced back at me in horror, then chucked his gun behind him in the direction of his brother and took off at a dead run. In the dense foliage, he was soon out of sight. These woods were the one part of Carlton that hadn't changed much from my youth. He would soon reach the "nature walk," a five-mile path that wound through the area and had at least a half-dozen outlets. His brother, who appeared to be a young teen, stood frozen with indecision. I lunged toward him. When he caught sight of my charge, he let out a "Who-o-oa," then started to run away.

I leapt over a pair of ankle-twisting fallen branches, only to land on a patch of marshy, uneven ground. My sneakers made "thwock" noises with each step as the mud only reluctantly released my feet. Yet my fury at the thought of my mother almost being shot had me so motivated I wasn't about to let a mud hole slow me down.

Just when it felt as if my lungs would explode from overexertion, I caught up to him and managed to get a firm grip on his T-shirt. He grabbed on to the nearest tree trunk, which caused me to lose my grip and stumble sideways into some bushes. I scrambled to my feet, expecting to have to resume my chase. But, with a flopping gesture of resignation, Tommy's son held his ground. He was standing among the trees in a spot relatively free from underbrush.

He was panting hard, and I had to double

over to catch my breath myself. The leafy, mushy ground swam in my vision. I had to battle the urge to collapse in exhaustion.

"It was . . . Joey . . . not me," the boy said in little bursts of breaths. "Joey pulled . . . the trigger."

"Why were . . . you trying . . . to shoot my mother?" I asked in my own indignant puffs of air. I gathered all my energy reserves, took a huge breath and straightened, glad to see that I had an authoritative inch of height on him. "What the heck were you thinking?"

He looked up at me, briefly caught the full force of my furious glare, then averted his eyes. Though he and his brother now spent considerable time at Lauren's — right next door to my parents — I had yet to be formally introduced to either of Tommy's sons. Aside from the hair color and the faintly freckled complexion, he didn't look like his father. He had that blobby, undeveloped appearance of a young teenager, his shoulders and chest narrower than his waist and hips. He had a receding chin and a mouthful of braces. "We, um, thought she was a raccoon."

"My mother? A raccoon? Oh, come off it!"

"But that's what happened." With his gray eyes open wide, he held his palms out in a gesture of innocence. "We were just messing around with the gun, and we spotted a coon, so we followed it, and we fired at the next gray and white thing we saw. Turned out to be Mrs. Peterson's hair."

"And I'm sure she'd be thrilled to hear her hair described that way. But there was an entire person attached to the hair. So even if she'd been wearing a Daniel Boone cap, it's inconceivable that you could have made such a mistake. Especially not during full daylight. When no self-respecting raccoons would be traipsing through people's yards, I might add. What's your name?"

"Jasper. But like I said, it was Joey who pulled the trigger."

"How old are you, Jasper?"

"Thirteen. My *older* brother is fourteen." He emphasized the word "older," as if that let him off the hook for his role as accomplice.

"Molly?" came my mother's voice in the distance.

"Over here," I called back. "Are you okay?"

"She's fine," Simon answered.

I gritted my teeth at the sound of his voice.

"I helped her up."

A regular Sir Galahad. With James Bond delusions. I returned my attention to the boy. "Well, Jasper, thirteen is certainly old enough to know better than to fire a gun at another person. You two just shot out the window in my daughter's room!" I retrieved the pellet gun from where Joey had chucked it. "I'm taking this thing, and I'm not giving it back to you. I'll turn it over to your father, but as far as I'm concerned, you two aren't responsible enough to ever use it again."

Jasper stuck out his unimpressive chin in defiance. "It's Joey's gun. Besides, all we can kill with that thing is blue jays and starlings. It's too weak to even shoot through a squirrel's hide."

"My mother's hide isn't as thick as a squirrel's. And you could have given her a heart attack, or she could have been injured from falling glass! I have two young children. I can't allow every idiot with a gun to be shooting into my yard. Somebody already got shot to death. Don't you realize that?"

Jasper nodded. He now appeared to be on the verge of tears, but I was on a roll.

"What if the police had been back here, watching my house? They could have spotted you and Joey with this pellet gun and shot you dead on the spot."

"Where are you?" Mom called. I could see the top of her head above some foliage she was pushing aside. And it looked nothing like a raccoon.

"Right here," I answered.

"I helped her up and she's all right," Simon called a second time. Did he expect a merit badge?

"I've got one of the shooters with me." I put my hand on Jasper's shoulder and said firmly, "Come into the house. We're calling your father."

"But what about Joey? He's the one who —"

"We'll leave that to Sergeant Newton to handle."

When our paths intersected, Mom was in the process of brushing Simon's hand off her arm. She spotted us and promptly leveled one of her patented glares at Jasper. "What do you have to say for yourself, young man?"

"Sorry, Mrs. Peterson. I mistook you for a raccoon."

"Oh, bullshit," Mom said, which was stunning, as this was the first time she'd ever cursed in my presence. "What were you doing?"

"I . . . We . . ." Jasper paused, his self-composure breaking to pieces in front of us.

"Joey did it. We were keeping an eye on the place, because it was all so weird the way that Helen Raleigh turned out to be a man in women's clothing, and we —"

"What?" my mother cried, looking right at me. "A man in —"

"Let him finish. I'll explain later."

Simon Smith, I noticed, had not flinched one iota at Jasper's revelation. Simon was currently separating his plaid short-sleeve shirt from the thorny grip of a bramble. The fabric was so thin and worn-out that if he wasn't careful it would rip.

"We couldn't see very well from where we were hiding," Jasper continued. "We thought you were one of his friends and were digging up something important. So Joey fired over your head to scare you off. He didn't mean to hit the window. My dad said last night that Mrs. Masters was gonna be staying over at your house, so we thought nobody'd be there. When we saw somebody, we kind of freaked out."

I glanced at my watch and groaned. "Mom, the school bus has arrived by now. I'm sure they'll go over to Lauren's house, but the kids will be confused and won't know why nobody's at your house."

"I'll go," Mom offered. "By the way, in addition to the new window, we'll need yet another pumpkin plant. When I dove down" — she glared at Jasper — "I landed right on top of it."

I tossed her my car keys and she loped out of the woods.

Simon Smith, who had been watching all of this with considerable interest, now stepped forward to place his pale, bony hand on Jasper's shoulder. Though Simon was a tad taller, Jasper was so much sturdier than the old man that if Jasper chose to, he could plow right over him. The three of us were soon out of the woods and heading across my chewed-up lawn. Jasper shrugged Simon's hand free and led the way.

"What's all this nonsense about Helen Raleigh being a man?" Simon Smith asked me under his breath.

I studied him in profile. His professed ignorance was not convincing. "You already knew that, didn't you?"

"No, I most certainly did not." Simon's outrage at my suggestion was clearly phony.

"Oh, right," I grumbled. "You have all of this high-tech surveillance equipment on Helen's house, but you never realized she was a he."

Simon pursed his thin, wrinkled lips, then said, "Didn't have cameras *inside* his house. Never saw him with his clothes off."

Jasper awaited us on my front porch, but I still wanted to learn more about Simon's relationship with Helen. Simon had concocted this whole front of being a retired CIA agent rather than admit to his ordinary background. Hoping to use his fragile ego to spur him into revealing something, I asked casually, "Not much of a spy, are you?"

"What's that?"

I crooked the gun under one arm and opened my door. Jasper went inside ahead of me, but Simon stopped on the top step, staring at me wide-eyed. I stepped out of my muddy shoes and set them on the porch, then retrieved my mail from where my mother must have stacked it by the door. While flipping through the bills and ads, I said with a shrug, "I mean, here you are, a trained professional spy, watching this person. And you don't even figure out what *sex* the person is?" I turned my back on him and went inside.

"So what if I did know? What of it? I didn't have a damned thing to do with the murder." He stood in the doorway, holding open my screen. He lifted his chin proudly. "I take it you can handle things from here, so I'll be heading home now. Call if you need me." He let the door bang behind him.

I turned toward Jasper, who immediately

150

met me with "You're not really gonna call my dad, are you? He'll *kill* me. We won't ever do anything like this again, and you can keep Joey's gun to guarantee it."

Jasper looked like a scared little boy, and it was all too easy to imagine my son in his shoes — which were, I noted, muddy and were leaving dark brown marks with each step.

"Yes, Jasper, I am going to call your father." He sagged with my words, and I tried to disguise how bad I felt for him as I continued, "But I can guarantee you this: You are going to live through this experience. Let's hope you learn from it, as well. And please remove your shoes before you take one more step."

After calling Tommy, I ripped off the cardboard backing from a packet of construction paper and fastened that over the broken pane with masking tape. Then, having decided to make this as unsocial a visit as possible, I had Jasper sit at the dining-room table with me to await his father while I paid my bills.

It was at least half an hour before a solemn-faced Tommy Newton arrived in his squad car. His only words to his son were, "Get in the backseat. We'll talk later."

151

Jasper silently brushed past us, retrieving his messy shoes en route. Once Jasper was safely in the car with the door closed behind him, Tommy blew out a disheartened sigh. "Sorry I took so long gettin' here. Been looking for Joey. Still no sign of him."

I handed Tommy the gun. "There's a good place for kids to hide where the roof of your garage meets up with the roof of your house. Lauren and I used to hide up there as kids. You can climb the maple tree in back to get to it, and there are only a couple of vantage points where you can spot someone up there."

"Uh-huh. Worth a try." He headed down the porch steps. "Sorry 'bout all of this. Your mom okay?"

"Yeah. The only casualty was a window and a pumpkin plant."

"The boys'll cover your expenses. Just let me know how much it comes to. Tack on a few bucks for punitive damages, as well."

"Tommy," I said, just as he'd started down the walkway, "what's happening with those hunters you've got in custody?"

"To be honest, I got some doubts. They still swear up 'n' down they hadn't fired a shot since the night before and were nowhere near your property."

"What about footprints? There are

marshes and bogs all over the place. Someone trekking through the woods off of the path would have to have left some."

Tommy shrugged. "That's certainly what you'd expect to find, all right. Only trouble is, there weren't any."

When I arrived, the children were seated on either side of my mother on her antique couch. My parents had bought that couch and restored it years ago. The fabric was gold, as smooth as silk, accented by the dark wood carved in an ornate pattern of leaves that ran along the base and up the front of the armrests. It made me nervous to see that the guinea pigs — and especially the notorious Spots — were on Karen's and Nathan's laps, a mere hop away from the seat cushions. They were making quite a racket with their squeaky purrs.

Mom straightened as I entered the room. "Well," she said, smiling. "Karen, Nathan, aren't your cartoon shows on right about now?"

I swallowed a groan. Her intent was to get them out of the room so she could grill me.

Karen looked from Mom to me, then, sensing something interesting was up, said, "I think I'll take a day off from cartoons today."

"Me, too," Nathan promptly chimed in.

Mom sighed, then looked to me for support, but I pretended not to notice and sat down on the love seat opposite them. I was in no hurry to explain why it was that Tommy's son knew Helen Raleigh was a man, but my mother didn't. Instead, I did my best to learn how school went for the kids today. As usual, their answers were all one word apiece, no matter how inventive my question.

Finally Mom said, "So. That was quite an interesting cat that Jasper Newton let out of the bag. Wasn't it?"

"Yes, well, Tommy asked me to keep some things confidential."

"I'm sure he didn't mean for you to keep secrets from your own mother," she sniffed.

"What secret?" Nathan asked.

With Tiger gently held against her chest, Karen scooted off the couch to the floor and said casually, "That the woman who got shot in our yard was really a man."

"Where did you hear that?" Mom and I asked simultaneously.

"At school today," Karen said happily. "Everyone knows."

"Well, I didn't," Mother said, sounding more hurt than ever. She pursed her lips, picked up an emery board, and began to file her nails.

"I'm sorry, Mom. I was just following Sergeant Newton's instructions."

She ignored me.

"Someone's coming out to replace the broken glass the day after tomorrow. Tommy said his sons would reimburse me."

"That's nice." Mom's tone was frosty.

"Somebody broke their glasses?" Nathan asked.

"Sergeant Newton's son broke my window by mistake," Karen explained. She noticed my puzzled expression and added, "Grandma told me."

"Is Peter okay?" Nathan asked.

"No, I'm sorry, sweetie. Peter didn't make it. How about you and I go out together next week and pick out Peter the Second?" Actually, Peter the Third, but no sense going into that now.

Nathan's expression fell, but he nodded.

"Nathan?" Karen said. "If I were you, I'd have Dad take you to the plant store, not Mom. Peter might live longer."

On that note, Karen let her guinea pig run around, then Nathan lost his grip on Spots, who leapt to the floor. Immediately the two furry animals started to do a mating dance around each other. They'd had ample opportunity to discover that they were of the same sex, but hope springs eternal in males of all species, including guinea pigs.

"Look! They're playing ring around the rosie!" Nathan shouted with glee.

"What are they doing, Mom?" Karen asked.

"They're each hoping the other guinea pig is a female," I tactfully explained.

"The guinea pigs have been living on your cul-de-sac for too long," my mother muttered under her breath, filing furiously away at her nails. Shaping them into points, perhaps.

"Do they want to get married?" Nathan asked.

"Yes, though that's called mating for animals." The two little cavies were still purring at each other, but were now, to put it in euphemistic terms, playing an unsuccessful game of leap frog.

"Let's separate the two of them so they don't develop some sort of identity crisis, shall we?"

We got the squeaking guinea pigs back into their own cages, and now I insisted the children watch their hour of cartoons. In the meantime, I had a heart-to-heart with my mother. She admitted she couldn't fault me for following police instructions, and I told her about the hunters Tommy had arrested. We agreed that if hunters were truly venturing this close to the Sherwood Forest subdivision, things were very amiss indeed.

I decided to take some action, but the only immediate "action" I could come up with was to find out who was in charge of guarding those woods against hunting. That led to my calling the Fish and Wildlife division, which eventually got me only as far as having a phone conversation with a park ranger. The ranger assured me they were well aware of the shooting that had taken place on my property and were going to step up security to prevent anyone bringing a firearm into those woods.

While this was better than nothing, it wasn't much better. It occurred to me, after I'd hung up and brooded over the phone for a while, that Mom had connections with some sort of nature group that regularly met in those troublesome woods. If I asked about the group now she'd know my ulterior motives. I could get the name during dinner.

In the meantime, I went downstairs to my temporary office. Needing an outlet to vent my frustrations, I drew a teacher in her classroom, hands on hips as she locks eyes with a student — who looked suspiciously like Jasper Newton. The teacher says, "Well, Billy, for twenty years now I've told my classes there's no such thing as a stupid question. But *your* question has just proved me wrong."

Jim seemed tired and a bit cranky when he arrived home that evening. During dinner, after the children had excused themselves and raced upstairs to play, I asked Mom about the group. They were a group of botany enthusiasts — called "Fond of Floras."

"Oh, that sounds fascinating," I lied, resting my elbows on the cherry wood table. "Maybe I should join them, on a trial basis."

Both my mother and Jim looked at me as if I'd just suggested I intended to flap my arms and fly to the moon.

"How would I go about joining?" I pressed on, undaunted.

"They meet at the west entrance to the park at noon on weekdays," Mom said slowly. "They hike for half an hour, recording the types of vegetation they spot, then they stop for a picnic lunch, and hike out afterward. But I dropped out of the group because they were so boring."

Jim set down his fork and stared across the table at me. "You want to join a group of amateur botanists? Molly, who do you think you're kidding?"

"Whom," I corrected.

"You think this group of wildflower enthusiasts may be packing rifles?"

"No. But the shooting occurred in the early afternoon. They might have seen someone."

"And, of course, it wouldn't occur to you to leave this matter to the police."

"I've heard officer after officer on TV say they can't do the job alone, that they need responsible citizens to help police their community. So I think —"

"I'm free for lunch tomorrow," Jim interrupted. "I'll go with you."

My mother looked at him in surprise. He shrugged. "Molly fancies herself as the friendly neighborhood sleuth, and I figure, if ya can't beat 'em, join 'em."

Chapter 9

Put Those Back
Where You Found Them!

"Grandma's" school bus stop was just two driveways down from Lauren's house. The next morning, since the weather was so nice, I ignored my children's groans that being seen at the bus stop with their mother was "*so-o-o* embarrassing" and waited with them. To my pleasant surprise, Lauren came out with Rachel just as the bus arrived. Lauren looked a little under the weather and was wearing a plain purple T-shirt and jeans instead of the usual attractive, semiformal attire she wore to the office.

"Heading out to work soon?" I asked her as we waved good-bye to our children.

She shook her head. "Remember how I called in sick yesterday when I wasn't?" Her voice sounded awful and her nose was red and sore looking.

"Uh-oh. You actually came down with something?"

She nodded, rolling her eyes. "Instant

karma got me but good." She coughed into the crook of her arm. "But, on the positive side, I managed to turn this into a life's lesson for Rachel. 'See how Mommy's suffering?' " Lauren said in a Mister Roger's voice, wagging her finger at me as if I were her nine-year-old. " 'Mommy told a lie yesterday. See what happens when people tell lies?' "

I laughed at Lauren's embellishment. She sneezed and blew her nose. She had what looked like half a box of tissues in her hand. We began to walk slowly toward our homes.

"When I called in, the principal told me the other part-time secretary wanted more hours on her paycheck anyway." She paused at the base of her driveway. "I'd invite you in for a cup of coffee, but I'm so germ-ridden you'd be safer keeping your distance."

Despite this sound logic, I so wanted to spend some time with my friend that I replied, "Oh, I like living on the edge. Besides, if I'm going to catch it from you, you were more contagious yesterday when we were together than you are today."

"True." She sneezed again. "But I'm more pathetic and miserable today," she said in a froggy voice. "Then again, you know what they say about misery loving company." She wiggled her eyebrows.

Lauren led me inside her house and poured me a cup of coffee, which I drank while we sat on the padded bar stools at her kitchen counter and chatted. Tommy had found Joey hiding on the roof, precisely where I suggested he look. I mentioned to her that it was reassuring that teenagers of a different sex and generation could still follow the same patterns she and I did when we were teenagers. That reassurance was short-lived, as Lauren promptly reminded me of some of the stunts we pulled as teens. She went on to tell me that Tommy had been so angry, he'd grounded his sons till further notice. He'd told them he didn't feel they had the maturity to be trusted alone and wouldn't burden Lauren with their guardianship, so he'd taken them to their house and said he was going to hire an after-school baby-sitter.

I winced. "A baby-sitter for a thirteen- and fourteen-year-old? That must have humiliated them to the core. Do you think he'll actually go through with it?"

"Not for long," Lauren replied. "He has an elderly neighbor who used to watch the boys when they were younger. Tommy will probably insist they help her around the house till school's out at the end of the week. They're counselors at summer camp, which starts in two weeks. I doubt he'll make them miss that, unless they screw up a second time."

Lauren had a painful-sounding coughing attack. She really did look miserable. Unlike *my* daily routine, she put on light touches of makeup that flattered her pretty, round face. But her only remarkable features this morning were her sore nose and parched, cracked lips. Even her brown hair had lost its normal sheen, its shoulder-length cut now looking as though it had a permanent case of static electricity. She cleared her throat, then asked, "How are your kids handling all of this?"

"We've done a pretty good job of answering their questions as they come up, while making sure they know we've got everything under control. Which, of course, is a crock. I aged two years yesterday when I thought my mom had been shot. Nathan has been more concerned about the loss of his pumpkin plant than anything else. Child psychologists would probably tell me he's redirecting deep-seated fears."

I reflected momentarily on my mental image of the two children as they headed to the bus stop this morning. "They're such opposites."

"Karen and Nathan?"

"Nathan's afraid to take risks. Sometimes his posture is so forlorn — shoulders slumped, head down, as if he's walking through a never-ending storm, and there's nothing I can do to shield him. And Karen's essentially skipping along joyously through life. She's like the heroine in a Disney cartoon, all goodness and light, friend to all the wounded forest creatures. I'm afraid she's developed the perfect-child syndrome — that she'll develop an eating disorder or run off with a drug addict on a motorcycle when she's in her teens."

Lauren gave me a sad smile. "That's one of my worst nightmares, too." She refilled my cup. "I'm so glad I invited you over this morning," Lauren said, blowing her nose. "Now I'm not only sick, I'm depressed."

I chuckled. "Solving a murder is so much easier and better defined than parenting. That's why I can't force myself to keep out of Helen Raleigh's murder. The thing is," I said, resting my head on my hand, "Tommy said there were no footprints from the main footpath to my property line, where our man Helen was shot from."

"Which tells you what?"

"The killer had to have approached from our end of the woods, where there's that hill to the left and the ground stays firm. He or she got into the woods directly from our cul-de-sac itself, or, more likely, to escape being seen carrying a rifle, the person parked alongside that road on top of the hill."

"Kings Way? The one that dead-ends into the west entrance of the park?"

"Right. The killer would have had only a short distance to travel to reach my property line through the woods."

"But how would someone have known Helen was going to be in your yard?"

"Helen's car was parked right outside my house. Anyone in the neighborhood would have known."

"Especially Simon the Schizophrenic Snoop," Lauren added.

"He supposedly wasn't home. Unless . . ." Thinking out loud, I continued, "He claims he was called out on a bogus errand. Helen taped up his camera lenses, and he's supposedly got it all on video, so that part of his story must be true. But he could have gone into the woods from his backyard, and nobody would have seen him."

"But wouldn't *you* have seen him drive away afterward, since his alibi was that he wasn't home?"

"Oh. That's right," I said, thinking. "He could have driven around the corner earlier and parked back on Kings Way. In fact, the more I think about it, that almost has to have been the escape route. I've got to build myself a map here, so I can figure this out."

I built a simplistic relief map of the surrounding area, using an upside-down saucer as the hill to the west of my subdivision with a knife alongside it as Kings Way, a place mat as our entire Sherwood Forest housing development, a napkin as my property, a spoon as the cul-de-sac, and a fork as the footpath in the woods. Then I used a salt shaker as Helen and a pepper shaker as the killer. Moving the shakers through my map, I could still see no other scenario. Somebody would have seen the killer run through their yard after the shooting if he'd come out of the woods into the development, and there would have been footprints if he'd escaped via the footpath that led deeper into the woods.

"There are only two possibilities," I said. "Either someone from my immediate neighborhood spotted Helen or her car, drove over to the knife and parked, trekked down the saucer, shot him, then trekked back up the saucer and drove off, or someone in the woods had been watching my napkin, waiting for the opportunity to shoot the salt shaker."

"You're sure it wasn't a hunter who

parked along the knife and didn't realize they'd ventured right onto the edge of the napkin?"

"It's remotely possible, but Helen was wearing bright clothing and was right next to the house." I moved my cup onto the napkin beside the Helen salt shaker to serve as my house. "It would've had to be a moronic and blind hunter."

We sat in silence for a moment. At the mention of Helen's clothing, the murder scene had become all too real to me again . . . the gunshot ringing out, the blood. I shuddered at the memory of Helen's wig and lifeless face suddenly appearing on my window-well cover.

Lauren said, "I'm going to ask Tommy, casually, of course, if he's talked to anyone who lives on Kings Way about cars parked there."

"That'd be great. Jim and I are joining the 'Fond of Flora' lunch group today. I want to see if any of them have seen anything suspicious around our end of the woods."

"Suspicious? Such as a guy wearing camoflauge clothing and carrying a smoking rifle?"

"Yeah. That'd be perfect."

By the time the noon hour rolled around,

I was dressed in my best notion of what a flora fan-a should wear: sneakers, full-length jeans — in case any of the flora had spearlike projectiles — and a green T-shirt, so that my fellow FFs would think that was my favorite color and hence the affinity for foliage. I slung the strap of a pair of high-powered binoculars around my neck. My hope was that the tour group would think I was a combination birder/floraer. The binoculars were actually to scope out how far away from my property the killer could have been to still spot Helen near my house.

To my surprise, Jim arrived right on time. This was something of a miracle, as tardiness is to Jim as joke telling is to me. My mother had packed us sack lunches. That was sweet of her, but I began to worry that if we stayed here much longer, she'd be laying out my clothes for the morning.

As we headed to the park, I told Jim to pull over on the shoulder of Kings Way so we could look for evidence to support my theory. I raced out and noted, to my disappointment, that the farmhouse directly across the road had large, dense trees that blocked the view of our car. The killer could have parked right in this spot, and the car would have been seen only by someone driving down this dead-end to reach the park. I checked the shoulder for telltale tire tracks. There were tread marks all over the place.

We drove the rest of the way to our meeting place, parked, and walked up to the only other people there. They were indeed the Fond of Floras. Except for one couple who looked to be in their forties, the six additional members were all white-haired folks: four women and two men.

A thin-haired, to put it kindly, elderly woman introduced herself as "Judy, our tour leader" and, "as new members to our little group!" asked Jim and me to introduce ourselves and state the reason we were here today.

Jim and I exchanged looks. The introduction part was easy, but we could hardly admit we were here to look for murderers, rather than wildflowers.

Jim then piped up with, "I'm Jim Masters and this is my wife, Molly." Then he held out his hand to me as if he'd done his half of the talking, now it was my turn.

"Yes. We . . . have always felt a kinship for plants. And we're hoping to . . . see some new ones today."

Jim furrowed his brow, an expression that meant, "That was really stupid," and I raised my eyebrows back at him in response

169

— a silent, "Well? You could've jumped in there anytime." To which Jim raised one corner of his lips, which meant, "You got us into this, not me!" and turned his back on me. One of the joys of long-term marriages. Now we were utterly ticked off at each other, having argued without exchanging a single word.

Our tour leader, Judy, then said, "Welcome to the Fond of Flora club. Remember, Mr. and Mrs. Masters, we don't pick anything."

I'll be sure to keep my fingers away from my nose, I thought sourly. If nothing else, maybe this outing would inspire a cartoon gag — a mother, presented with a handful of wildflowers, admonishing her children to "Put those back where you found them!" Or maybe not.

Judy turned and started to walk along the branch of the main footpath that led directly away from the Sherwood Forest subdivision.

"Could we possibly head this way instead?" I suggested, gesturing in the general direction where I was pretty sure my house was located.

"Oh, sorry, Molly," our tour leader said in a happy voice. "We've gone that way for the last three weeks. Today we're heading this way."

My heart sank. "You're sure you don't want to make it four weeks in a row? I'm sure there's just tons of flora back there. Maybe even a fauna or two."

"Too bad you didn't join our group last month. This way, everybody." She gave a sweeping gesture of her arm and led us the wrong way.

I followed glumly, but quickly reminded myself that the major purpose of this outing was to ask other FFs if they had seen anyone prowling around near my property. During a three-week tour of that vicinity, the chances of one of them having seen someone were somewhat reasonable.

Jim was conversing with a man who, I soon overheard, was the spouse of our fearless leader. Unlike his wife, he had a full head of hair. The two launched into a discussion of radio shows. To my knowledge, Jim had no interest in radio programs unless it was a sports broadcast, yet he did have a wonderful knack for making whomever he's conversing with feel that they're utterly fascinating. Unwilling to feign interest in radio shows myself, I quickened my step and caught up with Judy.

"Look at the lovely trilium!" she announced. We paused to appreciate the little reddish, triangular-shaped flowers.

"Yes. They're great," I responded automatically. I sincerely like wildflowers in general and triliums in particular. It's just that I had my own agenda today. "So, Judy. How often does this group meet out here in the woods?"

With another sweep of her arm, we left the trilium and sallied forth. She didn't answer. Assuming she was hard of hearing, I started to repeat my question, when she said, "Monday through Friday my husband and I come out here, as do Bob and Betsy Fender." She glanced back and indicated whom she was referring to. I followed her gaze, curious to see what the Fenders looked like. They were the relatively young couple. We exchanged smiles. Judy continued, "Unfortunately, the others can only join us on Wednesdays."

"We have bridge club every other weekday," a particularly ancient-sounding voice chimed in from behind us.

The path led us down a hill and into an area that, with another two or three inches of rain, would qualify as a pond. Grassy lumps that resembled miniature haystacks provided us a tentative path through the standing water. I knew from childhood experience that you had to be careful to step on the exact center of each bog or you'd soon be wringing out your socks. "Watch where you step, everyone," Judy said, pointing. "Skunk cabbage."

Those dull green, fleshy plants brought back fond memories for me. As children, Lauren and I used to kick them intentionally, releasing their odor full force. Even with the plants left intact, a skunklike smell permeated the already marshy-smelling air.

As soon as we reached terra firma I told Judy, "I live right back that-a-way, in Sherwood Forest. We've had some . . . trespassers who seem to come from the woods and cut through our lawn. Have you seen anyone hanging around the woods the last couple of weeks?"

"No, I don't think I've seen anyone at all." She stopped and pointed. "Look, everyone. Jack-in-the-pulpit." She lowered her voice and whispered to me, "But you might try asking the Fenders."

I wondered why she whispered this. Perhaps it was out of reverence to the nearby jack-in-the-pulpit. Or maybe, for some reason, she didn't want the Fenders to overhear her suggest that I speak to them. I waited until they caught up to me.

Betsy Fender was short and chunky with dull brown hair in frizzy curls that reached to the nape of her sturdy neck. Her husband, Bob, was tall and thin except for a potbelly. He had a receding hairline, horn-rimmed glasses, and a dark, bristly mustache in such severe need of a trim that it reached past his bottom lip. They both wore high-top sneakers and khaki-colored hiking shorts and tops. We made small talk — he was some sort of computer consultant, she made sleeping bags on an industrial sewing machine in her basement.

In the meantime, we learned about several more wildflowers, which Judy had her husband log into her notebook. At what I hoped was an appropriate point in my tedious conversation with the Fenders, I asked if they'd spotted any possible prowlers in the area, especially near the westernmost cul-de-sac. They said no, except for some teenagers, "truant from high school, no doubt."

"So. You live on Nottingham Court. Which house is yours?" Bob spoke with such intensity that I automatically stepped back from him. "The solid white one? Tan with white trim? *Surely* not the gray with maroon trim!"

"That's the one," I answered slowly, all sorts of warning flags going up at Bob's having identified my house as if to say it was haunted. Bob and Betsy exchanged a look of alarm. "Did you know Helen Raleigh, by any chance? She's the woman who used to own the house before us."

"Oh, yes," Bob answered, his features tight with anger. "We knew her all right. She had an enormous vegetable garden. We spoke to her about it, but our words fell on deaf ears."

"Another ignorant plant killer," Betsy replied, clicking her tongue.

"Excuse me?"

"The woman was a plant killer, like so many others in our society," Bob said.

Plant killer?

"Lunchtime!" Judy trilled. The other FFs promptly set about readying picnic blankets and such. Betsy asked me if I'd join them, which I accepted, despite my common sense, which was shouting at me, "Run fast! These people are maniacs!"

I helped her spread a wool blanket in the requisite large red-and-white picnic plaid. "I don't understand what you mean by calling Helen a 'plant killer.' Are you vegetable-rights activists, or something?"

"We're fruitatarians." She and Bob pulled plastic-wrapped sandwiches from their backpacks.

"We only eat dairy products, nuts, fruits, grains. Those things that don't involve killing purely for the sake of our sustaining our own bodies." Bob held out his lunch for me to inspect. His voice and demeanor had reverted to the earnestness he'd portrayed when we first met. "These, for example, are cheese and tomato sandwiches."

"I see. So you're opposed to —"

"The consumption of carrots. Potatoes. Lettuce, as it's commonly harvested." Bob plopped down onto the blanket and Betsy followed suit.

"There's no reason the whole plant has to be killed." Betsy's voice was confident and animated.

Uh-oh. Vegetable vigilantes.

She looked up at me and patted a spot on her blanket, indicating I should sit. "You're welcome to share our lunch if you forgot your own."

Just then, Jim handed me my brown paper bag containing my lunch. He was obviously preparing to introduce himself to the Fenders and join us, but I was so perplexed by their philosophy I ignored him. "But . . . you don't consider taking all of the tomatoes off of a tomato plant maiming?"

Jim did a double take at me as I said this, then changed course and headed off to sit with Judy and her husband. The coward. I sat down as far away from the Fenders as possible without revealing my uneasiness. I had no idea what Mom had packed for me, but I doubted it would pass the fruitatarian standards, and I had no idea what kind of a reaction that would cause on the part of the Fenders. If he showed as much hostility toward me and my lunch as he had at the mere mention of Helen Raleigh and her gardens, I could be in trouble.

"We do our best to respect the rights of the tomato plant. We always leave some tomatoes intact." I watched him take a bite of his sandwich, curious as to how he could avoid a mouthful of mustache. He parted his mustache, using his fingers like windshield wipers for mustache hair. Grossed out, I turned my vision toward Judy.

"After all, one does have to eat *something*. Don't you agree?"

"Yes. Sure."

Bob and Betsy gave me a smile as if they had converted me to fruitatarianism, but of course, I only meant that people had to eat — which was a no-brainer.

I grabbed my sandwich out of my bag. What luck! Peanut butter and jelly! I bit into it proudly.

"The lumber industry kills trees." Bob jerked his chin in my direction. "You should rethink your use of paper bags."

So much for my juice box. I pulled it out, stabbed the straw through its designated foil dot, and took a drink. "You must live in a brick house. Is all your furniture plastic?"

"We had our home custom-made. Our house is brick, as a matter of fact, and we hired a contractor with the special instructions that all of our trim was to be recycled wood or cut from branches."

"You met Helen Raleigh to discuss her garden?"

"Absolutely," Bob answered, setting his jaw. "At least most people have corn, peas, green beans. Those aren't so bad."

"The basic plant isn't killed, you see," Betsy continued on her husband's behalf.

"Yes, I understand your point."

"Exactly." Bob grinned at his wife and said, "She understands. Helen Raleigh, however, treated us like . . . raving lunatics. We were using our guaranteed right to free speech. We have a different opinion from the majority. But that doesn't mean you have to abuse us."

I felt a sharp prick on my forearm and swatted a mosquito. As I wiped the tiny carcass off of my palm, I realized what I'd done. Indeed, both Fenders were staring at me in horror, as if I'd just killed a tiny puppy. According to their philosophy, I should have just broken off the mosquito's nose.

"Helen *abused* you?" I heard footsteps and glanced back. Jim was approaching. I tried to catch his eye to signal that this wasn't the best time to interrupt my conversation, but Jim was looking down.

Betsy scoffed. "Mrs. Raleigh was the most abusive gardener we've ever met. Wouldn't you say so, dear?"

"Absolutely. Definitely."

"So you knew her well?"

"Hi. I'm Jim Masters. Molly's husband."

"Bob and Betsy Fender," said Bob, shaking Jim's hand.

"They're fruitatarians," I warned quickly before Jim made himself too comfortable in their midst. "They don't believe in the killing of either vegetables or animals for human consumption."

Jim grinned and said, "Are you —"

He was about to blurt about this being a joke, which would completely foil my attempts to learn more about the Fenders' relationship with Helen Raleigh, so I cut him off. "I think they have some very good points," I said, sending nonverbal signals to Jim that he was not to thwart my interview with these nut-eating nuts. "I, for one, plan to give up weeding my garden. After all, you can't decide that it's morally wrong to uproot and destroy vegetables, all the while content to lead to the wanton destruction of their weed brethren."

Jim was having a hard time fighting back a smile. He cleared his throat. "So, let me get this straight. It's fine to eat dairy products, fruit, wheat products, and so on."

"There have been very accurate, scientifically researched studies that show how distressed plants are — and by the way, Betsy and I like to refer to them as plants, not vegetables, that —"

"Right," Betsy interrupted. "You wouldn't refer to a calf as a veal cutlet, after all. Referring to plants as vegetables implies their only function in this world is as food."

Bob shot a look at his wife, which seemed to telegraph "shut up." "As I was saying, studies have shown that plants actually send out pain signals when —"

"Broccoli screams when its head is cut off," Betsy interjected. Bob harrumphed, and she gave him a wan smile. "Sorry, dear. I didn't mean to interrupt."

"The sap flows, just like blood from a severed head." His eyes, already enlarged by his thick lenses, widened as he spoke. I fought an involuntary shudder. "So our point is that we have to be kinder, gentler to our plants. That a plant life is every bit as valuable to that plant as an animal life is to that animal, or a human life is to a person."

"If, as you say," Jim said, "vegetables feel pain, despite having no nerve endings, isn't it —"

"Just because the composition of their bodies is different from ours," Bob interrupted, his voice once again betraying a fierce and unexpected burst of anger, "is no reason to conclude that they don't feel pain! An alien who lands on this planet may not have nerve endings either, but can you guarantee that he won't feel pain if you hit him with a baseball bat?"

Jim merely furrowed his brow and gave no answer. At length, he continued, "Still, isn't it kinder to put a veg— a plant to a swift, painless death than to keep . . . plucking its nuts and fruit off?" Jim grinned. "You've got to admit, Bob, it would hurt if someone were to pull off *your* —"

"Jim!" I admonished. He stopped abruptly and lifted his eyebrows at me, but I ignored him and focused my attention on Bob. "I'd like to hear more about your confrontation with Helen Raleigh."

"That woman has the mouth of a trucker!" Bob growled.

Betsy widened her eyes and edged toward me as if she were about to relate her favorite anecdote. "We were merely walking along the edge of the woods when she happened to be digging in her garden. We called hello, and she was a little startled, I guess. We must have surprised her, coming out of the woods behind her house like that."

They must have emerged from right where the shots had been fired, I thought, as Betsy continued, "Bob was just trying to inform her of the callousness of her gardening ways. Most times, people just don't stop to realize that plants have the right to life, too."

"She threw a cantaloupe at me!"

"At least it was a fruit," Jim muttered.

"We were so glad to see she'd sold that property," Betsy continued. "We remarked to each other just last week how nice it was that the new owners weren't into vegetable gardening."

"You'd probably like our kids," Jim said. "We can't get them to eat vegetables to save their lives."

"Good for them," Bob said.

"Okay, team," Judy called out, rising. "Time to go."

Jim hopped to his feet and held out his hand to help me up. As I took it and got up, he gave my hand a firm squeeze and said, "Let's not monopolize Bob and Betsy's time, okay, dear?" As he spoke, he gave me a look that meant, These people are insane! Let's get out of here!

Though I shared Jim's assessment, I needed to know more about their relationship with Helen before I felt justified in calling Tommy Newton to turn them in as possible suspects.

"Oh, for heaven's sake," Betsy said, grinning broadly at Jim and me, "we don't mind in the least."

"Quite the contrary. Really," Bob seconded.

"I must say," Betsy said with a chuckle, "I'm utterly delighted to have met another couple with whom we have so much in common!"

Chapter 10

Take Turns Blowing on His Face

"So, what else did Helen Raleigh do to you poor folks?" I asked with as much sincerity as I could muster.

Jim gritted his teeth and groaned — though quietly enough that it was unlikely the Fenders heard. I ignored him as I kept my vision locked on Betsy. I hoped my expression looked suitably guileless and sympathetic.

The two Fenders exchanged unreadable glances.

Bob pulled on his wallpaper brush of a mustache. "Nothing else, really. But that's simply because we never gave her the chance. She aimed that cantaloupe right at my face!" Bob's whining voice sounded like that of a little child, tattling on an older sibling.

We started our trek homeward in earnest, with tour-guide Judy in the lead and the four of us at the tail end. "Look at the lichen," Judy called out, gesturing at a rotting log. "Notice the size and color."

I made the appropriate appreciative murmurs as I stepped over the lichen-laden log. "That's terrible," I said to Bob. "Did you file assault charges against her?"

"No, though we certainly could have."

"We're so lucky!" Judy cried. "Look, everyone! A bloodroot in June!" She pointed and veered off course to waddle up a hill toward some small, white flowers. The others ahead of us followed.

"We saw the bloodroot last week, didn't we, Betsy?"

She nodded.

"Let's just go straight, then." The four of us continued along the path. Bob turned to me. "That former home owner of yours broke the frame of my glasses in two. I sent her a bill for my replacement frames, but she didn't pay. We decided to turn the other cheek."

"So you didn't talk to her again? Or insist that she pay for your glasses or doctor bills?"

"No," Betsy answered. "We try to lead by example. If someone can't see the error of their ways, there's nothing you can do but wait and hope the person comes around eventually."

"That could be a motto for the way we live our lives, couldn't it, Betsy?"

"It sure could," she said proudly.

"A regular Joan of Arc," Jim whispered.

"Toadflax!" came Judy's distant voice.

Though we stayed with the Fenders for the rest of the tour, we learned nothing more about their relationship with Helen. Apparently, some foul language and the one melon chucked at Bob was the extent of their face-to-fruit dealings.

Once we had finally shut the doors of our Jeep behind us, Jim immediately said, "That was fun. We should do lunch more often." He started the engine. "Along with our good friends, Bob and Betsy Fender-bender."

I thought for a moment. "Can you imagine them in the vigilante role, willing to murder a human being for the sake of saving the life of a vegetable?"

"Not Betsy," Jim answered, looking behind his shoulder to back the car out of its space. "I can't picture her handling a rifle, let alone pulling the trigger. That Bob's another matter. The guy's certifiable." Jim furrowed his brow as he shifted into gear. "You didn't have to be so nice to them. How are we going to discourage them from thinking we've become friends for life? These people know where we live!"

"We'll just have to move into my parents' house permanently."

Jim shot me such a horrified look, I had to laugh. "Just kidding."

At my request, he dropped me off in front of our house, then left to return to work. I planned to stay at home just long enough to make sure everything was all right, then walk to Mom's.

As I started up the walkway, I spotted Simon Smith on an aluminum extension ladder. He appeared to be removing the dome that housed one of his cameras. Curious, I walked toward his cedar fence and watched him. He was wearing the same baggy brown pants and faded plaid short-sleeve shirt as yesterday. He spotted me and sent me an evil glare.

"I hope you're happy," he shouted down in his raspy voice. "Your lawyer served papers on me. So I'm complying. Even though this is my own damned house."

My *lawyer?* According to Roger Lillydale, Sheila's license had been suspended. Maybe she had a partner working for her. "You mean Sheila Lillydale?"

"Yeah. You got more than one lawyer on my back?" Without waiting for my response, he continued, "She came over this morning with a batch of legal writs and rats. She told me I could either remove the cameras or get 'em confiscated." He turned his back on me and resumed his task.

"And she told you I'd hired her?"

Simon gave no response.

"What did the papers she gave you say?"

He rotated a little to shoot me a quick glance in profile from his high perch. "Don't play Miss Innocent with me! She's acting on *your* behalf."

Not necessarily, I thought. "Have you got a copy of those papers I could take a look at?"

He stopped his work and looked down at me. "In case you haven't noticed, I'm busy right now. Get your own damned copy. And tell that Joanne Abbott friend of yours to back off, too. Woman's a lunatic. I already got the cameras on her side down, but is she grateful? Ha! Threatened to wring my neck."

Simon turned back to his task, but continued to grumble to himself about how the women in this neighborhood had all conspired against him. I pivoted and headed across the street to the Lillydales'. No one was home.

Though Simon never looked at me, I got the feeling he was paying close attention to my movements as I crossed the street again, unlocked my front door, and went in. First,

I went upstairs to Karen's room to check whether or not the cardboard we'd taped over the hole in her window was holding. It was, and I went back downstairs. The house was quiet and in the same state I'd left it in yesterday. I decided to ignore the possible phone tap and to call Sheila at the business number she'd given me. I located Sheila's business card, sat down at the built-in desk in my kitchen, and dialed.

She answered on the first ring. As soon as I identified myself, she said, "Oh, Molly. I was about to call you. I had my secretary type up some documents that stated you were bringing a complaint against Mr. Smith unless he removed his cameras and —"

"Yeah, that's precisely what he told me happened. He's removing them even as we speak."

"Wonderful. I'm glad I could get such expedient results for you."

"I am, too." *Except . . . was our part in this actually legal?* How I could tactfully inquire about whether or not she had been disbarred? "I ran into your husband at the mall yesterday."

After a pause, Sheila said, "He was supposed to still be in Boston. What time was this?"

"Early afternoon. About one-thirty, I guess."

"I see." Her pitch had dropped a couple of notches. "He came back to town early and didn't let me know. No wonder he didn't call me last night. Was he with another woman?"

"No, but he . . . kind of implied he was waiting for someone who never showed up. I hope this isn't upsetting news."

"It is," she said in a voice choked with emotion. "That's not your fault, though. I'm glad you told me. At least now I know where he is."

"I may as well just tell you this straight out. He told me you'd had your law license revoked. Is that true?"

"No! How dare Roger tell you that!" Her anger was so intense the phone seemed to grow hot in my hand. After a pause, Sheila spoke in calmer tones. "It's true that I butted heads with an obstinate judge last month who *threatened* to yank my license, but we got everything worked out. Roger's selective memory must have omitted that part. You can check my story against the records of the New York State Bar Association if you'd like."

"I'm sorry about the problems you and Roger are having. I don't know what else to say, Sheila. Thank you for handling Simon Smith for me so quickly."

For a couple of minutes after hanging up, I stayed seated and mulled which of the Lillydales' stories was more plausible. My answer was both and neither, in equal measure. Maybe they both were telling the truth as they knew it. All I could tell was that, lately, I didn't care much for either of them. I might actually have to take Sheila up on her suggestion to check her story.

There were few things less enjoyable in this world than having to deal with government bureaucrats, not knowing whom to speak to or what questions to ask. I could just imagine trying to do that in person while dragging the children around with me.

The thought of running errands with the children gave me an idea for a silly cartoon. On a blank sheet of typing paper, I sketched a drawing of a frantic-looking woman with one hand on the steering wheel, the other gripping the back of a child's shirt. The child is hanging out the passenger window to hold onto a dog's legs, and a second child watches in horror from the backseat. The woman says, "This is the last time Fido falls out the window! From now on, when he wants more air, we take turns blowing on his face!"

While I locked up, intending to head to Mom's house, I decided to first check on Simon's progress removing his cameras. Both were down, but as I trudged across my yard, something else caught my eye.

Were those new holes in my yard? I went over for a closer look. There were three newly turned areas of soil and a slight mound of dirt by the back corner of the house on the side yard. I stared at it. Tire treads from the Bobcat had now been partially covered in two distinct places by loose soil. These dirt piles couldn't possibly have come from the one little pumpkin plant my mother had planted yesterday. I didn't notice the new holes and dirt piles then. Someone had dug up my yard again in the last twenty-four hours.

Simon! Those cameras of his were still up last night, so he probably had the trespasser on tape!

I rounded his fence and cut through his front yard to ring his doorbell. No answer. But I was quite certain I'd heard some noise from inside. I rang again. Though his image was distorted, I could see him through the narrow etched-glass window that ran parallel to the edge of the door. He was standing in the entranceway looking through the glass at me, as if waiting to see if I'd go away.

I leaned on the buzzer. Simon finally yanked it open.

"What do you want, Mrs. Masters? I took the cameras down. You want me to move my damn *house* now?"

"No, I need your help." Simon merely sneered, so I added in somber tones, "I need to take advantage of your professional expertise."

That got the desired reaction from him. He lifted his chin and said, "I'm listening."

"Someone's been digging in my yard since yesterday afternoon."

Simon grinned slowly, revealing crooked teeth. Then he made a hissing noise that gradually grew into a full chortle. He slapped his thigh in delight. His pants, I noticed, had permanent-looking bumps from his knobby knees. "I was hoping you'd notice that, Mrs. Masters. And I bet you'd like to know who that person was, wouldn't you?"

"Yes, I would."

Simon continued to laugh, wiping his eyes at the humor of it all — which was totally lost on me. "Happened late last night. Got the whole thing on tape."

"Could you show it to me? Please?"

He shook his head, still smiling broadly. "Nope. Not unless you send me a written apology, cancel all legal proceedings against me, and climb up there yourself to reinstall my camera equipment."

"I'm not going to do that!"

"Then *I'm* not going to give you my tape." He started to close the door in my face.

I reached out quickly and pushed the door back against him. "Fine. Be that way. I'll call the police and tell them you're withholding key evidence in the murder of Helen Raleigh."

"You do that," he said, letting go of the door to wag a gnarled finger at me, "and I'll erase the tape before they get here!"

"Then you'll be destroying evidence. That's a federal offense. You'll go to prison."

Simon growled, then pounded his fist into his palm and cursed about the "damned dames in this neighborhood." In that moment, he looked like Rumpelstiltskin, set to tear himself in two. He threw up his palms and gruffly said, "All right, then, damn it! I'll give you the damned tape! It's the neighborly thing to do, after all."

He pointed to my feet on his cement front porch. "You stay right here and don't take one step into my house. Man's got to have his private space."

After a minute or two, Simon returned

and handed me two tapes. "These are from both cameras. They show the person digging from different angles." Again, he wagged a bony finger in my face. "Don't forget to buy me new tapes. And don't go getting me cheap ones. I only use top of the line."

He started to close the door again, but I asked gently, "You said this happened last night?"

"Yep. The time's recorded in the lower-right corner. Motion detectors automatically activate the camera, so you don't have to scan through a batch of tape of your empty yard."

"Yesterday, you said you got the Newton boys on camera. Are the recordings activated by anyone walking around, clear back in the woods, too?"

"Er, no, it's got to be motion in your yard, near your house. It was your mom out there planting that set it off yesterday. In the corner of the screen you can see the barrel of the gun poking out and the shot being fired."

"How about last night's recording? Wasn't it too dark to make out anything?"

"There's enough light from the street lamp and the beam from my floodlights. It's dark, but you can make out some things.

Tell you this much, it was a man. A tall man. Frankly, till you came over here ranting and raving about it, I just figured it was your husband."

"Well, it wasn't." I indicated the tapes and said, "Thanks. I'll turn these in to the police, but I'll be sure to replace them."

"Damn well better," Simon said and slammed the door behind me.

In my assigned role as a responsible citizen aiding the police, I knew my first step should have been to turn the tapes over to Tommy immediately. I was too curious. Instead I raced home, popped them into my VCR, and scanned backward as I watched a tall man whose back was turned rapidly undig three holes in my yard. Then I watched it from start to finish in slow motion.

I could see why Simon had assumed it was Jim. The man, wearing a dark jacket, jeans, dark shoes, and a fedora, had my husband's tall, thin build. I twice replayed the entire section of tape from the moment the man walked onto my yard until he left, having taken nothing with him. He never picked anything up out of his holes, so whatever he was looking for went unfound. Which was what? Surely not the poodle's body. Money? Gold? Jewelry?

I popped the second tape in, and this one

showed the man's face in a partial profile. Though that at least revealed he was a caucasian, it was just too dark a recording to make out any identifying details. It could have been Roger Lillydale. Could also have been Jim. Or the President, for that matter. Maybe the police would have one of those devices that zoom in on sections of film.

But what could he have been digging for? The police had plowed up the whole area and found nothing.

Perhaps Helen had fed the poodle a map of where the "treasure" was buried, then deliberately killed the dog before its digestive tract could dissolve the directions. That theory might have been a tad far-fetched. But maybe Helen fed the dog a key to a locker that held great riches.

The phone rang. By the sneeze on the other end, I knew it was Lauren before she'd had a chance to say hello. "You're not going to believe this," Lauren went on. "I had lunch with Tommy today and met him in his office. Some paperwork was on his desk and I happened to glance down and see it."

"Yeah, yeah. Remember whom you're talking to here. You don't have to make excuses for snooping to *me*."

"I know, but I feel guilty for doing this to Tommy."

Too anxious to hear what she had to say to come up with a solid argument for her, I merely said, "Ah, guilty, shmilty. What did you find out?"

"Tommy ran a check a few days ago on the social security number the guy claiming to be Helen Raleigh used on documents during the sale of your house."

"Aha! The dragster's identity revealed at last!" I grabbed a pen. "So what was his real name?"

"If the police have that information already, I wasn't able to learn it from the paper on Tommy's desk. There really was a Helen Raleigh with that social security number, though. She was an innocent bystander who got killed during a robbery of a jewelry store in Los Angeles three years ago."

"No kidding?"

Lauren blew her nose, then echoed, "No kidding."

"Three years ago. That was just a couple of months before the man disguised as Helen first purchased this house."

"You got it. But don't let on to Tommy that you know any of this. Or he'll figure out I was the leak and be furious with me."

"The Mr. Helen Raleigh who bought this house must have been the robber and took

198

her wallet after shooting her," I said, thinking out loud. "Otherwise, how could he have known her social security number? Still, you'd think the original loan officer on this house would have run checks and found out Helen Raleigh was deceased."

"Sure, but my guess is it takes a while for those things to clear. Then when it does, your Mr. Helen says, 'Obviously, since I'm alive, there's been a mistake.' And if the house payments keep coming in on time, the whole question about social security numbers falls through the cracks."

"Did they ever recover the goods from the robbery?"

"I have no idea. You'll have to find that out for yourself. Using, I might add, some method that doesn't involve asking Tommy directly about the robbery, since you're not supposed to know about that."

"I wish *he'd* told me about this. He's probably been sitting on this information since Monday afternoon, when I gave him my copies of the real-estate transaction."

Lauren chuckled. "Let's not forget that you're *supposed* to be a disinterested private citizen."

"Oh, that's right. How silly of me to forget. Listen, Lauren, I really appreciate your help."

"Don't mention it. And I mean that literally."

"I won't tell Tommy how I found out about this. In fact, I'm going to the library right now to uncover this information on my own. I'll just tell him I happened to think to run Helen Raleigh's name through the library, and I'll pretend that I'm doing him a huge favor in sharing the news of the robbery with him."

"Yeah, right," Lauren muttered.

"Some man was digging up my yard last night. So, if the man who pretended to be Helen was in fact a robber who had given his partner the slip . . ."

"You think there're stolen jewels buried in your yard someplace?" Lauren asked.

"I'm not sure. But I *do* think somebody else thinks so. The same somebody who shot Helen Raleigh."

Chapter 11

Gesundheit

My new theory was that my former house owner, posing as Helen Raleigh, had been one of the jewelry store robbers. But, if so, why steal his female victim's identity? Maybe he had given his partner the slip and reasoned that his partner would surely never look for him disguised as a woman living in a small suburb in upstate New York. Apparently, the charade had worked for three years. Had the missing partner then found and killed my former home owner? Wasn't it equally possible that the murderer was one of my suspicious-acting neighbors? What about Bob Fender, the vegetable vigilante? What if Bob was the former partner, who'd made up all the hooey about plant rights as a ruse?

Deep in thought, I drove to downtown Carlton where the library was located. Which is not to say Carlton *has* a "downtown" in the classic sense of the word. It's more accurate to call it the busiest and most centrally located intersection within the immediate area.

The library was a good-sized brick building. When I was growing up, Carlton had no library. My mother had to drive us to a neighboring town. Of course, back in those days, Carlton had no fast-food restaurants or grocery stores, either. Those days were long gone. As were the days of lengthy searches involving card catalogs and stacks of old, yellowed newspapers. The library's CD-ROM database included articles from both *The New York Times* and the *L.A. Times*. This crime having occurred in L.A., I should be able to reference it with no trouble.

I parked, then darted through the overly air-conditioned lobby to the nearest empty computer terminal, called up the newspaper database, and typed "Helen Raleigh." Nothing. Not even an obituary. I keyed in "jewelry." And then I selected from the subtopics of "store" and finally "crime." That brought up thirty article headings in descending chronological order. I paged to the end, where a heist from three years ago was likely to be located.

Judging from the newspaper article abstracts, a couple of stories dated June three years ago seemed to concern that particular crime. A bystander had been shot to death and a half-million dollars in diamonds had been stolen. I jotted down the specific editions and page numbers to locate them on microfilm.

I had the small, narrow room that contained the library's microfilm all to myself. One wall supported the gray metal cabinets where the small boxes of film were filed in chronological order. I found both reels from the *L.A. Times* that contained the articles I wanted to read, sat down at one of the five machines opposite the cabinets, and quickly threaded the machine.

Only the bottom two-thirds of the page were displayed on the screen, and I couldn't figure out how to see the top third. I was too embarrassed to seek help. Numerous signs urged patrons to ask for assistance threading the film, but nary a one went on to read: Also ask for help if you can thread the machine but are too stupid to figure out how to view the top of the page.

After pushing and pulling on everything as discreetly as possible — this despite the fact that I was getting frustrated enough to hurl the entire thing through the wall — I eventually banged into the right section of machinery. With the date and page numbers visible, I easily found the first article about the robbery, printed that page, and read:

> . . . A woman patronizing the store was
> shot to death when she stumbled upon a
> robbery in progress. Police are with-
> holding identification of the woman
> pending notification of next of kin.

The two white males, I went on to read,
wore stocking masks to disguise their faces
and were able to escape. They shot and
wounded a security guard and drove off in a
white pickup truck that had been stolen earlier that same day. I needed a picture of the
two men. There was a grainy photograph of
the jewelry store, but no composite drawings of the suspects.

A subsequent article in the next day's
paper reported that the robbers had eluded
police and were still on the loose, and that
they had escaped with half a million dollars
in diamonds. This article reported that the
victim's name was Helen Raleigh, a thirty-
five-year-old who was a newlywed and had
been going into the jewelry store to have her
engagement ring appraised. The suspects
had stolen both her ring and her purse. A
clerk at the store was quoted as saying:
"They shot that poor woman dead, just because she happened to be in their way." It

showed a small picture of the real Helen Raleigh. She did have short black hair, but was much prettier than my former home owner. Still no pictures of the suspects. Blast it! I needed a picture to see if the partner could be anyone I knew.

A third, more recent article recapped the same information in the previous two reports and stated that three other jewelry heists, each in different locales along the West Coast, had been perpetrated by two men wearing stockings over their faces. The FBI had theorized that the robbery of the three jewelry stores could have been perpetrated by the same suspects. If so, they had amassed two million dollars' worth of diamonds.

There, finally, was a series of composite sketches of the suspects. A pair of drawings from the three heists supposedly showed similarities in features. The only similarities I could detect was they all had chins like Jay Leno. The Helen Raleigh I knew and disliked was not recognizable in any of the drawings. Under no circumstances could I say that either drawing looked like Bob Fender, or anyone else I knew.

"Molly," came a deep voice from behind me. I jumped and whirled around in my seat. "I thought that was you."

It was Joanne's husband, Stan Abbott, my neighbor on the other side of Simon. "Stan. Hi. You startled me." I turned back to the viewer and rotated the rewind knob to its highest speed before he could read the screen. "What are you doing here?"

"My office is right across the street. I come over here sometimes during my lunch break."

"Rather late for lunch," I said, glancing at my watch, which showed it to be half-past two. Shoot. The kids would be home from school soon, and I still needed to speak to Tommy Newton. "Were you researching something?"

"No, just happened to be wandering through the library."

Right. Wandering through the microfilm room at the back of the library. Not exactly the route most people would choose for a daily stroll. During their two-o'clock lunch break.

I met Stan's gaze. He seemed to be watching my actions with considerable interest. Stan Abbott was built like a pink Pillsbury Doughboy. He was pudgy and an inch or two shorter than his wife, but always wore clothes that fit him so perfectly they had to be tailor made. He had a broad face, light brown hair, and widely spaced teeth that gave him a goofy — though engaging — smile.

"Going through microfilm, are you?"

"Yes," I said, stuffing this reel into its box. "Old newspaper articles."

He picked up the box the first reel was in and glanced at the side, which identified the two-week period this tape spanned. "Old *L.A. Times* editions, hey? Does this have something to do with Helen's murder?"

"What makes you ask that?"

He didn't answer, just handed me back the tape as if he hadn't heard the question. "Have you heard the scuttlebutt?"

"Scuttlebutt?"

Stan nodded. "The rumor around the neighborhood is that Helen Raleigh was actually a man."

"No!"

He held up his palms in an exaggerated shrug. "That's the rumor." He grinned and shook his head. "Why would anyone do that? Dress like a woman for all that time. Kind of gives you the creeps."

He gave me a look that implied I, too, should be horrified at the prospect, but I was used to dressing like a woman — at least upon occasion. Besides, there were fates much worse than disguising oneself as a woman and living in an upper-middle-class suburban neighborhood. Perhaps one such fate had caught up with Mr. Helen. Plus, if he had shot to death the real Helen Raleigh, he'd met with the fate he deserved.

"Did . . . Helen seem to be hiding from someone?" I asked.

"Hiding from someone?"

"Yes. Was she . . . or rather *he* jumpy, reluctant to meet new people, that sort of thing?"

"Not es—" He stopped, then stroked his chin as if lost in thought. "Now that you mention it, yes. I just naturally took it for shyness, but that could have been exactly why Helen acted that way. Maybe Helen was hiding from the authorities."

"You knew Helen for three years, didn't you?"

Stan nodded.

"You never suspected she was a man?"

"No. I mean, why would I? How could anyone suspect that the woman who happened to live two doors down from you was really a man? Of course, I practically never saw her, except when she was outside working on her lawn or gardens. She did seem to operate that mower of hers pretty proficiently, now that I think about it."

"And mowing the lawn struck you as a masculine discipline?" I asked, bristling. I'd

208

mowed many a lawn in my day and had surrendered that task to my husband only because he felt it was important to cut grass in a diagonal pattern. Jim has never once suggested we *vacuum* in a diagonal pattern, and, to this day, I failed to see the difference.

Stan missed my intonation and added, "Was pretty terrific with hedging shears, too."

The mention of hedging shears brought to mind Betsy Fender's declaration, "Broccoli screams when its head is cut off," and I felt a shiver of revulsion as I pictured contorted facial features on a broccoli sprout. Though light-years from becoming a "fruitatarian," it would be a while till I served broccoli again. The Fenders would be pleased.

"She did have that, you know, deep voice, and thick ankles," Stan continued. "I always thought she was . . . one of the homeliest women around. No offense. I know you women don't like to be compared to one another in terms of your looks."

As he said this, his vision dropped to my chest, which was one part of my anatomy I certainly didn't appreciate having held up for comparison — so to speak. But I let the matter slide and said, "I heard that a couple of the men on our cul-de-sac had been interested in her."

Stan grimaced. "Really? There was Simon Smith, who took a definite shine to her, but who else?"

"I'd rather not say. No sense in spreading unfounded rumors."

"No. No sense in that." Stan's brow was furrowed, as he no doubt mentally ran through the other men on our cul-de-sac, which left only Roger Lillydale and Mr. Cummings, my next-door neighbor currently in Europe. "Hard to fathom either —" He broke off, then gave me one of his goofy smiles.

I rose and said, "Good seeing you, Stan. I'll bet you're glad Simon took down the cameras on your side of the house."

"We're all glad of that." He licked his lips as he stared at the reels in my hand. "What did you say you were looking for?"

I pretended I didn't know he was referring to the newspaper articles and said, while refiling the tapes, "Just a little privacy and peace of mind, like everyone else. Say hi to Joanne for me."

I strolled across the library, wondering whether or not I believed that Stan had simply happened to bump into me. I had parked along the street. If he worked nearby, it was more likely that he spotted my Toyota and was nosy enough to come look for me. Just as I turned the corner to leave, I glanced back and was disconcerted to see that Stan Abbott stood motionless, watching me.

There was a public phone in the lobby. I called my mother, told her I was at the library, and asked if she could please watch the children. I specifically mentioned my current location because my mother was such an avid reader that a visit to the library was the be-all, end-all alibi as far as she was concerned. The truth, though, was that I'd already finished. Together with my two tapes from Simon and my printouts of related newspaper articles, I drove to the police station. Now to pretend to Tommy that I'd discovered on my own the information our mutual, runny-nosed friend had actually given me.

The thought of Lauren in her current sneezy condition brought to mind a cartoon I could draw. A woman has both hands clasped over her mouth, her eyes wide with horror as she stares in front of her where a second woman appears to have been blown backward into a tree by a tremendous wind — her hair is straight back and the tree is stripped of leaves. A man standing next to the first woman simply says to her,

"Gesundheit." Perhaps the card could be marketed as a get-well card.

Tommy's pint-size office was in its normal cluttered state. Tommy was paging through a thick file when I knocked on his glass door. He gestured for me to come in. While I did so, he folded up the file and put it away in a four-drawer cabinet directly behind him. The photo of Tommy's sons and their deceased mother had migrated to the opposite side of his desk. A picture of Lauren was now in its place. I wondered if the relocation of the photographs had been inspired by Tommy's recent altercation with the boys' irresponsible use of their firearm. And was a pellet gun technically considered a firearm? A fire pinky perhaps.

"Tommy, I have some important news about the case." I'd opted to go for the direct approach, rather than first chatting with him about his boys as I would have under most circumstances.

"Uh-huh."

I sat down on the marginally padded folding chair that faced his desk. "You're not going to believe this, but I came across some articles in the library computer system that tell us who Helen Raleigh's imposter really was."

"That so?"

"Yeah. I think the imposter was a robber of a jewelry store in Los Angeles."

Tommy's facial expression was inscrutable. "Uh-huh. And how exactly did you happen to discover articles about a robbery in California?"

"I figured out that with all of this burying of various things in my yard, there had to be some sort of treasure there, which was probably stolen. So I searched for unsolved robberies. Here. I'll show you the copies I printed up." I pulled out the photocopied articles from my purse, smoothed them a little, and handed them to Tommy. While he read them, or at least pretended to read them, I also removed the two tapes from Simon and set those on his desk in front of me.

Tommy scanned the last of the articles, and I was now fairly certain he was merely making a show of reading them, as I happened to know he was one of the world's slowest readers and this had only taken a half minute at best. "Uh-huh. And you searched through the numerous entries and came up with this one, that identifies Helen Raleigh as a victim? That's incredible." Again, he kept his expression blank, but I knew he was thinking that I had to have gotten this information from Lauren. In fact, it wouldn't surprise me to learn that he'd left the file open in front of Lauren because he *wanted* to pass the information on to me, and hadn't been at liberty to do so through conventional means.

"Yes, well, the important thing is that last night, someone dug up my yard again, and Simon Smith caught the guy on tape." I patted the tapes in front of me to accentuate the words.

"You've got an image of the guy's face?" Tommy asked, failing, for once, to mask the excitement in his voice as he snatched up the tapes.

"Well, no, not his face, exactly. You can see a little of his jaw, though."

"Uh-huh." Tommy sounded deflated. He set the tapes back down.

"You know, Tommy, I can't help but notice that you don't seem very surprised by any of this. So that means you must have already discovered Mr. Helen's former occupation. Tell you what. Let's trade surveillance videos, shall we?"

" 'Scuse me?" Tommy said with a sigh. He leaned back in his chair and crossed his thick arms across his chest.

"Surely, in this day and age, you've got the video recordings from the jewelry store's video cameras, right?"

"Yep. But the film is grainy and hard to decipher. Plus the robbers were wearing stockings over their faces."

The image of robbers wearing stockings distracted me momentarily. Stockings were so less common than pantyhose. It would probably cut down on the fear factor for robbers to stuff their heads into pantyhose and leave the empty shriveled nylon leg dangling. "Have you got one of those contraptions that could zoom in on the face recorded on my tapes?"

Tommy scoffed. "You think we've got that kind of high-tech equipment here? This is Carlton. We'll have to take 'em to a crime lab in Albany and let their technicians see what they can do."

Tommy, I noted, had slipped into his friendly country-cop vernacular. "Will you let me look at your tape of the jewelry heist?"

"Nah. I'd have to deputize you first."

"Really?" I perked up at that suggestion. I would love to be made some sort of police deputy. "Oh, Tommy. I thought you'd never ask!"

He gave me a little smirk, but said in flat voice, "Fact is, I got nothin' to gain by showin' you the tapes."

"But I'm your best witness. Except for

215

Roger Lillydale, I knew Helen Raleigh the best. I might be able to pick her out, I mean *him* out, on the tapes of the robbery, even though she's wearing men's clothing. *He's* wearing, rather." My story wasn't true, but I was really curious about what Mr. Helen had looked like when he was a male bank robber.

"That's all right, Molly. But thanks for offering. And for bringing these tapes. I'll let you know if we get anywhere with 'em." He opened his center drawer, snatched up a handful of pencils, and jammed the first one into the electric pencil sharpener on the shelf beside his desk. "Thanks for stoppin' by."

Tommy's nonchalance bothered me. He hadn't poked fun at me for all of my *he* vs. *she* verbal flubbings. That was out of character. I sat there and watched until Tommy had sharpened the last of his pencils. Still, he kept his eyes averted as he blew the dust off of each of them. "You already know who Helen is, don't you?" I asked.

Tommy replaced the pencils in his drawer, laced his fingers, and only then met my gaze. "One of the two masked gunmen fit 'Helen's' general physical build, and he had possession of the real Helen Raleigh's wallet. He was tentatively identified as

Frank Worscheim, a habitual criminal. The second gunman was never identified, but was caucasian, trim, and approximately six feet tall."

"And what about the fingerprints of Helen Raleigh's corpse?"

"*Which* Helen Raleigh?"

"The male Helen who owned my house. Were the fingerprints Frank Worscheim's, or weren't they?"

"Yep. They were Frank Worscheim's."

"So there's no 'tentative' about it," I said testily. "You've IDed him. And what about the poodle?"

"No known criminal record for the poodle."

"Ha. Ha. What I meant was, did you do an autopsy on the dog?"

"It, uh, had been in the ground a bit too long for that. Even Tupperware has its limits as far as keepin' things fresh."

"As my daughter would say, 'Eeww! Sick.' Could you at least tell if the dog could have been run over by a car?"

"Yep. Likely cause of death. Why?"

"That's how Roger Lillydale told me the dog was killed — that Helen's imposter had accidentally run over him in the driveway. But I was thinking that . . . Frank might have shot the dog, for some reason. Maybe the dog's body was just a cover, so that if Mr. Helen had been caught in the act of digging his yard, he could claim he was burying a dog, when he was actually trying to dig up the jewelry underneath."

Tommy shook his head. "We already had to dig down more than three feet to find the dog. If the guy dug a whole lot further, it'd be like digging a well. And we went over your property using a powerful metal detector. It would have detected gold from the jewelry. Didn't come up with a thing. Not countin' your water and gas mains."

"Maybe the settings had been removed so the diamonds wouldn't get traced as easily." A revelation hit me. "What if . . . what's-his-face used the dog as a . . . whatchamacallit? What if he stuck the dog right on top of something he'd hidden? Nobody would think to dig below the dog, right? Did you?"

"Er, no, once we uncovered the dog, we stopped digging."

I rose and grabbed the doorknob. "Now's the time, then. Are you coming with me?"

"S'pose you're going to dig again, one way or the other."

"Yeah."

Tommy stood up and locked his desk. "Let's go, then."

"You're coming, too? Cool. You can help me dig."

Tommy followed me to my house in his cruiser. I toyed with the idea of speeding just to see what he'd do, but quickly decided he might go ahead and ticket me.

After grabbing a large shovel from the garage, we headed to the yard. "So, my theory is what we're looking for is a couple of feet or so below the dog. That Frank Floorshine —"

"Worscheim," Tommy corrected.

"Whatever, had deliberately placed the poodle's body directly over the diamonds so anyone digging would stop there and not think to keep digging."

"Uh-huh," Tommy merely said.

"I remember exactly where the dog was, because I noticed it was exactly where my son had planted a pumpkin plant. And it's right where my mom put in the new one."

The new plant was still decidedly flat and its branches, vines, or whatever you called those green thingama-bobs on plants, were partially broken. So I dug up and tossed the plant without hesitation. I took another couple of shovelfuls of dirt and tried to mentally calculate just how many of these I would have to dig to develop a four-feet deep, three-feet in circumference hole. I could estimate that it would be more than ten and less than a hundred.

"Oh," someone called from the sidewalk. "Good afternoon, Molly."

I turned. It was Joanne Abbott. She must have noticed Tommy's cruiser and come outside to investigate. She took a few steps toward me, nodding at Tommy in greeting, then returning her attention to me. "I see you're digging again. Are you looking for something buried in your yard?"

Tired of these "just happened to be passing bys" on the part of her and hubby, combined with the thought of some ninety-seven more shovelfuls of dirt to go, I was in a less-than-gracious mood. "It just seemed like such a nice afternoon for digging holes. Don't you think?"

She held onto her large nose as if to stifle a sneeze. She gave another glance Tommy's way, then said to me, "Don't forget about the home-owners' meeting tonight. We have a lot of important things to discuss. Did you see that Simon took down his cameras?"

"Yes."

"Well, I won't keep you. Good luck with finding the . . ." She let her voice trail off as if she expected me to jump in there with the name of the mystery object.

"Thanks. I'll see you tonight."

Tommy watched all of this with a mild look of amusement, but said nothing.

I aimed the spade and hopped onto it, jiggling so that it sank in. The soil was still loose enough that getting the shovel pushed in was the easy part. Lifting and tossing was much harder. As I worked away, I paused to note that Tommy was sitting in the shade of the house, watching me.

He grinned at me and said, "Farewell to Pumpkins. Is that the name of a movie, by any chance? Seems to ring some sort of bell with me."

"Are you going to help me dig or just sit there, cooling your heels?"

"Hey. I'm here as an officer of the state of New York. Not an old high school buddy. Keep that in mind."

"And officers don't dig holes?"

"All the time. In fact, most of the time that's my job. Diggin' holes. Or trying to make sense out of existing ones."

"Good." I held the shovel toward him. "Because I think this job requires a professional. This is no easy task. I'll bet you could dig a lot faster than me."

"Prob'ly could. But you're doing fine."

As I wiped some perspiration off my brow, a movement from the window next door caught my eye. "Simon's watching. I'll bet

221

he's pretty surprised that I'm doing all the work."

"Don't exactly see him rushing out here to give you a hand."

I returned to my digging, still determined to shame Tommy into taking over for me. I started singing a line from an old song from my childhood. I didn't know the words, but it went something like, "Yoga Boat Men. Huh!" I sang that over and over, and tossed a shovel full of dirt over my shoulder with every "Huh." Eventually, my song annoyed Tommy so much he yanked the shovel from my grasp and took over for me, which was, of course, the whole idea. He further pointed out that the word was "Volga," after the Russian river, not "Yoga." Picky picky. I liked "Yoga" better.

It proved much more pleasant to sit in the shade and watch someone else work. "Stupidest thing I've ever done," Tommy began to grumble, as he dug deeper and deeper with no luck. By now he was standing in a hole up to his waist. "S'pose I'll keep going long enough and you're going to say, 'Oops. I meant to have you dig six feet farther from the house.' "

"Oops. I meant to have you dig six feet farther from the house," I obliged.

He gave me the evil eye. He was sweating

profusely now in the hot sun and dirt was clinging to the glistening skin on his forearms and face. "Got a septic tank you want me to put in, so long as I'm —" He broke off as the shovel made a dull thud. "Wait. Think I've hit something."

He began to work rapidly, clearing the dirt away with his hands. At length he lifted a cube about one foot long on each side. It was a Tupperware tub. We both fell silent. The container didn't seem to be very heavy.

I cast a nervous glance at Simon Smith's window. Though there were no immediate signs of him, I said, "Let's block my neighbor's view."

We angled ourselves shoulder to shoulder away from Simon's windows. Tommy pulled off the blue plastic lid. Inside was a small bluish gray laundry bag. Tommy untied it, peered inside, then poured the contents back into the tub.

The sparkling sunlight reflecting off thousands of diamonds was blinding.

Chapter 12

Wait Till the Meeting Actually Starts

My nerves were jittery that evening as we sat at my parents' cherry wood table. My appetite was all but gone, though my mother's deliciously seasoned baked chicken with carrots and potatoes was normally one of my favorite meals. In Mom's lone concession to the hot weather, she'd also served juicy, bright red tomatoes fresh from her garden.

Mom was in her customary spot at the foot of the table. Trying not to become entrenched permanently in the patterns of my childhood, I had claimed the normally vacant ladder-back chair next to her and given Jim my sister's seat, which, more recently, had become Karen's spot. At first, Nathan had objected to the change. He loved routines almost as much as my mother did, but I'd managed to appease him by giving him Dad's honored position at the head of the table.

We all dutifully listened as Karen told us at great length about her tadpoles, whose tails were only a quarter-inch long. That quarter inch was all that separated us from needing to build a terrarium, complete with live insects. Actually, *two* terrariums because Karen, always good at sharing, had bequeathed three of the frogs to Nathan, who was determined to keep his new pets in his room. Neither child was willing to accept my compromise of one frog apiece and the rest set free.

"So, Jim," my mother said during a pause, "what's new at your office?"

Jim launched into a lengthy answer rife with acronyms and numbers. My eyes glazed over and my thoughts returned to the image of all of those diamonds. Moments after we'd uncovered them, Tommy had confessed to me that he'd known for two days that Mr. Helen was really Frank Worscheim, convicted felon, but had kept the information private because he didn't "want to compromise the investigation." No sense in letting me, his girlfriend's best friend whom he'd known most of his life, in on the fact that a convicted felon's *partner* was on the loose. Searching for stolen diamonds. *On my property.*

I stabbed at a piece of chicken with the full force of my frustration. I nearly bent the tines as my fork clanged onto my plate.

"Your dinner isn't too chewy, is it?" Mom asked, peering at me, a worried expression on her face.

"Not at all. Everything's delicious. I just wasn't looking where I was forking."

I jumped a foot when the phone rang.

"Must be a sales call," my mother said and rose to answer on the kitchen phone. She was soon saying, "Yes, she's right here," into the handset, and I got up from the table, expecting the worst. Another corpse in my yard, perhaps.

On the phone, it took me a moment to re-arrange my thoughts — another mother from Karen's class had merely tracked me down to ask how my plans were going for the school party tomorrow afternoon. I have a lot of trouble saying no — I can say the word, but unfortunately, it's usually fol-lowed by the phrase, "I don't mind." Try convincing a lawyer or an accountant that creating greeting cards and cartoons was "work," and that I didn't have any more time to put together a class party than they did.

I shrieked into the phone in a white lie, "Oh, no! The party's tomorrow! I can't be-lieve I forgot! What am I going to do?"

After a short pause, the woman gallantly offered to do this party for me, since I'd "spearheaded the last seven parties our children have shared for the past two years." I thanked her profusely and assured her that, since this was the last minute, this one party counted as a year's worth of work, so I'd be "homeroom mom" again next year to repay her.

Jim watched me as I reclaimed my seat. "Did you just volunteer to be homeroom mom again next year?"

"Yes, but I —"

"We may not even *be* here next year. My temporary assignment's supposed to end soon."

"What?" Nathan cried, dropping his fork. "We're moving?"

I shot a dirty look at Jim, who had forgotten our vow not to discuss the quixotic "end date" of his "temporary" assignment in front of the children. "I'll believe that when it happens. Besides, what's Carlton Central going to do? Tell me I can't leave town because I promised I'd be homeroom mom?"

"You aren't actually going to leave Carlton, are you?" Mom asked. Though she hadn't dropped her fork, she'd stopped eating and her tanned features had paled. "I thought you liked it here."

"I do like it here. But I love Boulder."

"I don't want to move!" Nathan shouted. "I want to stay here!"

"You said the same thing when we moved from Boulder, remember? And everything worked out that time, and it will work out —"

"I don't want to move!" Nathan repeated, louder, his cheeks so red his freckles all but vanished.

"Neither do I," Karen said, pushing her seat back from the table and crossing her arms. "Rachel's my best friend, and I'm not leaving her."

"Our house in Boulder is rented through the end of the summer, so we'll be here another three months no matter what. In the meantime, let's just finish dinner before we start packing. Okay?" Besides, I thought, my annual commitment for Carlton Central to run a scholarship committee required my physical presence several weeks out of every summer. I'd be summering in Carlton for several years to come, even if Jim's "temporary" assignment ever actually ended.

The phone rang again. I rose. "It's probably the movers wanting to know our schedule," I grumbled.

"What?" Nathan cried again.

"Just kidding." I snarled "Hello" into the phone.

"Managed to trace the diamonds,"

Tommy began with no preamble. "They were from all three heists along the coast, just as you'd suspected. Thought you'd like to know."

"Thanks," I said frostily, still angry at Tommy for having withheld information from me that could have endangered my family. "By the way, were any of the jewelry stores offering a reward?"

"I'll look into that for you." He paused, then said, "Reason I'm calling is to warn you. We located Frank Worscheim's next of kin, finally. Was from L.A. originally, and his mother flew out and IDed the body. So we had to let the press know the victim's identity. His name'll be in tomorrow's *Times Union*. Expect some reporters to hound you for more info. Also had to let 'em in on the fact we recovered the stolen diamonds."

He paused, letting this sink in. *Expect some reporters,* he tells me. In our little town, a convicted felon, with a stash of stolen diamonds buried in the yard, was killed while disguised as a woman. *Gee, Tommy. Do you really think any reporters will think there's a story there?*

"But it occurred to me there's a chance this former partner of the victim's — if that's who was diggin' holes at your place — could think you or Jim might still have some of the stash. You follow?"

Of course I "followed." The same thing had occurred to me hours earlier — that if this former partner was crazed enough to shoot Mr. Helen, he could come after one of us. But I had a roomful of eavesdroppers at the moment, so I merely said, "Yes." My head was pounding. I massaged my temples with my free hand.

"So I was thinking. For your own safety, maybe you and your family should consider leaving town."

There are moments, thankfully brief, in which I hate my life. This was one of them. As calmly as possible, I said, "Thanks for the suggestion, Tommy," and hung up.

"Here's the thing," I told Jim as we drove to the home-owners' meeting later that night. "Frank, aka Helen, didn't dig up the buried treasure, sell the house, and flee the area. Why not do that if some partner you'd fleeced had finally caught up with you? Why didn't Frank-slash-Helen dig up the money when he still owned the house? Why stick around and merely keep an eye on the place, hoping to prevent the new owners from finding the stash?"

"Maybe the ground was frozen," Jim said as he flipped on the turn signal. "So he was forced to wait until the spring to sell."

"Or maybe Frank had a new partner he was working with now. Perhaps someone in the neighborhood."

No, I decided on second thought, that made no sense. He already had the diamonds and had, apparently, run out on one partner. Why share the spoils now? "You know what I think happened?"

Jim was paying attention to his driving and gave no response — not that he had any choice but to listen to me.

"I think Frank suspected that Simon had gotten wise to him. What else *could* Frank have concluded when he saw that Simon had installed surveillance cameras? In fact, maybe Simon really was onto him. He might have been blackmailing Helen, or rather Frank, and it took Frank a long time to get the opportunity to lure Simon away from his house so that he could dig up the diamonds surreptitiously."

We pulled into the parking lot. "Quite a turnout," Jim said as we slowly circled, looking for a space. "I thought your mom said hardly anyone came to these things."

"How would *she* know? She's never been to a single home-owners' meeting in the thirty-plus years she's lived here." I shouldn't complain about that, though. Her choosing not to go tonight allowed us to use her as a baby-sitter. Still feeling under the weather, Lauren had elected not to join us either.

Jim finally found a space. As he pulled on the parking brake, I asked, "So, do you think I'm right about Simon Smith and Frank Worscheim?"

"I think you should leave this up to the police to investigate."

"Oh. Okay. I'll do that."

Recognizing my sarcasm, he chuckled and escorted me through the asphalt lot to the church where our fellow Sherwood Forest home owners were holding their annual meeting. The outside of the church was a rather ugly white stucco. I'd never been inside before and was surprised to find it quite nice. The ceiling was slatted wood that resembled the inside of a ship's hull. The pews and hardwood floor were in a complementary light grain. A long, white-skirted table was located in front of the room, where Joanne Abbott and three men I didn't recognize sat conversing with one another.

I scanned the room for faces I recognized, but, other than Joanne, I recognized only her husband in the corner. Stan's thick neck and pudgy form were recognizable even at a distance. This lack of friendly faces out of the hundred plus that were here was an unpleasant surprise. There was a general din of hostile voices. Part of that was no doubt caused by the heat. The crush of bodies made the quarters stuffy, despite the spinning overhead fans and open windows.

Ignoring our off-putting surroundings, Jim greeted everyone we angled past with his customary charm and friendliness. He received nods or solemn hellos, nothing more. The pews were filled, but we found two folding chairs in the back.

In front of us, Joanne's group discussion had grown quite animated. The scene could easily lend itself to a cartoon gag, where a group of people at a table marked "Executive Committee" are involved in a brawl. In the audience, a woman wearing a startled expression listens to the woman beside her, who says, "Oh, they're simply choosing their seats. Things won't heat up till the meeting actually starts."

I turned to the middle-aged couple beside me and said, "This is my first meeting. Do you normally get a turnout like this?"

"Are you kidding? Not hardly," the female half of the couple answered. Her husband merely smirked.

"You must take your mailboxes seriously around here."

"Mailboxes?" she repeated.

"That was the main topic to discuss, according to the newsletter. The architectural committee has recommended that home owners replace their metal mailboxes with wooden ones, and they're putting the matter up for a vote tonight."

The woman furrowed her brow. "I don't know anything about that. I just heard that some transvestite was shot dead in someone's yard. And I want to know what they're going to do about it."

"Do about it?" I repeated, feeling the blood drain from my face.

She nodded, setting her jaw. "We hear it's a young, seedy-looking couple who just recently bought the house."

"Whoever lives there must be running some kind of a crack house!" her husband exclaimed.

Seedy-looking? Crack house? This was not going to be your typical, friendly get-together of a few neighbors. I glanced at Jim. His forehead was dotted with perspiration and his dark brown eyes had flown wide.

"Maybe it's not too late to escape," Jim whispered to me. We both looked back at the heavy oak double doors. People who'd come in behind us were standing two deep, right in front of the doors. There would be no leaving inconspicuously. We turned around again. I had butterflies the size of eagles in my stomach. Oh, well. At least the rumor had pegged us as "young."

"Are you two new in the neighborhood?" the man asked, looking right at Jim.

"Yes. Though my wife actually grew up in this neighborhood. Didn't you, dear?"

"Uh, sure." I forced a smile. "I like to think I've grown up. All told, I've lived in this neighborhood for twenty years now. In total law-abiding peace and tranquillity."

The man looked puzzled at my response, but Joanne Abbott pounded a gavel before he could ask what I meant. I had forgotten that she was acting association president, filling in for the president — our mutual neighbor who was still on vacation in Europe.

"Let's bring the meeting to order. First on our agenda is —"

"To hell with the agenda," some male voice cried. "We need to know what's going on with that homosexual who got stabbed on somebody's doorstep."

"Let's keep our facts straight," Joanne said, raising a placating palm to the audience. "That was no homosexual, as far as anyone knows. That was my neighbor, Helen Raleigh, who rumor has it, though it's just a rumor, was actually a man. And Helen was shot, not stabbed, on Jim and Molly Masters's yard. Isn't that right, Molly?"

All eyes scanned the audience. My mouth felt dry. I cleared my throat and mustered a smile. "Yes, that sounds about right."

The couple in the seats nearest to mine squirmed and inched their chairs farther away.

"So what was this person *doing* getting shot in your yard, I'd like to know!" I didn't recognize the speaker, but he had a Stalinish mustache and was nobody I felt like messing with.

"Doing? He was just lying there, *bleeding.* It's not as though he asked my permission to get killed on my property. Had he done so, I certainly would have told him no."

"Why are you yelling at my wife?" Jim asked pointedly. "She didn't kill anybody!"

"How do we know that?" some red-faced man said from three rows up. "I heard you're running a crack house out of your basement."

"Puh-lease!" I cried. "I create greeting cards, not drugs."

"Our property values are going to drop if people keep getting shot here," an elderly voice cried.

"Greeting cards?" one of the male board

members next to Joanne repeated.

Maybe I could divert everyone's attention by launching into a sales pitch for Friendly Fax. "Yes. They're completely harmless. Some of them aren't quite as humorous as I'd like, but they're not even offensive to anyone."

"Plus, has everyone seen their yard?" the man with the big mustache exclaimed. "I've seen better-looking dumps!"

"Do you evaluate dumps for your profession, or is that your hobby?" I couldn't help but ask.

He clenched his jaw.

"You do have to admit, though, Molly, you're somewhat of a Typhoid Mary," Joanne said into the microphone. She raised one corner of her pink-painted lips. "Or, a Typhoid Molly, as it were."

I stared at her in surprise.

"In the entire forty-year history of this subdivision," Joanne went on, "no one was ever killed here until you moved back here two years ago. Since then, we've had two murders."

"Our property values are going to go down!" the same elderly voice cried out from the crowd.

Calm. I needed to stay calm. "Surely, Joanne, you're not saying you blame *me* for the former owner of my house's murder. Or for a neighbor's tragic death two years ago. It's just a coincidence. Other people have moved into Sherwood Forest in the last two years. Are you going to accuse them of jinxing the place, too?"

"Of course not," Joanne puffed. "But my point is, we used to have such a wonderful, peaceful neighborhood. And this murder took place in *your* yard."

Desperately, I scanned the seats ahead of me for Sheila Lillydale. For once I fully felt the need of her legal skills to defend my rights.

"Two doors down from *your* house," Jim said, rising and pointing at Joanne. "My wife was inside our house, heard the gunshot, and rushed out to try to save the victim. It was a terrifying experience. None of you has the right to vilify her!"

"Actually, *you* might have the right," I told Jim as he sat back down. "Wasn't it in our marriage vows 'to love, honor, and vilify, when appropriate'?"

Jim ignored my attempt to lighten the tension. In the meantime, Joanne pounded the gavel unnecessarily, for Jim's words had silenced the room. "Mr. Masters is absolutely correct," Joanne said, now using appeasing tones. "None of us is accusing you or your wife of any role in this, other than that of an unfortunate witness. Isn't that right?"

The male board members immediately agreed with this.

The woman beside me said, "That must have been dreadful for you. I don't even know what I'd do in that situation. I think I'd faint." She turned to her husband. "Don't you, dear?"

"She'd faint, all right," the husband said. "Probably puke, as well."

The board member closest to Joanne grabbed the microphone and launched into a speech about how it was "good people like Mr. and Mrs. Masters we all need to encourage and support in our little neighborhood." That it was "neighbor helping neighbor" and "backyard barbecues" that kept this town the "good, safe place to live."

I murmured into Jim's ear, "Next they'll launch into a chorus of 'My Country 'tis of Thee.'" I was thoroughly perturbed at Joanne Abbott. First she insinuated that I was responsible, then had the nerve to act as though everyone were being just as reasonable as could be.

"I'm sure we all appreciate the trauma you've been through, Molly, and we admire your bravery in trying to save Helen Raleigh's life. Don't we, everyone?" Our feckless leader looked down her Roman nose to scan the audience. "Let's give Molly Masters a big hand."

Everyone dutifully began to clap. This time *I* rose. Cutting off the applause, I said to Joanne, "First you call me a Typhoid Mary, then you lead everyone in clapping for me? Which is it, Joanne? Are you running for political office or something?"

For an instant, Joanne was nonplussed. Then she said in gratingly calm tones, "I merely gave a voice to the many grumblings I've been hearing, so that I could allow you the opportunity to defend yourself publicly."

"Thank you so much, Joanne." I put my hands on my hips and eyed the sea of faces that surrounded me. They dropped their eyes as I met each gaze. "If any of you think that I am a bad or dangerous element in this neighborhood, all I ask is that you have the guts to discuss it with me face-to-face. And not" — I glared at Joanne — "from behind a microphone."

Jim rose and said quietly, "Let's get out of here."

The room was completely silent. I started to follow Jim, then paused. "By the way. You know that nondescript aluminum mailbox I've got now? I'm getting an eight-foot-tall clown statue from a fast-food restaurant and installing a mail slot in it. The statue's made of wood, so I know you'll all approve."

Jim put his arm around me and escorted me to the car. Neither of us spoke as we got in. Jim started the engine and said, "I guess we might as well start looking now."

"Start looking?" I repeated, thinking he meant we should start searching for a new house and leave this neighborhood.

"It could take us quite a while to find an eight-foot-tall wooden clown."

The next morning was Thursday. I was biding my time at our house, waiting for the repair person for Karen's window.

I came out onto my porch at the sound of a truck pulling into my driveway. To my surprise, it was a lawn-service vehicle. The driver was staring at my side yard as he got out of the vehicle.

"Holy moley," he said, starting to wander toward the side yard as he spoke.

"No, the name's Molly, not Moley." By now, I was so sick of hearing about my chewed-up yard that I had no patience for this, especially not if this was some sales ploy to encourage me to fork over the bucks to save my lawn. "What can I do for you?"

I followed as he wandered onto my yard, staring at the dirt as if I hadn't spoken. "And here I thought Helen Raleigh was exaggerating about how messed up her lawns were."

"Oh," I said, suddenly remembering. "You must be from the lawn service that Helen had scheduled. Helen doesn't live here anymore. I do. I meant to —"

"You're going to need all new sod. This is gonna cost extra, you know."

"I meant to call and cancel. I don't need your services."

He snorted and pushed his green cap back on his forehead with a thumb. "Beg to differ, lady. But, hey, it's your house."

"Did you use to help Helen Raleigh maintain this property?"

"Sure did. I just took care of spraying for weeds and fertilizing, though. She always took meticulous care of the gardens and stuff." He scanned the chewed-up area as if in awe of how badly the place had deteriorated in three months.

"Do you ever recall coming out and finding piles of dirt or recently dug up areas, or anything?" I strode in front of the hole where we'd uncovered the diamonds. Indicating it with a sweeping gesture, I asked, "Especially right in this general area?"

He chuckled. "She used to stand right about where you are now and keep an eye on me. She explained she had herbs in this garden and didn't want me getting near it with my spray can. She was a real gardening fanatic, let me tell you."

"So you never saw it dug up, as it is now?"

"Like it is now? Not by a long shot." He started to return to his truck.

"But you *have* seen it partially dug up?"

He shrugged. "Helen must've really been into turning the soil in her herb garden. That often had exposed topsoil. But the lawn was always meticulous." He ran his eyes over me. "Till you moved in. Good luck restoring it. You might want to consider —"

"Could you please just give me a written estimate? Maybe I can make some phone calls and find out if the party responsible for these damages will pay to have you fix this mess."

An hour later, I was in the midst of a thorough vacuuming of my daughter's room to ensure Karen wouldn't step on a glass shard. The glass repairman had come and gone, having replaced the window in Karen's room. I had gotten a bid from the lawn service and passed it along to Tommy, who agreed that his department should pay for it.

I asked again if he could take it out of the reward money, and he merely laughed and said he had money budgeted for situations such as mine.

I dusted and then moved the desk and shelves. As I did so, the section of the room's wall-to-wall carpeting nearest the baseboard came loose at a seam. This particular carpet problem had inspired us to place the desk where we did — slightly off-center from the window and on top of the bad seam. I knelt and pulled up the loose carpet, figuring I should clean under this section of the carpet as well, since I was so near the window.

The padding looked as though it had been sliced unevenly. Upon close inspection, I realized that this wasn't a seam in the carpeting after all. Someone had taken a sharp knife and deliberately sliced through both the carpeting and its pad. Curious, I knelt and grabbed a handful of pad and carpet and pulled them both back, revealing a triangle of the plywood flooring underneath. A foot-long square had been cut out of the plywood and patched back in, with a hole drilled close to the edge of the square. For all the world, it looked like the proverbial "loose-floorboard" hiding place. I stuck my index finger in the hole and removed the small section of flooring.

There was a four-inch gap between the plywood of the second floor where I now knelt and the top of the first-floor ceiling below. It was empty. Frank must have hidden something here at one point, though. Apparently he hadn't cared whether or not his hiding place was a cliché. Perhaps this had been the original hiding place for the diamonds, though what could have motivated him to move his hiding place outdoors was beyond me.

A diamond could have accidentally rolled away from its stash. I grabbed a flashlight and angled the beam as far into the hole as I could see. No glitters or sparkles greeted me. Though not optimistic about my chances of finding anything, I lay flat on the floor and reached as deeply into the area underneath the plywood as possible. It was more likely that I'd touch a mouse than a diamond. Half an arm length in, I felt a piece of paper and managed to pinch it between my second and third fingers. I pulled it out.

It was a letter, dated the middle of June last year. I read:

Dearest Helen,
My love for you will never die.
For your heart I must always try.

I only wish I could reveal myself to you.
In this case, that would never do.
And so my love must remain secret.
Yet my heart is yours, you can bet.

                     Your secret admirer

"This is the worst love poem I've ever read in my life," I murmured to myself. Then the handwriting rang a bell. I reread it. The line: "I only wish I could reveal myself to you" was nearly identical to something I'd had anonymously faxed to me earlier this week.

It was time to pay my crotchety, stoop-shouldered neighbor another visit.

Chapter 13

I Forgot to Have Our Mail Held

Simon Smith answered his door immediately. A section of his white hair in the back stood on end like a flag on a mailbox. For the third day in a row, he wore the same clothes. The outline of his sleeveless, scoop-necked undershirt could easily be seen through the thin fabric of his faded blue, tan, and white plaid shirt. He said nothing by way of greeting, merely stood there blinking at me, reminiscent of a tortoise poking his head out of his shell.

Wanting to ease into what would be an embarrassing subject for him, I forced a smile and said, "Good morning. I didn't see you at the home-owners' meeting last night."

He scoffed and muttered, "Batch of women sniping at one another. I got better things to do with my time." He placed his bony hands on his equally bony hips. "And I got things to do *now*. What do you want?"

So much for subtlety. Yet, if my theory

was correct that Simon had blackmailed Mr. Helen after having discovered his true identity, Simon was nobody to take lightly. In fact, I could picture him killing Helen just because she turned out to be a he, which threatened the precarious self-image Simon had concocted for himself. Under the circumstances, I wondered if confronting him head-on about his relationship with Mr. Helen the wise thing to do. It certainly wasn't the *nice* thing to do, at any rate.

"Well?" Simon prompted in his raspy voice. Then he made a hacking noise and spat out some phlegm a few inches from my feet. I automatically stepped back. He chuckled at me — thus sealing my decision to go for the jugular.

"I have something that belongs to you."

"Oh?" Simon raised an eyebrow. "What's that?"

"A love letter, written by you to Helen Raleigh." I held it up for him to see, but was far enough away to elude his grasp.

His jaw dropped. "What are you blathering about? I'm a spy, not a poet!"

"Oh, really? Then how did you know it *was* a poem?"

"I . . . I didn't. I . . . just assumed." Angry red splotches had formed on his cheeks. We both knew I'd caught him.

I started to carefully refold the sheet of paper. "We'll just see what the police have to say about who wrote this, once they analyze the handwriting."

He tried to snatch it out of my hand. "Give that to me!"

"So it *is* your poem, isn't it?"

"No! I just don't want you to spread vicious rumors about me to the police!"

"Vicious rumors? Such as that you were courting a man dressed as a woman?"

His eyes bulged. "You've got no right —"

"Did you kill Helen?"

"No! I would never kill anyone!" He paused, then ran a palm over his unruly hair, which popped back up at attention an instant later. "Even when I was working for the CIA, I never actually killed anyone. Wounded a couple damn commies, but I never killed nobody."

"Is this why you started running the surveillance on the house? Because you were so humiliated when you found out Helen was a man, you wanted to humiliate him right back?"

He stomped his foot and sputtered about for a moment, then pointed a gnarled finger. "Get off my porch! If you so much as step one foot on my property again, I'll —" He stopped abruptly.

"You'll what? Shoot me?"

He stuck out his chin in defiance, but his eyes were wild with panic.

"Were you blackmailing Helen Raleigh?"

"Blackmailing her? Ha! No damned way!"

"It seems to me that you had each other in quite a stalemate. You reveal his suspicious activities, he destroys your macho reputation by allowing it to get out that you were attracted to a cross-dresser."

"He couldn't destroy *my* reputation without —" He stopped, realizing he'd said too much. "You can't prove any of that!"

"Did you learn Helen's real identity?"

"No."

"Aha! You knew Helen Raleigh was an assumed identity! So you admit you knew she was a man!"

He grabbed his head with both hands. "Stop! You're confusing me!"

It was about time I confused somebody other than myself.

I backed away as he stepped out onto the porch, directly onto his own spittle.

"You're giving me that poem if I have to chase you from here to hell!" He lunged at me, but I dodged him. I gasped and started to reach out a protective arm as he nearly fell down his porch steps, but he managed to grab his banister and steady himself.

"Surely we're both too old for this nonsense," I said with a sigh. How old *was* he, I wondered. Sixty? Eighty?

The bit of physical exertion in this steamy heat seemed to drain the last of his resolve. He met my gaze with his watery eyes and said humbly, "Let me have the poem. Please."

"I can't. It's evidence."

He sighed and kicked at a leaf on his porch. "I didn't kill him. But I should have. He led me on, letting me go on thinking he was a gal. The man was a damned scum bag."

A scum bag? Did *real* CIA-retirees actually talk like that? "How did you find out he was a man?"

He sighed, eyes averted, his thin, dry lips trembling. "I was on my roof one night, taking down the Christmas lights. Caught sight of him through his bedroom window, coming out of the bathroom."

Taking down the Christmas lights? More likely it was simply one of Simon's spying operations. He'd probably watched over Helen's place every night — the lovesick neurotic that he was. "That must have been quite a shock."

"Damn near fell off the roof." His face

251

and entire body sagged before my eyes. He looked like a skeleton, a tired old man. "Please, Molly. I got nothing in this world. Took all my life's savings to buy this place. I got no family. No friends. Just my reputation. That's all I got left. I'm begging you. Give me that poem."

Though it made me feel terrible, I knew I couldn't give in. I could not hand over something that could provide a motive for Mr. Helen's murder without first getting an okay from the police. Yet it seemed so heartless of me to refuse Simon's pleas. After all, the poem was his gift to someone else, now deceased. Still, for all I knew, his current state of despair could be an act. "I can't. It's evidence in —"

"But it's *not* evidence! I didn't kill her!"

"How can I know that for sure? I have to turn this in to the police."

He gestured at the eaves where a camera used to be. "None of this had a damned thing to do with his death. Leastways, not so far as —"

"Molly? Simon? What's going on?" a male voice called from behind me.

Simon gasped audibly, and I whirled around. It was Stan Abbott. "Nothing's going on, Stan," I replied as calmly as possible. "Are you taking the day off?"

252

"Working at home today. Hooked up by modem. I could hear you two going at it clear back in my office. Is everything all right?"

"We were just having a difference of opinion, that's all," I replied.

"Ain't none of your damn business, Mr. Abbott," Simon hollered.

"We're fine, Stan. Really."

Stan stayed his ground. "You sure?" He crossed his arms and rested them on his flabby stomach.

"Sure, she's sure. Don't she look it?"

While I tried to don a "sure" look by setting my jaw, Simon leaned toward me and said in a stage whisper, "Come inside."

I weighed the thought of which of these men I felt safer with and opted for Simon. Not because he was less dangerous or less likely to have killed Frank aka Helen, but because I would stand better odds in hand-to-hand combat with the skinny, creaky Simon than with Stan, who could render me helpless simply by sitting on me. I followed Simon into his foyer. He swiftly shut the door behind us, then stood staring out the window at the front sidewalk. Simon finally turned toward me.

"Did he leave?"

Simon nodded and muttered, "Damn

snoop." He was so unnerved, he looked to be on the verge of tears. I averted my eyes and glanced at my watch.

"Listen, Simon, I'm sorry, but I've got to get to school for my children's end-of-the-year activities. I'll be home by three. Why don't you come over to my house sometime after that, and we'll discuss this matter then?"

"Your house? No way. Too dangerous. Meet me back here."

I shook my head. "The kids'll be all wound up. It wouldn't be fair of me to leave them with my mother. Meet me at my parents' house at three-thirty. The address is twenty-twenty Little John Lane."

He eyed the poem in my hand. "You . . . er . . . gonna keep this between just the two of us in the meantime?"

Sergeant Newton would have a fit if I agreed to that. Not to mention throw me in jail for withholding evidence. On the other hand, it was just a poem, not a smoking gun.

At the thought of a murder weapon, a realization hit me: I had just told him my mother's address. He was likely to ransack either my home or my mother's house to search for this poem while I was gone. "I can't make you any promises, Simon, but I won't mention it to anyone in the immediate neighborhood." I put his poem in the pocket of my shorts. "In any case, I'm keeping this *with* me, in a safe place, where no one else will see it."

He rubbed at his pale, wrinkled forehead. "Damn. I . . . All right. Maybe we can work out a trade."

"A trade?"

"Your useless evidence for my real goods. I . . . began the surveillance once I found out Helen was a man, to see what he was up to."

Whoa! He had evidence? "Actually, I don't have to leave for a few minutes yet. We can talk about —"

He shook his head. "I got to think things over first."

"But —"

He opened the door for me.

I should immediately call Tommy and let him know about this supposed evidence. Then again, Simon might be bluffing. I'd know for sure soon enough. I obliged him by stepping out. "We're definitely going to have a talk this afternoon, though, right?"

"You're damn right we'll talk." He slammed the door shut.

Stan Abbott was no longer standing vigil. It was strange, I thought as I walked toward home, how Stan or Joanne Abbott always managed to pop up at the most inopportune times for me. Maybe Simon hadn't been the only neighbor who'd bugged my house. I clicked my tongue and mentally chastised myself. Now I was getting downright paranoid.

I hesitated as I neared my front porch. My mother was sitting on the step. Her back was straight and her tall frame looked as stiff as a folded ironing board. She gave me a solemn nod and said, "I was just out for a little walk and stopped by your house. I happened to notice you weren't inside it." She jiggled her keys — one of which was to my front door — as she spoke to make it clear that she had gone inside looking for me.

"I was next door." Mom's lips were pursed. She was harboring a good deal of anger toward me. I now remembered that I'd told her I'd be back at her place two hours ago.

"Well." She rose and stayed on the step, putting me at a considerable height disadvantage. "It's always a relief to discover your child is alive, after all." She added in softer tones, "I see the window in Karen's room got fixed."

"Yes, the repairman left not too long ago."

She ran her fingers through her short salt-and-pepper hair. "Your father called earlier this morning. We both feel that you need to leave town. You and Jim can take the kids down to our Florida condo."

"But . . . that would be hard to arrange, and besides, I don't want to go."

"When your father gets back on Sunday, you're going to have a hard time convincing him you should stay."

Her patronizing attitude was getting on my nerves, even though it was somewhat justified. "What is this? The old, 'Wait till your father gets home'? I'm an adult, Mom. That line hasn't worked on me since I was five."

"Actually, it never worked." She sighed, then her lower lip began to tremble. Despite her not-so-subtle martyrdom techniques, Mom was not the trembling-lip sort. She had my full attention. "I know you have more important concerns than your poor old mother's feelings, but you'd —"

"Mom!" I cried. "I'm sorry I caused you to worry, but for heaven's sake! It's not like I climbed out the window to spend the night carousing! Don't you think you're overreacting just a little?"

"Kind of makes you want to get far, far away from me, doesn't it?" She dangled a pair of keys until I reluctantly held out my palm. She dropped them into my hand.

Judging from the palm-tree key chain, they were to the Florida condo. "Think about it." She headed down the sidewalk toward her home.

"Wait, Mom."

She looked back at me.

"You're going to the kids' parties, aren't you? We may as well carpool."

"Sure."

That passed as a heart-wrenching emotional exchange in my family. We strolled in companionable silence.

The built-in telephone on my fax machine was ringing when we reached my parents' house. I told my mom I'd be right back and trotted down the stairs, hoping this would be a job order.

I winced as I spotted the fax from my office doorway. Another fax with blackened margins. I checked the sender tag. Sure enough, it was from S. Smith. Poor Simon. He wanted to send me another anonymous message and still hadn't figured out that this method didn't work. I grabbed the handwritten fax and read:

Dear Mrs. Masters,

You are making a terrible mistake. I've tried to warn you before. Now it may be too late. You have fallen for your neighbor's masquerades. That could cost you dearly.

Sign me,
A concerned friend

"Well, that's a relief," I muttered to myself. His punctuation of "neighbor's" indicated only one of my neighbors posed a threat to me. Lately I'd been starting to think in terms of a conspiracy — that somehow we'd managed to move into the one cul-de-sac where all the local bad guys lived. Not that one could trust the punctuation of someone who wrote such atrocious poetry.

Assuming Simon was warning me in earnest — which was an enormous assumption to make — Simon could only be referring to one of four neighbors: Stan or Joanne Abbott, or Roger or Sheila Lillydale. Until very recently, I'd had almost no interactions with Stan, so Simon couldn't accurately accuse me of "falling for his masquerade." Joanne had been an absolute witch at the meeting last night, so she wasn't pulling anything over on me — though Simon may not have heard about that incident yet. Then there were Sheila and Roger Lillydale, neither of whom I trusted at this point.

I dialed the number of the sender that had

shown in my display. I recognized Simon's raspy voice as he answered on the first ring.

"Simon, what is this? What do you mean by 'neighbor's masquerades'?"

"I, uh, who is this, please?"

"It's Molly Masters, as if you didn't know."

"I haven't the damn foggiest what you're blabbering about!"

"I received your fax. I dialed you using the sender's number shown on my display. I want you to tell me what's going on. Stop playing these silly games with me. Which neighbor? What masquerade?"

"Maybe you should heed what the damned fax is saying, 'stead of worrying so much about who sent it to you!"

The line went dead.

As Mom and I pushed through the lobby doors of Carlton Elementary School, I spotted the principal, on his way out. The two of us had gone to high school together, though our social circles rarely crossed anymore. We greeted each other warmly and joked about the mound of paperwork he had yet to conquer, then Mom and I split up, agreeing to swap places in half an hour. She went to Nathan's class party and I headed toward Karen's classroom, since I'd spent most of my time during the last party in Nathan's classroom. Contrary to my children's opinions of me, I truly did try to be fair to them.

The classroom was currently filled with parents and younger siblings. Just outside the glass outer door, the students were lining up along the windows after recess. Karen's face lit up when we spotted each other and she waved at me, as did two of her friends.

Standing by the door, Karen's teacher looked unusually harried. Her vision fell on the two-liter bottles of fruit punch in my arms. "Oh, thank goodness. You brought the beverage. I was afraid we'd have to let the kids drink melted sherbet."

Sheila Lillydale stood near her stepson Ben, apart from the hubbub of parents chattering and preparing rows of cookies. I helped another mother stir the fruit drink into the slushy sherbet, then went over to Sheila, who leaned against the wall near the blackboard.

I said hello, then asked, "Did you hear about all the excitement at the homeowners' meeting?"

She looked right through me. "I don't know what you're talking about. However, this is hardly the time."

"Excuse me?"

"Let's not be discussing your legal problems during a party in our children's classes." She cast a nervous glance past my shoulder.

Surely she hadn't meant to be hostile to me. I hadn't done anything wrong, and we'd been on good terms the last time we spoke. I followed her gaze to where her handsome husband, Roger, appeared as though he were listening to our every word.

The bell rang and the teacher opened the door, allowing the children to rush inside. After several minutes of general pandemonium, I found myself standing near Roger, as we waited for the children to serve themselves treats across the room.

"Hi, Roger. How are you?"

He appeared to be affronted that I'd even spoken to him. He cleared his throat, then leveled a finger at me, and said, "You had no right to tell my wife something that I told you in confidence!"

I was totally taken aback. "Tell her *what?* I don't recall your having *told* me anything in confidence, let alone my having blurted it to Sheila."

"So that's your game, is it?"

"What game? I don't know what you're talking about. Apparently, we've had some sort of massive misunderstanding. If I said something to your wife you wanted me to keep quiet, I wish you'd tell me what it was so I can apologize."

"Sheila's right about you." He gave me a look of blatant hatred. Sheila must have described me as a garden slug. "We're trying to patch things up, for our son's sake."

"I'm glad to —"

Sheila, suddenly directly behind me, interrupted, "I already said this wasn't the place to have a discussion of this nature."

Good Lord. This was like suddenly being surrounded by people shouting at you in a foreign language. "I honestly can't understand what's going on here. Sheila, can we step out into the hallway and discuss this?"

Sheila took a halting breath and cried, "*You're* the one who's —"

Roger cut her off and stepped between us. "I'm warning you, Mrs. Masters! Stop harassing my wife! Come on, honey. Let's get out of here."

My cheeks were blazing. I turned around and realized that all of the children plus their parents were staring at me, aghast, especially poor little Ben. The teacher, in a gracious gesture, clapped her hands and said, "If everyone's gotten their treats, you should all be sitting at your desks."

I sought Karen's eyes and she rushed over

and gave me a hug. "What's the matter with Mr. and Mrs. Lillydale?" she asked. "Why were they yelling at you like that?"

"I don't know, sweetie. Let's forget about it so it won't spoil your celebration."

At the first opportunity, I went over to Ben Lillydale and crouched beside his desk. His big blue eyes met mine, and I said, "I'm really sorry, Ben. The last thing I wanted to do was upset your parents and ruin your party."

He looked away and pushed his chair back from his desk. "They're always mad. It's not your fault."

Before I could think of a response, he found an excuse to head across the room and left me sitting on my heels by his desk, trying not to cry.

The four of us arrived at my mother's house at three P.M. As anticipated, the children were so excited it was all I could do to disguise my own emotional state from them. It just didn't seem fair to them to have me upset over that insane, nasty exchange I'd had with the Lillydales.

I immediately checked the tray on my machine for more faxes from Simon. To my pleasant surprise, I had received a fax from a prospective customer. A woman requested an idea for a bon voyage card for some friends going to Yellowstone.

I had a half hour till Simon would arrive, and there was no telling when I'd have another opportunity to work — no doubt the kids would find me soon. I drew a family hunched together in their car, the man and children looking scared out of their wits as an enormous bear on the roof of the car is scraping at the windows. The mother, however, looks calm as she snaps her fingers and says, "Oh, shoot! I just remembered I forgot to have our mail held."

I had just finished inking the cartoon when the power went out. A few seconds later the power returned. But my mother called, "Molly? Can you come upstairs please?" Judging from her quaking voice, all was not well.

A moment later, I discovered the cause of my mother's distress. While I'd been working on my drawing, Karen and Nathan had gotten their summer vacation off in typical sibling style: Nathan had spit his gum into Karen's hair. She retaliated. I now had two sobbing kids, with gum wads firmly enmeshed in their hair, screaming and threatening each other.

We separated the children, and my mother unceremoniously snipped the gum out of Nathan's hair while I used the ice-cube method on Karen. I'd heard that peanut butter works well, but neither Karen nor I were especially anxious to give that one a whirl. We opted to keep the children as far apart as possible and sent Nathan into the backyard while Karen went upstairs to take a shower.

Afterward, it occurred to me that Simon was forty minutes late. I called his house, but got no answer. Since the man almost never left his house, that must mean he was en route. Sure enough, the doorbell rang.

"I'll get it, Mom," I called. I swung the door open without looking through the window first. To my surprise, it was Lauren, looking tense. Her nose was still red and chafed, but her eyes looked a little brighter, as if she were starting to recover from her cold.

I greeted her and looked past her shoulder. "I'm expecting my next-door neighbor, Simon Smith. He was supposed to be here over half an hour ago."

"That's why I'm here," Lauren said somberly, maintaining her post in front of Mom's doorway.

"What do you mean?"

"I got a call from Tommy. He checked your house and realized you weren't home.

He asked me to come see you and make sure you were all right."

"Why? What's wrong?"

"Simon Smith had an accident. He was on a ladder and fell onto the high-voltage wires. He's dead."

Chapter 14

We Lost the Duck L'Orange

Lauren's stunning announcement gave me a horrible feeling in the pit of my stomach. Simon Smith was dead. I had just spoken to him a couple of hours ago.

Why was he up on some ladder when he was supposed to be *here?* Had someone murdered him to stop him from giving me incriminating evidence?

"Are the police calling it an accident?"

Lauren nodded. "Tommy said that, by all appearances, Simon simply lost his balance."

"Simon *Smith?*" my mother asked from behind me. She'd been in the kitchen, but she had obviously overheard our conversation and had wandered in to learn more. "Molly, wasn't he that evil little man who'd been spying on you?"

"He wasn't evil, Mom," I immediately fired back. "He just had a few loose screws."

"Maybe so, but he kept pawing me after Joey Newton fired that beebee gun at me."

Mom furrowed her brow. "He claimed he was just trying to help me brush the dirt off my clothes."

"Well, he's dead now, so let's give him a break."

Lauren gestured toward her house and said, "I guess I'd better —"

"Thanks for telling me, Lauren. Would you like to come in for a while?"

I knew Lauren felt the slight tension between my mother and me. "No, I need to get back to Rachel. She's so excited about school being out she's bouncing off the walls. You know how that goes."

Needing to get away for a moment, I said, "I'll walk you out," and led the way outside. Part of me knew I couldn't blame my mother for her callousness over Simon's death. After all, I had never said anything nice about him to her. With good reason. But now that I knew I'd never speak to him again, my thoughts returned to his telling me so forlornly, "I got nothing left. Just my reputation." I battled feelings of guilt, remorse, and fear. *Accidental* falls could easily be faked. If someone had killed Simon to prevent him from presenting me with evidence, where could that leave *me*, except as the next intended victim?

I stood on the sidewalk with Lauren, the

late-afternoon sun beating down on us. She put her hand on my arm and said, "Are you okay?"

"Yeah. This is just such a shock." I winced and added, "No pun intended." I stared in the direction of my cul-de-sac. "I have to talk to Tommy. Simon said he was going to give me some information about Helen Raleigh's killer. That's why he was coming over to Mom's to meet with me."

"So he died minutes before he was going to give you some evidence?"

I nodded.

Lauren searched my face for a moment. Her pretty features bore deep worry lines. "Molly, please stay out of this. Lock yourself and your family in your parents' house and don't come out until the killer's behind bars."

"I can't do that. I have information that will help the investigation. Simon could have climbed up to his roof to retrieve evidence he'd hidden there that could identify the killer."

"I guess you do need to talk to Tommy." Lauren pursed her slightly chapped lips and ran her fingers through her hair. "Why don't you send Karen and Nathan over to my house? Rachel would love it."

"Okay. Thanks. But whatever you do,

don't let them near any chewing gum."

Lauren did a double take at that, but then merely took me at my word. I dashed back inside, told Mom what I was up to, gathered up the children, ushered them over to Lauren's, and headed off.

Minutes later, I surveyed the "crime scene." The police had cordoned off Simon Smith's house with the yellow and black-lettered plastic tape that I was altogether too familiar with by now. The tape ran from the front corner of Simon's privacy fence on our side, around a maple tree on Simon's front lawn, to his petunia-adorned lamppost, his mailbox, some other less-recognizable type of tree on the far side of the lawn, to the front corner of the fence on the Abbotts' property line.

Since Simon had apparently been fiddling with the fascia at the side of his house, the "accident" scene itself would be within Simon's privacy fence. I wished I could see for myself what was going on over there. Though if Simon had been in the process of retrieving some evidence, odds were the killer had taken it from him. And even if Simon *had* died while clutching some major clue — such as a piece of paper that read, "The name of the murderer is _____," Sergeant Tommy probably would notice it without my assistance. But still . . .

I walked slowly up to the foot of Simon's walkway, where the baby-faced officer was standing guard. He remembered my first name and greeted me. I'd forgotten his name, but called him "Officer" and asked if he could send Sergeant Newton over to my house as soon as possible.

Though it felt a bit voyeuristic, the first thing I did when I unlocked my front door was rush upstairs to my bedroom to look out the window at Simon's side yard. The angle was such that I could see Simon's lawn by the base of the house. There was nothing: no chalk lines, dead body, fallen ladder. Simon must have been on the opposite side of the house when this happened. Somehow that was slightly reassuring. My property wasn't such a murder magnet after all. A death had occurred next door, yet alongside someone *else's* property line.

The doorbell rang and I trotted down the stairs. It was Tommy, who immediately held up his hands as if to placate me. "Know what you're about to say, and you're wrong. This was an accident, Molly, not murder."

I clicked my tongue as I opened the screen door for him. "You've already made your mind up? That's not very good police technique, is it? Aren't you supposed to keep an open mind?"

He gave a big sigh as he entered. "Oh, I s'pose." He shuffled over to the tan velour recliner that the children and I refer to as "the big chair" and plopped down. He looked tired, the front of his red hair damp with sweat. I crossed the room to the couch and took a seat myself.

He slowly met my eyes, as if out of obligation. "Okay, Moll. You tell me. How come you think Simon Smith was murdered?"

I gathered up Simon's poem and the faxes he'd sent me, and explained about how I'd located the poem in a small opening in the floor in Karen's room.

Tommy read everything twice, then said, "Let's go take a look at this hiding place of yours."

I led him upstairs to Karen's room. Tommy whipped out a flashlight from his belt and shined the beam into the opening. "Guess I'd better get someone out here to enlarge this hole, just in case there's somethin' else hidden here."

"No!" I shouted.

Tommy looked at me as if surprised by my outburst.

"Sorry, but I'm putting my foot down while there's still a floor to put it on. If you want to send someone out here with a peri-scope, that's fine. But you're not going to tear up my house. You've already bulldozed my yard. It looks like a dump out there." This was my property, so I felt completely free to exaggerate.

"Fine. We'll examine the house as unob-trusively as possible. With the under-standing no one's allowed to cut or drill any new holes without your knowledge."

"Without my *prior* knowledge and con-sent."

"Yeah, yeah. Whatever." Tommy gave me a dismissive wave and led the way back downstairs.

As I trudged after him, I promised myself that nobody was coming into my home to look for evidence without my being present. "How do you think Simon wound up acci-dentally electrocuting himself?"

"He was boarding up the fascia where the cameras used to be. He apparently leaned out too far and the ladder tipped over. He grabbed on to the power lines that run past his house."

"And this happened on the side facing the Abbotts, right?"

Tommy gave a small nod. "Apparently the ladder slid. He grabbed the wires for bal-ance."

"No way. It's too enormous of a coincidence that he died right before he could give me something he claimed could identify Mr. Helen Raleigh's killer." In fact, Simon had merely told me he'd give me "real evidence." Close enough. "Besides, he was an electronics whiz. He should have known he'd be better off falling from a ladder than grabbing a power line."

"Molly, we get an accident like this every few years. I guarantee you, it's the natural human reaction. You feel yourself falling, you grab hold of whatever you can. Even a high-voltage wire."

"Maybe so, but someone *could* have pushed the ladder into the lines. The only people who might have been able to see over Simon's fence to tell what really happened are the Abbotts. Have you talked to them yet?"

"We will as soon as they get home."

Aha! They weren't home! Those two popped up at all sorts of odd times to overhear snippets of my private conversations regarding Mr. Helen's death. Then they managed to be gone when their neighbor died alongside their house. A little too convenient, in my opinion.

Tommy intercepted my thoughts and said, "Don't go jumpin' to conclusions."

"*You're* the one who's leapt to the conclusion that it was an accident."

Tommy held up his palms. "All right, all right. It's possible he was pushed, Molly. We're lookin' at the evidence. And if he was pushed, we'll catch the guilty party. But, Molly, you've got to accept the fact that it's also possible it was just an accident."

"No. It couldn't have been an accident."

"Why not?"

My voice was thick with barely suppressed emotion as I replied, "Because he wouldn't have been up there in the first place if it weren't for my having insisted he remove the cameras."

"That doesn't make this your fault."

I averted my eyes and stared out the window at Simon's house. "Oh, no? Then why do I feel so guilty?"

After Tommy left, I sat on my porch chair on the deck, sipping an iced tea, trying to put my thoughts in order. I was so frustrated, I had to force myself to stay seated instead of pacing. Why hadn't I insisted on hearing whatever Simon Smith had to say? Because, I answered myself, what rational person would believe that a real-life witness would actually die right before revealing the killer? That was the stuff of TV cop shows.

And, in retrospect, there was no guarantee that Simon wasn't merely blowing smoke. It would have been completely in keeping with his character to have manufactured evidence, simply to appease me and get his embarrassing poem back.

For that matter, *Simon* could have been Mr. Helen's murderer. He could have been careless on that ladder because he felt so guilty. If so, Mr. Helen's murder might never be officially solved.

My brow was furrowed as I mentally ran through the bizarre, tangled threads of clues. Who was the tall man in the fedora digging up my yard? Why were Sheila and Roger so angry at me? Out of the mire of unanswered questions came an idea for a cartoon. Pencils were always strewn around my house, and I spotted one on the other side of the glass patio table. I snatched it and began to draw on the nearest paper available — my napkin.

A couple dining out watches in surprise as a duck flies out of the kitchen, through the restaurant, and toward an open window. A snooty-looking waiter says, "The Duck L'Orange has apparently escaped. However, we offer an exquisite array of condiments for your dining pleasure."

Afterward, I stared at my drawing, trying

to decide what the cartoon said about my current state of mind. Perhaps I felt a bit like the flabbergasted woman in the restaurant — wondering what the heck was going on while my seemingly sane world goes topsy-turvy. Or maybe I felt like the duck, desperate to escape impending doom.

A flurry of motion in the bushes that lined my backyard caught the corner of my eye. I looked up, then gasped and barely stifled a scream as someone suddenly burst through the woods and into my back lawn.

A man smiled and waved wildly. "Molly! Hello! Betsy and I were just on a little stroll, when we happened to spot you."

Bob Fender. That reminded me: I'd forgotten to tell Tommy Newton about him as a possible suspect.

Betsy appeared a step behind. While they tromped their way toward me, I scanned my immediate surroundings to see how I'd rate as far as conspicuous vegetable consumption went. I pocketed my pencil and napkin to spare myself a lecture about the wanton destruction perpetrated by the lumber industry. Were tea leaves harvested so that the roots were left intact? Probably. My tea-logged slice of lemon would also pass their inspection. Just so long as they weren't currently lobbying for ice-cube rights. Mine were melting rapidly in the heat.

I forced a small smile, but didn't rise from my position on the patio chair as the Fenders neared. "Bob. Betsy. This is a surprise. What brings you out to my little neck of the woods?"

"Oh, we often take little strolls after Bob gets done with work." Betsy fluffed her curly, dull brown hair. They were wearing identical khaki shorts and shirts, with heavy hiking boots. They looked as though they were on a safari.

"Uh-huh," I murmured, then recoiled. I was starting to sound a bit like Sergeant Tommy.

"There were quite a few police vehicles out here when we first walked by," Bob said. The bristles of his unkempt mustache moved with the wind of his breath. "Is everything all right with you?"

Ignoring his question, I asked, "How long ago was this?"

Bob grabbed hold of the frame of his glasses and repositioned them, looking at Betsy inquisitively. "Maybe half an hour ago, wouldn't you say, dear?"

"That's about right. Neither of us wears a watch."

"Why not? Does Timex exploit vegetables?"

A hurt look flashed across Betsy's features.

"Sorry," I said. "It's been a frazzling couple of hours. My next-door neighbor just had a fatal accident, an hour or so ago. You weren't in the neighborhood at that time, were you?"

"No," Bob said. "Why? What happened? Which neighbor?"

I gestured at Simon Smith's property with a jerk of my head. Keeping an eye on Bob, I said carefully, "My neighbor fell into the power lines and was electrocuted."

"Oh, dear," Betsy said, clutching her hands to her chest. "The poor man."

Gotcha! "How did you know it was a man?"

She and Bob exchanged nervous glances. "It . . . I just . . . assumed. You said your neighbor fell onto the power lines. What would a *woman* be doing on a tall ladder?"

"Oh, I don't know. Taking down her Christmas lights, perhaps. Painting trim. Cleaning the gutters. I've climbed ladders for those reasons. Haven't you?" In point of fact, my only motive for climbing onto our roof during the last few years had been to fetch objects the kids had thrown up there. But no sense muddling the gist of conversation.

Betsy, still looking nervous, took a step back. "No, those are all Bob's jobs."

"Did you know my neighbor?"

"No," Bob answered, a bit too quickly in my opinion. "We already told you. We just happened to bump into the former owner of your house. We don't know any of your neighbors."

Betsy cleared her throat. Her ditsy smile was looking all the more lame. "I'm sorry to hear about . . . your neighbor." She put her hand on her husband's shoulder. "Bob, let's get going. Molly is obviously not in the mood for visitors."

"Have a nice evening," Bob mumbled.

"Thanks. You, too." They traipsed hurriedly through my backyard and reentered the woods without a glance back.

Hmm. Did I believe Betsy's explanation? Given my prelude about a neighbor falling onto high-voltage wires, a majority of people might have assumed I was referring to a man. But why did they both seem so ill at ease?

A warm breeze rustled the leaves. I scanned the woods, wondering if the Fenders were watching me, cloaked in leafy shadows. I no longer felt comfortable on my own deck. The doorbell was ringing as I slid open the glass back door.

I took a quick look out the peephole, but didn't recognize the man's face, however, distorted by the wide-angle lens. Curiosity bested my common sense. I opened the door a crack, but left the chain in place.

The man wore a nondescript brown suit. With the perverse thought that, the way things were going in my life lately, I may need to identify this man in a lineup, I studied him. He was tall with wavy dark hair, ordinary looking except for the ridge along his eyebrows and receding chin. Maybe forty or so.

He smiled and gave me a polite nod. "Afternoon, ma'am. I'm from the *Herald*. Could I speak to you for just a minute or two, please?"

Uh-oh. The press. "The *Herald*?" The name meant nothing to me, but there were a lot of "*Heralds*" in the nation. "Just a moment." I released the chain and opened the door cautiously, fully prepared to slam it shut if he did anything suspicious. I looked beyond his shoulder, expecting to see a television van, but saw only a blue car parked near the base of my driveway.

"Are you Molly Masters?"

Not wanting to give out any information, I decided to keep him on the defensive. "You're here to discuss . . . the shooting?"

"That's right," he said, his face lighting up as if trying to impart to me how brilliant he thought I must be to have figured that out. "May I come in?"

"No, I'm sorry. For one thing, I don't let strangers into my house. For another thing, I have nothing to say to you or your paper."

This morning's newspaper account had been, thankfully, brief. Under a headline and lead paragraph about "Stolen Diamonds Recovered," it had explained about the diamonds having been buried, recapped previous reports that Helen Raleigh, a former home owner in the Sherwood Forest subdivision, had been shot while on Raleigh's former property, and that the shooter had used a high-power rifle and had been in the woods at the time. For the first time, this article went on to announce that Helen had been a man named Frank Worscheim, a one-time convict of a bank robbery in California and suspect in the series of jewelry heists.

"I understand your concerns, Mrs. Masters, but —"

"That reminds me. How did you know my name?"

He widened his eyes for the briefest of moments, then returned to his smug smile and replied, "I'm an investigative journalist, ma'am. That's my job. As I was saying, we could sit out here on your porch if you'd prefer. This will only take a couple of minutes."

Maybe it was paranoia on my part. Maybe it was the product of an overactive imagination. In any case, he looked like the man shown digging up my yard in Simon's video. Granted, most of the male population of the world looked like the person in that video. But still, why take chances?

"Can I see some ID, please?"

He straightened and gave me a Cheshire-cat grin. "You sound like a bartender. I can assure you, I'm over twenty-one."

"No doubt, but I'd like to know for sure that you're really a reporter before I talk to you."

He shrugged and held out his hands. "All right. If you don't trust me . . ."

He let his voice trail off as if expecting me to back down, but I stared at him, un-flinching. He set his jaw — unimpressive though it was — then reached into his back pocket and pulled out a black leather wallet. He whipped out an ID card, which he held out to me between his index and middle fingers. I took it from him.

To my surprise, the card listed him as working for the *Toledo Herald* and not a local paper. His name, listed under the picture, which appeared to have been taken recently, identified him as Arnold Rhodes. "You're from a newspaper in Ohio?"

"That's right," he replied, retrieving his ID card. "A bank robber with a stash of diamonds buried in someone's yard in the heart of suburbia is pretty big news. Throw in the fact that the robber passed himself off as a woman for a couple of years, and you've got yourself a front-page, twenty-four-point blockbuster."

"Really?" I muttered, though my mind was rapidly assessing type sizes. I'd gotten my bachelor's in journalism. Unfortunately, that had been so long ago, I could no longer remember the headline sizes of major stories.

"You betcha." He slipped his ID card back into his wallet and pocketed it. "So first, I'd like to ask how long you've lived here. Surely you don't consider that an invasion of your privacy, do you?"

I stared at his face, memorizing its every detail. There was something I couldn't quite put my finger on that made me untrusting and uncomfortable. Perhaps it was the intensity of his mannerisms. The way he stared at me. Unfounded paranoia or not, for all I knew, this supposed reporter could have been the unidentified partner of Frank Worscheim.

"You say your name is . . ."

"Arnold Rhodes."

"And you've worked for the *Toledo Herald* for how many years?"

"Two." He chuckled. "Aren't I supposed to be asking you the questions here?"

"Listen, Arnold. This isn't a good time."

A police car was just pulling out of the cul-de-sac behind us, and Arnold glanced back. "I suppose you've had quite a bit of commotion here lately."

"Yes, in fact, why aren't you interested in what's happened next door?"

"Already interviewed the investigating officer. And I find your story much more compelling. So could you at least tell me how long —"

"No, I've really got to be going now. Sorry. But if you come back here tomorrow at this time, I'll answer your questions."

He smiled, but his impatience was written all over his features. "Fine, Mrs. Masters. I'll do that. I'll see you tomorrow, then." He pivoted and got back into his car.

I went back inside and grabbed a phone book. After locating the area code for Toledo, Ohio, I dialed information, parting the curtains to peer at the street. The car was gone. At the operator's predictable prompt of "What city?" I answered, "Toledo. The *Toledo Herald*, please."

After a pause, she said, "There's no such listing."

Chapter 15

My Happy Meal is in the Car

Three police vehicles were still parked in the cul-de-sac. I raced next door, where the sound of male voices told me Tommy and his men were still milling about. Though I knew my actions would perturb some uniformed officer, I leapt — or rather stepped with a modicum of gracefulness — over the yellow police ribbon strung between Simon's mailbox and his wrought-iron lamppost.

I donned a purposeful stride to appear as though I belonged and crossed the front yard. The hinge creaked as I opened the gate and peered around. A pair of male officers were using a tape measure and a third was taking notes. There were no dead bodies in the immediate vicinity, but a long aluminum extension ladder on the grass lay at a diagonal from the house. Automatically, I glanced up. The power lines that I'd barely noticed before now looked dark and menacing. Before I'd taken two steps, the officer looked up from his notebook and pointed at me with his pen. "Hey! You're not allowed in here."

I spotted Tommy, whose red hair made him stand out even at a distance. He was at the far corner of the yard talking with a man in a white shirt and tie. "Sergeant Newton," I called, "could I speak to you for a moment, please?"

Tommy's surprised look quickly changed to a glare. While the other officers went back to what they were doing, Tommy marched over to me and grumbled, "I swear, Moll. You got the persistence of a horsefly the way you keep buzzin' around me."

"Does that mean you think of yourself as a horse?"

Ignoring my comment, he brushed past me and, as he shut the gate behind us, muttered, "What's up?" The furrows on his freckled brow implied this had better be important.

"Have you spoken to any reporters recently?"

"Depends. *How* recently?"

"Within the last hour."

Tommy shook his head, and I quickly filled him in about the bogus reporter who'd claimed to have spoken to "the investigating officer."

Tommy snatched his pad from his pocket.

I grinned, knowing I'd been vindicated. Not only was this important enough to interrupt him, it warranted an entry into his official notes. "What type of car was he driving?"

My momentary sense of pride vanished. I'd paid no attention to the car and had only gotten one quick glance at it from the side. "It was a medium shade of blue."

Tommy raised an eyebrow. *"Blue?* You call that a *type?"*

"Well? I don't know anything about cars. It had two doors. One on each side."

Tommy rolled his eyes. "Hatchback? Sedan?"

"It had four wheels, a regular trunk in the back, and a hood in the front."

"A blue sedan. Now we're getting somewhere. 'Course, if it had something other than four wheels, we'd stand a better chance of makin' a quick ID. Notice if it had New York plates?"

"No, but I'll draw you a picture of the guy. The car, too, if that'd help."

"Fine." He put a hand on my shoulder and gave me a gentle push toward Simon's walkway. "But do it from *inside* your house. I'll swing by and pick it up before I leave here."

Feeling rebuked, I stepped back over the yellow tape. This time one of the hems of my baggy shorts caught on the cordon, and I had to reach back and free myself or risk twanging the tape. Tommy was grinning at me, but had the decency to quickly turn away.

Back in my deserted home, I sat in my living room so I'd be close to the front door and went right to work on sketches of the man and his car. My drawing of the car was so generic Tommy would find it useless, but I remembered the man's features clearly. He had a caveman ridge to his brow and a receding chin, which lent him an almost cartoonish inverted-triangle-shaped face. By the time my drawing was complete, Tommy still hadn't arrived. I needed to pick up the kids from Lauren's soon. I toyed with the thought of going next door again, but dismissed the notion. Tommy didn't deserve the satisfaction he'd glean by reprimanding me for yet another interruption.

Impatient and frustrated, I doodled and eventually wound up drawing a cartoon. An exhausted-looking woman wearing a T-shirt and jeans sits in a posh restaurant. The waiter looks scornfully down at her as she says, "My children and my Happy Meal are in the car. I just want to sit here for a minute and fantasize."

When the doorbell rang, I hopped up to

answer, portrait in hand, expecting it to be Tommy. It was Bob and Betsy Fender. My face fell. I did, however, manage to refrain from uttering the phrase that had popped into my head: *What the hell do you people want from me?*

"Hello, Molly," Bob said with a sheepish smile. Betsy, too, wore an embarrassed expression. She stood directly behind her husband, her plump cheek pressed against his upper arm. From my vantage point, it looked as though Bob had a second head stuck to his sleeve. "May we come in?"

"Well, actually —"

"This will only take a moment." Betsy had cut me off before I could pull out the ever-popular — and, in this case, reasonably accurate — excuse of my being on the way out. She continued, "We want to apologize."

"Apologize? For what?" While I spoke, I visualized them as Tommy's buzzing horse-flies. In the Fenders' case, they were more like fruit flies.

Bob opened the screen door and, uninvited, they both stepped inside. I deliberately took only a half step back, so the three of us stood on the small rectangle of Spanish tile alongside my living room. Betsy now merely clung to his arm, no longer using him as a human shield. They exchanged a glance, and Betsy gave Bob a slight nod.

"Betsy and I have been talking. We decided that —"

"We realize we've come on a bit strong," Betsy interrupted. "We can't expect you and Jim to adopt our lifestyle immediately. But, as friends, we need to compromise."

Friends? Was the Fond of Floras their version of a personals ad? Wanted: couple for long-term relationship. Meat and vegetable eaters need not apply.

Tugging on his bushy mustache, Bob began again, "So we decided —"

"We want to have you and your husband for dinner."

That was either clumsy sentence structure, or the Fenders had converted from fruitatarians into cannibals. They may as well have, for all of the likelihood that I'd say yes. Let alone convince Jim to join me in their stew. I waited, hoping one of the Fenders would specify a date so I could decline more graciously. They merely searched my eyes, hopeful expressions on their faces.

"Thank you for the lovely offer, but I'd have to check with my husband. And I'm pretty sure he'll . . . point out to me that we're . . . moving to Florida soon." I'd muttered the first thing that popped into my mind, but was now slightly appalled with myself. I was somewhat used to my mouth working faster than my brain, but normally I didn't tell an outright lie just to get out of an unpleasant social occasion. Maybe this was an aftereffect from having two acquaintances die in less than a week.

"Permanently?" Betsy asked, her bland features taking on a basset-hound look of disappointment.

I shrugged. "Everything's up in the air at this point."

"You're lucky," Bob replied wistfully, jiggling his dark-rimmed glasses. "Florida has some of the best citrus fruit in the world."

"I'm so sorry to hear you're moving," Betsy said. "At least we can still look forward to seeing you on Monday."

"Monday?"

Betsy's gray eyes widened in surprise. "Yes, of course. The Fond of Floras. Don't tell me you aren't even going to that?"

"I'll be too busy packing," I lied, spreading my hands to demonstrate that I was a mere victim of circumstance. Once again, in for a penny, in for a pound. Still, I mentally chastised myself for not being honest with these people: I'm sorry, but you're kooks and my husband and I dislike you. No offense.

Tommy appeared at the screen door. The Fenders whirled in surprise at his sudden deep voice as he met my eyes and said, "Didn't realize you had visitors. I'll come back."

"No, no," Betsy cried in something of a chirp. "We were just leaving."

"Right," Bob mumbled through his mustache. "Excuse us, Officer."

They brushed past him and headed down the front walk at a near sprint. Was their nervous energy the product of guilt, or just of their unexpectedly encountering a policeman?

Tommy, too, was curious enough to ask, "Who were they?"

"I've been meaning to tell you about them," I began. I handed him the drawings, a bit soggy at the edge as a result of having been in my hands for so long. I still had not ruled out the duo as having something to do with the murder. "This could take a while. Maybe you'd better have a seat."

Tommy sighed.

That evening, Jim, Mom, Karen, and I were playing a spirited game of Parcheesi in my parents' family room, with Nathan rooting loudly for "anyone but Karen," when the doorbell rang. My mother went to answer, and to my surprise, Joanne Abbott swept into the family room a step or two ahead of my mother. Joanne's cheeks were flushed. Her forehead was damp and crossed with worry lines.

Without preamble and in front of my entire family, Joanne put her hands on her hips, glared down at me at my seat on the floor, and said, "How dare you accuse us of pushing Simon Smith into the power lines!"

"I did no such thing," I said, scrambling to my feet. Beside me, Jim rose as well, and I knew he would protect me from bodily harm, if necessary.

"Those were my words exactly to the police!" Joanne spat back at me.

"Great, but since I *didn't* accuse you of pushing the ladder, there's no reason for —"

Joanne jumped as the doorbell rang.

"— you have no reason to be angry at me," I continued and headed toward the foyer.

Joanne's husband, Stan, was standing on the front porch. Through the screen, he asked, "Is my wife here?"

"Yes. She seems to be under the misconception that —" He held up his palm and brushed past me. He wore a tailored white shirt, knee-length shorts, and loafers with black socks that made his fat legs seem all the more pale. It looked as though he were dressed for work, but that someone had, unbeknownst to him, removed the bottom half of his slacks.

We joined the others. Joanne, red-faced and ready to kill, was pacing in a tight circle. She was wearing a white silk blouse and black slacks, and she had some sort of a dark jacket or sweater slung over her shoulders Batman-style. "You didn't have to come, Stan," she growled. "I told you I'd handle this!"

My mother, who tended to clean whenever she was nervous — hence the meticulous house — swept up our half-finished Parcheesi game from the Oriental rug. "Let's go have a seat in the dining room," my mother said. "Can I get anyone some coffee?"

Great idea, Mom, I thought sourly. Arm these irate people with hot liquid to scald me with.

Jim asked, "What's this all about, Stan?"

Stan shook his head and said in a monotone, "You've really gone overboard this time."

Since his eyes were focused on his shoes, I couldn't tell if he meant his wife or one of us had "gone overboard." Maybe he'd only just now noticed how badly he was dressed.

"Mom, could you take the kids upstairs, please?"

My mother shot me a worried look, but Karen and Nathan were so startled by the sudden onslaught of adult-sized tension, they merely took my mother's proffered hands and headed up the stairs with her.

Joanne was breathing so heavily her large nostrils were flaring like a bull's. As soon as I heard a door shut upstairs, I asked her, "Who told you that I'd accused you of killing Simon?"

"Some police officer."

"Sergeant Newton?"

"No. Some young kid in a uniform. He claimed to be an officer, but he looked fifteen or sixteen, at the most."

"Well, he's wrong. I didn't say anything at all about you. How could I? I wasn't even home at the time. I was here, at my mother's house."

"So," Jim said to Stan. He left the word hanging.

Stan met Jim's gaze, then rolled his eyes and set his jaw. Who was he rolling his eyes at — his wife or me?

In my most appeasing voice, I said, "I assure you both that I did not accuse you of having anything whatsoever to do with Simon's death."

Joanne put her hands on her hips and tossed her head back. "Then how did the officer know how upset I was about Simon's cameras? You were the only one who knew that!"

Since this was the absolute truth, I told her in no uncertain terms that I had said nothing to any officer about how either Abbott reacted upon learning about Simon's cameras.

After a few minutes of going over the same ground, Joanne gradually calmed down. Stan apparently felt his role in all of this was that of detached observer, for he said nothing whatsoever. Jim asked him whether the police had spoken to him, but Stan merely nodded, keeping his eyes on Joanne all the while.

Finally, as if suitably convinced that I hadn't committed some horrible act of betrayal, or whatever sin it was that Joanne thought I'd committed, Joanne looked at her husband and gave him a small smile.

To this, Stan said, "Okay, dear?"

She nodded.

He put his arm around her and said to us, "Sorry to bother you." Joanne, who was taller than Stan, dropped her head onto his shoulder. "This has been most upsetting for her, as I'm sure you can understand."

"Of course," Jim replied. I studied his face, momentarily persuaded that Jim was sincere in his claim that he understood. But his eyebrows were knitted, which reassured me that he was every bit as confounded as I was.

"By the way, how did you know where we were staying?" I asked Joanne.

Joanne didn't look at me. Her head still rested rather awkwardly on her husband's shoulder. Her cheeks were still flushed. "Sheila told me."

And how did *she* know? I let Jim escort them out while I dropped down on the couch. Maybe there were bugging devices throughout all of Sherwood Forest.

"Gee-Zeus," he said as he reentered. "What in heaven's name was that all about?"

"It occurs to me that we must be doing something dreadfully wrong. We're leading normal lives. We have our two children, our house, our lawn. Okay, we have a half-dozen frogs and a pair of gay guinea pigs instead of the requisite dog or cat . . . but still. We work hard at our jobs. Though I don't make much of a profit. Everyone in the cartooning industry knows the real money isn't in original art, but licensing and merchandise. So far, nobody's offered to put my mug on a cartoon. Cartoon on a mug. Anyway, the point is, day in, day out, we follow the rules."

Jim raised an eyebrow. I shrugged and continued, "Okay. *You* follow the rules, and I follow most of them. The ones that make sense to me. And yet, at times like this, I just want someone to tell me why. Why us? Why did our former home owner have to turn out to be a bank robber and jewelry thief who buried loot in our yard and then got murdered on top of it? Would it have spoiled some vast, divine plan if it had been in someone *else's* yard? And why was our next-door neighbor a Peeping Tom who thinks he's James Bond? Why did he have to die, right after he said he'd give me evidence?"

Jim patted my knee and snuggled beside me on the couch. After a long silence, he said, "I don't know. Fifteen years ago, I was sitting in the library at C.U., trying to decipher a complex power-supply circuit, when I happened to look up and spot this . . . skinny girl with long brown hair, the darkest eyes I'd ever seen, and a radiant smile that seemed to lift me right out of my chair. And sometimes I ask myself, 'Why me?' What did I ever do to deserve such good fortune? And I don't know the answer to that question, either."

"That's so sweet," I told him, my eyes misting and my voice choked with emotion. I resisted a perverse urge to facetiously pretend I didn't know he meant me. And to point out that that first meeting of ours was actually *sixteen* years ago. And that he'd been reading *Sports Illustrated* at the time. I gave him a deep kiss, which was interrupted by the sound of the door being flung open upstairs, followed by Karen's plaintive, "Mo-o-omm-eeee, Nathan poked me in the eye!"

"I did not! I was just patting her on the head and I missed! Accidentally!"

Jim and I chuckled. Our eyes met, and I knew he felt the same rush of gratitude that I did — that however high life might have stacked the cards against us, we were in this together. And that, at times like this, our love felt like nothing short of a miracle.

"Her eye is fine," my mother called from the other room. "I'll handle this."

"Okay. Thanks, Mom." It was never necessary to tell me twice that someone else would deal with my squabbling children.

I paused, thinking. "You know what's strange, Jim? I saw the Lillydales at the school party today. They were acting out-of-character and hostile toward me, just like the Abbotts. They've obviously been talking to one another, since Joanne claims to have learned my parents' address from Sheila. Somebody must be spreading lies about us. Of all of them, Joanne strikes me as the least rational. Maybe Joanne had hallucinated something about me and told them some crazy story. Maybe that would explain why everyone is suddenly so angry at me."

"Let's just keep a low profile for a while. Stay away from the house entirely."

While Jim was speaking, I got up and started rummaging in the cabinet by the phone for Sheila's business card. Though I located it, her home phone wasn't listed. I started flipping through the phone book.

"What are you doing?" Jim asked.

"Making a quick phone call."

I dialed the Lillydales. Roger answered. I greeted him pleasantly, but was met with silence. Not to be discouraged, I asked to speak to Sheila.

"She's at her office," he barked.

I glanced at my watch. It was almost seven-thirty.

"Listen, Roger, I really wanted a chance to talk to you about what happened this afternoon at school. I sincerely believe there's been some kind of a misunderstanding that —"

"I can't talk now." He hung up.

Chapter 16

Pardon My Faux Paws

I was still standing next to the telephone when Nathan charged down the stairs, followed, eventually, by Karen. Karen was not a happy camper. She drooped down the stairs one step at a time like a human Slinky, but I noted that she had both of her eyes, so I was inclined not to overreact.

I waited for one of them to ask if our guests had beaten us prior to leaving. Preoccupied with his own concerns, Nathan rushed up and gave me a big hug. A sure sign that he'd deliberately poked his sister and felt he needed an ally.

In the meantime, Karen shuffled over to join Jim on the couch, but curled up against the arm across from him. He murmured, "How are you doing, sweet pea? Is your eye okay?" and tried to rub her back. She gave an indignant growl and jerked away from his touch. Obviously, she'd decided to give everyone the cold shoulder.

My mother came downstairs. At the

bottom step, she paused, studied our faces, and said with a forced smile, "Did your friends leave?"

"Everything's fine. It must have been the shock of —" I stopped, determined to re-phrase my statement to avoid the pun. "They must have been deeply upset by our neighbor's accident and chose to vent their emotions at us." Although I also fervently believed that Joanne was either seriously off balance, or someone had been spreading lies about us.

Mom arched an eyebrow, but made no comment. A piece of paper was in her hand, which she lifted. "Oh, Molly," she said pleasantly as she brought the paper over to me, "earlier today I was cleaning the base-ment when this came for you. I meant to give it to you sooner, but I completely for-got."

She handed me a fax. I leaned back against the cabinet and read it. A prospec-tive customer wanted an eye-catching faxable flyer to advertise an upcoming office party. If possible, they wanted to see some-thing from me by four P.M. — more than three hours ago. The time stamp in the margin indicated they'd sent the fax at 9:43 this morning.

Annoyed, I glanced over the top of the

paper at my mother. "You got this off my fax machine and forgot about it?"

She patted her perfectly neat hair. " 'Fraid so. I must admit that I read it, though, and you can send them that cartoon of yours I just love. Remember? The one you sent to me a few months ago when we were in Florida. About the bears with the paws?"

"Oh, yeah." She was right. That cartoon might do quite nicely for this customer. "I'd forgotten about that one."

"I think I've got a copy of it in my desk." She opened the antique drop-lid desk in the corner and managed to retrieve the cartoon in all of three seconds. This was my mother's typical efficiency and didn't necessarily *guarantee* that she'd already located my cartoon this morning, when she first read my fax. "And if you want, you can include a note blaming me for your not getting back to them sooner."

Blame my mother? That'd sure impress a prospective customer with my professionalism. I excused myself and trotted downstairs. I used my low-tech security system of putting a large X over the cartoon and faxed it to them, not anticipating a response until tomorrow or Monday.

In the cartoon, a batch of bears are standing around at a cocktail party, mingling and sipping from martini glasses. All of the bears look virtually identical, except for one who's wearing what looks like enormous, furry gloves. A couple of other bears are looking at the gloves with disdain. One of these bears whispers to the other, "I don't know why they invited that guy. He has the world's worst faux paws."

When I returned to the family room, my mother was about to head upstairs. "I'm going to bed early tonight," she explained. "I've just started reading a wonderful novel, and I'm dying to get back to it."

"Okay. By the way, I'm curious as to how the Abbotts knew we were here. Have you ever met my neighbor, Sheila Lillydale? Her son's in Karen's class. Sheila's petite, very pretty, with long dark hair."

Mom smiled. "Oh, yes. We met at the school party for spring break. What a nice person. So perky and friendly."

Friendly to everyone but me. "Did you happen to tell her your address?"

"No, though I remember introducing myself as your mother, and I probably did tell her I lived in Sherwood Forest."

That would explain how she could have gotten the address. If she remembered Mom's last name, she could have looked up the address in the directory. I shifted my attention to the children, who were starting to antagonize each other again. Nathan had squeezed between Jim and Karen, and Karen was trying to shove him off the couch with her feet. "Tell Grandma good night, guys."

They mumbled good night. The moment Mom left the room, Karen started to cry.

"Does your eye still hurt, sweetie?" I asked her gently.

She shrugged. Nathan, however, immediately shouted, "It was just an accident! It doesn't mean she has to stay mad at me forever!"

Karen began to sob full force. "First he puts gum in my hair. Then he pokes me in the eye. Why do I have to have such a stupid brother?"

"I'm not stupid! You're stupid, you stupidhead!"

My son had better not follow in my footsteps. He was not going to get anyplace in the greeting card industry with such limited use of adjectives. Good emotional content, though.

I pried the children apart just before Nathan could land a blow, then unenthusiastically began my usual litany: You two need to separate — blah blah — time out to get control of yourself — blah blah. Some parenting counselor had recommended the technique, which I swear was designed to bore your children into submission.

Jim, in the meantime, was reading the newspaper as if none of us existed. How annoying.

With the children momentarily quiet and seated in opposite corners of the room, it occurred to me that this was the perfect opportunity to do some sleuthing. Sheila might still be at her office and, by speaking to her while she was away from her husband, I might be able to get her to tell me what horrendously upsetting thing it was she thought I'd done.

I swept up my purse. "I'm going to Sheila Lillydale's office. I should be back in an hour, at the most."

"Maybe we both should go," Jim protested, folding the newspaper.

"One of us needs to stay and get the kids to bed, and I've already got the car keys in my hand."

He glared at me, which I pretended not to notice. Just because you revel in the miracle of your love for your spouse doesn't mean you have to be nice to him all of the time.

Sheila's office was on the top floor of a two-story building with wraparound upper and lower decks. The main lobby was locked. Lights were on in an upstairs window. Maybe I could throw pebbles at the window and see if Sheila eventually looked out. As I walked around the building, I spotted an external staircase. I went up and pounded on a door marked, LILLYDALE, ATTNY. P.C. After a half minute of pounding, Sheila came to the door, looking very surprised. She was wearing a long-sleeved blue dress with a floral print that was very flattering on her small, trim figure. She rapidly unlocked the door and leaned out.

"Hello, Sheila. I know I shouldn't have barged in unannounced and everything, but your husband said you were here, and I was hoping we could get our misunderstanding worked out once we had a chance to discuss it face-to-face."

She hesitated only momentarily, then slowly nodded and held the door for me. She let it close behind me, then locked it. Her lips were fixed in a grim line, but she seemed at ease otherwise. She faced me and frowned. "I was going to call you in the morning, Molly, to apologize. You see, Roger and I had just had a terrible fight about you before we arrived."

"A fight about me?" I repeated. Seemingly I'd acquired of late the ability to inspire great emotion — all of it bad — among my neighbors.

"Why don't we go sit down in my office?" she asked. She led me through the nondescript waiting room and into a much more lavish area. This room was done in greens and earth tones, with plush wall-to-wall carpeting and oak wainscotting below an elegant wallpaper. There were no pictures hanging, but I eyed her diploma from UCLA. At least, I had to assume it was her diploma, since the name on it read "Sheila Benitez." Beside it was a second diploma certifying her law degree, this one from the University of California at Berkeley. She gestured at the pair of stuffed brown velveteen chairs that faced her desk. I dropped my purse beside the first one and sat down, surprised at how soft it was. I sank so far into it I half expected to bump my nose on my knees.

"It's a shame about Simon Smith," Sheila said, shutting the oak door. "An officer came here and told me about it a few hours ago."

"You haven't been home?"

"I've been so behind at work, I've been here since we left the party." She slipped behind her enormous black enamel desk and sat down in her equally large desk chair. Now I understood her choice of office furniture; her high perch more than negated our height differential. "Roger says you're dangerous and that I should drop you from my client list."

"Dangerous? Me?" I tried to scoot forward on my seat, without much luck. Roger should see me now. *No one* could pose a physical threat in Sheila's man-eating chairs.

She nodded. "He seems to think you killed Helen Raleigh."

"He's wrong. I didn't . . . What makes him think that?"

"Roger's point is that we've lived next door to the same people for at least three years without incident. Now all of a sudden both Helen Raleigh and Simon Smith are dead, after you argued with them." She paused and looked down at her hands. "And Roger says you were coming on to him during your encounter at the mall coffee shop."

"That's simply not true." Inside I was screaming about the injustice of such a wildly incorrect accusation, but I had to be careful not to place myself squarely between husband and wife. "I was . . . trying to be nice because he seemed so down in the dumps. Maybe he misinterpreted my be-havior."

Her face was a lovely but emotionless mask as she looked down at me. I couldn't tolerate being below her line of vision when I knew full well I was telling the truth. I rose, tossed my purse on the chair as a booster, and sat back down. By keeping my back rigid, I was now at her eye level. "Sheila, all I can tell you is I love my husband. I would never have an affair. And I would never kill anyone."

I paused, studying her reaction, which was inscrutable. "I came over here to clear the air, but I've been on the defensive ever since I walked in the door. Did you do that deliberately?"

She raised an eyebrow. "No, though I sup-pose it's a professional liability." Sheila leaned on her elbows and gazed directly into my eyes. "I got a call from Joanne a couple of hours ago. She's terribly upset at you. She wanted me to bring a suit on her behalf against you."

"Oh?"

"You don't sound surprised."

"When your life is going down the drain, you tend not to be surprised by a wet hairball or two. What did you tell her?"

"I told her that you had already hired me

on a separate issue, which, of course, I didn't divulge. I urged her as a friend, not as a lawyer, to discuss her problem with you before seeking a means of legal action."

"She came over to my parents' house about an hour ago. Did you tell her where I was staying?"

"No, how could I? I don't know where you're staying. She asked me if I knew your mother's address, so I'm assuming that's where you were."

"And did you give that to her?"

"No, she was so upset, I thought it best not to fan the fire. I advised her to wait until the morning to speak to you, after she'd had a chance to sleep on it."

Hmm. One of these women was lying, but it struck me as inconsequential either way.

"Joanne is not . . ." Sheila paused. "Ever since the miscarriage, she's —"

"Joanne had a miscarriage? When?" I'd had a miscarriage myself, many years ago during my first pregnancy. I was painfully aware of how devastating that could be.

"Last year. Well before you and Jim moved in."

"That's sad. But I don't get the connection between that and what's happening now."

"She tends to overreact and become emotional. The Abbotts have been trying to adopt a baby. Two weeks ago, the hospital called them and told them to come in and get their baby. They drove to the hospital, and the birth mother changed her mind. They were both crushed."

Two weeks ago. Could this have some connection to Mr. Helen's murder? Could he have been the baby's father and . . . This was getting ridiculous. Not everything in Carlton was tied to Mr. Helen. It only seemed that way. Nonetheless, that brought to mind another puzzling incident that *was* tied to him.

"Sheila, before I forget, there was a strange man who visited me at my house earlier this afternoon. Did you happen to see him or his car? A blue sedan?"

"No, why?"

"Frank Worscheim was an inmate in California." Again, she looked puzzled, so I explained, "That's the guy who'd disguised himself as Helen Raleigh. He had a partner in some jewelry heists."

"Oh, yes. I'd only had time to glance at the paper today."

"I was thinking that the two men might have met in prison. The guy who came to see me, claiming to be the reporter, might have been Frank Worscheim's partner."

"What did he say his name was?"

"Arnold something."

Though she showed no reaction, she repeated, "Arnold?"

"Why? Do you know him?"

"No, of course not."

"You seemed to recognized the name," I lied, merely testing her reaction.

She leaned back in her chair. "I'm simply troubled by your theory. The last thing any of us wants is the guy who shot Helen Raleigh prowling around in our neighborhood."

"Which Helen Raleigh do you mean? The Helen Raleigh who lived in disguise in my house, or the original one?"

She drew her eyebrows together as if puzzled. "Our former neighbor. Was the actual Helen Raleigh the victim of a shooting, as well?"

"Yes. That was reported in the same article. That Frank Worscheim killed her and then assumed her identity."

"The police know *Frank* killed her?"

Her wording bothered me. She called him "Frank" as if they'd been on a first-name basis — which they had been, but at the time, his first name had been Helen. In fact, all of her responses bothered me. I had a couple of close friends in Colorado who were lawyers — I'd known them before law school and tried not to hold their choice of professions against them. Two characteristics they had in common were uncanny memories for details and their voracious reading of the newspaper. I suspected Sheila was playing dumb, but I had no idea why she would do so. "The paper identified *him*, not his partner, as Helen Raleigh's alleged killer," I answered.

She gave me a sad smile. "That's very hard for me to believe. Helen . . . or rather, Frank, didn't seem like a murderer. I've met —" She broke off. "Is everything copacetic between you and Joanne now?"

"From my point of view it is," I answered halfheartedly, intrigued by what she'd almost said. My hunch was that she was going to say she'd met murderers before — perhaps while she was practicing law in California. "You went to school in California. Were you —"

She followed my gaze to the diploma behind her. "You're very observant."

"I've got good eyesight, too. Were you there during the jewelry heists?"

"The ones allegedly perpetrated by Frank Worscheim?"

I nodded, finding her wording annoying.

"We moved here five years ago. When did

the robberies occur?"

Yet another item already reported in the press. "Three years ago," I answered, still suspecting she already knew this. "Frank Worscheim had just been released from the California penitentiary. He'd done time for armed robbery. Would the court proceedings be on file in a local law library or anything?"

She had her poker face on again and said pleasantly, "No, you'd have to know which county he was tried in and contact that courthouse for their records."

Thinking out loud, I muttered, "Maybe Tommy can get a copy of the transcripts and see if he mentioned the name 'Arnold.'"

"Tommy?" she repeated.

"The investigating officer. Surely the police have access to trial information, don't they?"

She nodded. "Unless the judge had them sealed for some reason." She pushed back her silk sleeve to glance at a gold watch. My eyes widened as I, too, stared at her wrist. Just above the watch was a spectacular diamond tennis bracelet. Why wear such nice jewelry above your watch and hidden by your sleeve?

"That's a beautiful bracelet. May I see it?"

She gave me a stiff smile. "It's just

zirconias. I forgot I still had it on." She took it off as if to give me a closer look, but dropped it into her desk drawer instead.

"Isn't there some professional directory of lawyers?" I asked, feeling my cheeks warm with embarrassment over what I was thinking.

"Yes, the Hubble and Martindale Directory. Listen, Molly, I don't mean to rush you, but I'd really like to get home to my family. It's been a long day."

"Oh, sure."

Sheila walked me to the door and locked it behind me. As I started the car, I stared up at her office window for a moment. Some Coloradoans have an accent in which the word "lawyer" sounded like "liar." Fitting.

I drove to the public library. Reading her listing in the directory might not tell me much, but at least I'd find out if she practiced criminal law when she was in California.

The volume for the Hubble and Martindale Directory of Lawyers for New York State was several inches thick and weighed a ton. Lawyers for our county were listed alphabetically, and I quickly found the listing for Sheila Benitez Lillydale. At least she was licensed to practice law, as of last year when the directory was published.

The directory listed a one-paragraph biography of the lawyer. I glanced at Sheila's birth year and was surprised to see she was forty. She looked much younger than that. When I stopped and calculated, she'd gotten her B.A. from UCLA eighteen years ago, which was about right chronologically.

Her entry listed that she practiced "family law," and she had indeed been a public defender in Los Angeles for seven years.

Suddenly my mental flags snapped to attention. She'd been a public defender while Frank Worscheim was on trial for armed robbery. Granted, L.A. was a huge city and odds were astronomical against her having represented him then. But an old saying had popped into my mind: When you eliminate the impossible, the answer must lie within the realm of possibilities, however unlikely.

What if they'd kept in contact with each other after his trial? What if Sheila had deliberately misled me about her husband having an affair with "Helen Raleigh" — that all along, *she'd* been having an affair with him? If the tennis bracelet of hers had been a gift from him, that would explain why she kept it in her office.

I headed home, my mind in a whirl. Should I call Tommy Newton from my mother's house, or go straight to the police station? There was no rush. Sheila wouldn't have any reason to suspect that I might be on course for uncovering her clandestine relationship with Frank Worscheim.

I was only mildly surprised to see Sheila Lillydale waiting for me in my parents' driveway.

"I see you beat me here," I said, lowering my voice by a notch to make myself sound relaxed.

She didn't smile. "I was leaving the building, just after you drove away. I saw you turn into the library." Her tone was accusatory, and she was staring directly into my eyes.

"Would you believe I was looking for a book that was already checked out?"

She shook her head. "You were looking at the Hubble and Martindale Directory. You know, don't you." It was not a question.

In general, people tend to underestimate me. I'm not sure why — perhaps because I'm a sloppy dresser, or because I'm a basic introvert, hiding behind a class-clown facade. Rather than analyze it to death, I use it to my advantage. But Sheila had not made that mistake. She had seen through me and knew I wasn't buying her act.

I nodded. "You were Frank Worscheim's lawyer."

Chapter 17

This Does Not Meet Our Needs

"Let me explain," Sheila began. "I had nothing to do with his decision to move here. I didn't even know he'd gotten released from prison. Or that he pulled some more robberies. I moved here specifically to get away from him. I needed a new start with my family."

The light from the darkening sky was muted, but bright enough for me to see how tired and worried she looked. Even in the rapidly fading light, she indeed looked forty, not thirty or so as I'd assumed, having blamed the faint age lines around her eyes and lips on too much sun.

I was gradually developing a new picture of her — an aging beauty, perhaps desperately trying to hold on to her dashing husband. Or was it Mr. Helen she'd loved and lost? What if they'd been in cahoots, but she'd hired Simon Smith to spy on him? Simon's surveillance had revealed that Mr. Helen was set to run out on her, as he had with his former partner in the jewelry heists. So she killed Mr. Helen, and killed Simon to prevent him from revealing her crime.

"You'd had an affair with Frank while you were his lawyer?"

"No," Sheila retorted as if disgusted. She sat back on the trunk of her forest green BMW. "He'd become obsessed with me. That's why I wanted to move. I was worried about his . . . I was afraid of what would happen when he got his release. He used to write to me from prison. He thought *I* was in love with *him*, too, but it was this ridiculous infatuation that he'd built from nothing. Just before we moved, I went to visit him one last time. I told him there was nothing between us, that I never wanted him to contact me again. We moved here, and I didn't hear from him for months. I forgot all about him." She clenched her teeth. "But he must have tracked me down. He'd lived here for a couple of weeks, disguised as Helen Raleigh, before I even recognized him. Then I didn't know what to do."

She paused. I prompted, "You recognized him?"

"We were all outside, Ben, Roger, and me, and . . . Helen was out front gardening, so Roger said we should go say hello. Which we did. It was the way Helen was staring at me.

That smile. He twisted one corner of his lips up, in this young-punk smile of his he'd never outgrown. And I knew."

"Did you tell Roger right away?"

"I never told him." She shook her head wildly as she spoke, her eyes wide at the very thought of telling Roger. "If Roger had ever found out . . . he'd be so jealous. He'd think that I'd wanted Frank to move here. That we'd arranged it."

"So Roger never knew about Helen's disguise?"

"Never. Not until the story came out after Frank was murdered, that is. That's why we were so distraught at the school party. Roger eventually twisted things around to make all of our marital problems *your* fault, and I felt it wasn't prudent to try to argue with him."

"*My* fault? I don't get the connection. How could *I* have anything to do with *your* marriage?"

She sighed. "You're the one who's been stirring the pot. Fair or not, he's blaming you for the rancid ingredients."

Oh, baloney! Depending on which Lillydale you asked, Roger had either "left town on business" or "separated" with his wife *before* Mr. Helen was shot. Prior to that ghastly event, I hadn't been near anyone's kitchen, let alone stirred their pots. However, there

324

was no sense in arguing with Sheila about her husband's point of view. "So Roger knew about Frank Worscheim being an infatuated former client of yours?"

She pulled her barrette out and let her dark, shimmering hair cascade down her shoulders. "Roger knew he was a former client. That had been a pretty intense trial, and I'd been tied up with it for several months. But I never let Roger know about the phone calls and letters from Frank. Roger would have become incensed."

"So all that stuff you told me about Roger and Helen having an affair was a lie. Why?"

She tightened her lips in a slight, momentary wince, then searched my eyes. "I was testing you. I was trying to see how much you knew about Frank. Roger *is* having an affair. I just don't know who with. You seem to be his type."

That was a silly idea, but everything about Sheila struck me as being slightly off-center, so I wasn't surprised, nor affronted. "It certainly isn't me. Maybe Joanne Abbott."

"No, not Joanne. What makes you say her?" Sheila asked.

"She's the only woman left in the immediate neighborhood."

"She's not attractive enough for Roger."

"But you think I am? That's the nicest

horrible thing anyone's said about me. Why didn't you tell the police about all of this?"

"It makes me look guilty. And I didn't kill him."

I stared at her, incredulous. That was too lame an excuse to swallow, even though I could almost swallow the rest of her story. Withholding key evidence in a murder investigation was stupid and risky. As a lawyer, nobody knew that better than she. "You said you had an alibi. That you were in court at the time of the shooting."

"I wasn't. Roger was right. In part. I haven't been disbarred, but my license has been suspended."

"So you've been representing me illegally?"

"Not exactly. I haven't charged you. And my suspension should be lifted at the end of the month."

At which time she planned to charge me two hundred dollars an hour for past services rendered. From her jail cell. She seemed willing to freely admit to having told me lie after lie, then expected me to believe she was telling the truth that she hadn't murdered Mr. Helen. "Why was your license suspended?"

She squirmed. "I'd rather not discuss this, but I guess you deserve the truth." I had to fight back a smile at that line, as she continued, "I had a minor substance-abuse problem."

Oh joy. A murdering drug-abuser working illegally with a suspended license. Just what everyone wants in their high-priced lawyer. She could make most clients look squeaky clean.

"So where *were* you when Frank Worscheim was murdered?"

"Alone in my office."

The screen door banged open, and Karen and Nathan ran out, barefoot, otherwise wearing the same shorts and T-shirts they'd had on all day. "Hi, Mommy," Nathan said. "We're catching lightning bugs."

"Not tonight, you're not." I caught them as they tried to dash past me and cast a nervous glance at Sheila who regarded them with a blank expression on her face. She had no reason to hurt them, but after what I'd just learned, I didn't want my children anywhere near her. "I thought Dad was going to put you to bed by now."

"He's watching TV," Karen explained. "There's no school tomorrow, you know."

Sheila got into her car. "I'm going to the police station now to give witness testimony. You probably don't believe me, but you can call the police later to verify."

She drove off while I ushered the children inside. After almost an hour of stall tactics, the children were in bed, and I called Lauren. She told me that Tommy had gotten called out a half hour earlier and that he'd told her there'd been "a break in the case."

I gave Lauren my theory about Sheila killing Mr. Helen and then Simon. Lauren wholeheartedly and enthusiastically agreed that it sounded as if I'd solved the case. In the meantime, Jim had reentered the master bedroom where I was on the phone and kept interrupting with an occasional "What?" and "Hey!" He obviously felt I should have shared this information with him first before calling my best friend. That was one of those differences between men and women he should have adjusted to by now. Nonetheless, he left the room in a huff.

"Tommy just drove up," Lauren announced.

"Already? Ask him if he arrested Sheila. No, wait. Don't."

"Hi, darling," Lauren said. Her voice was muffled, so she'd partially covered the receiver, but I heard Tommy ask who she was talking to.

"Can you put Tommy on?" I asked Lauren, but Tommy growled hello so quickly I realized he must have snatched the phone from her.

"Did you arrest Sheila Lillydale for murder?"

"That'd be jumpin' the gun there, Moll. Those of us who are trained and earn a living as officers of the law tend to frown on such things."

I rolled my eyes. He just had to get his little digs in about how he was a policeman and I wasn't. "Don't you think it looks suspicious that Sheila didn't tell you she was Helen Raleigh's lawyer? Back when Helen was Frank Worscheim, I mean."

" 'Course it's suspicious. But that's all it is at this point."

"He came back for her, don't you see? Maybe they were in the whole thing together all along. I know Sheila claims Frank loved her and it was unreciprocated and he moved here unbeknownst to her. But ask yourself this, Tommy. If you were to try to convince some former girlfriend to leave her husband for you, would you do it wearing heels, falsies, and a wig?"

Tommy sighed. "No. Can't say as I would. Maybe he thought the way to her heart was to try to get in touch with his feminine side."

"Funny, Tommy. My point is, you wouldn't disguise yourself as a woman, as

Frank Worscheim did. *Unless* that was part of the original plan, to keep his identity hidden from Sheila's husband and from the former partner in the jewelry heist." Tommy made no comment, so I added, "Did she tell you she has a diamond tennis bracelet she keeps in her office?"

"Tennis bracelet?"

"She claims it's just zirconias, but I don't believe her. I'll bet that was a gift from Frank. Plus, she has no alibi for the shooting."

There was a noise on the line that sounded suspiciously as though Tommy were cursing under his breath. "Listen, Moll. We can always arrest Ms. Lillydale for withholding evidence if we feel she's a flight risk or posin' a threat. Rest assured, we're keepin' an eye on her. But bear in mind, Frank Worscheim shot Helen Raleigh, an innocent bystander. He stiffed his partner and ran off with all of the stash from a string of jewelry heists. We ain't exactly talking about a nice guy here."

"Granted. But that —"

"Know who most hardened criminals blame that they're forced to serve time? Not the judge or the jury. Not themselves for breakin' the law in the first place. They blame their lawyers. 'I'm here because my lawyer screwed up.' So maybe Frank Worscheim did, as you say, come looking for Sheila Lillydale. And maybe he intentionally moved into her neighborhood. But maybe that wasn't because they were former lovers, but because he wanted revenge for his having been in the pen."

I sat back on my bed and tried to put that reverse spin on my theory. If accurate, it could mean that Sheila had told me the truth tonight. "I guess that makes about as much sense as any of this does. Did you have any luck, tracking down the bogus reporter?"

"Faxed your likeness of him to L.A. to see if they could ID the guy. Nothing so far. Could be your run-of-the-mill crackpot. Wants to play investigative reporter. Cases like this bring 'em out of the woodwork."

"Do you believe that?"

He sighed. "No. I think you're right on this one. I think he's Frank Worscheim's former partner. I'm stepping up the patrols in your neighborhood, and I've got an APB out on his car and him. In the meantime . . . the boys 'n' me are movin' into Lauren's place. My house is just sittin' empty. You and your family could stay out there for a few days, or a few weeks. However long it takes us to catch this guy."

My initial reaction was "Yuck," but I kept the thought to myself. I had this vision of a little, rectangular house in dire need of cleaning. That wasn't fair, since Tommy was undoubtedly a better housekeeper than I was. Yet I felt like a turtle being offered someone else's shell, when all I wanted was my own. "I'll discuss it with Jim. Thanks."

The next morning was Friday, and the first day of the kids' summer vacation. Bad news kept rolling in. My cartoon about the horse and cowboy getting onto an elevator with live music had been rejected. They'd sent me a fax stating, "This does not meet with our needs." I coped with my resulting disappointment by designing another cartoon. A sad-looking William Shakespeare sits in a modern office and faces a man behind a desk, who hands him a stack of paper, the cover of which reads *Hamlet*. The man says to Shakespeare, "This doesn't meet with our editorial needs. Have you ever thought about trying your hand at . . . oh, rap music, perchance?"

Unlike me, Jim suffered no shortage of demand for *his* expertise. He had fallen behind in work and left at the crack of dawn. I needed to shop for groceries, and Mom wanted to go, too. So we loaded the kids in the backseat and started to back the car out of the driveway. Just then, a black minivan drove up and pulled in behind me, blocking my exit.

I craned my neck and saw Stan Abbott peering at me. Joanne was in the passenger seat. Stan got out of his vehicle, but left it where it was, blocking us in.

"Uh, morning, Stan," I called out the window to him. "We're kind of in a hurry." That wasn't true, except that when you're going someplace with your children, you're *always* in somewhat of a hurry, as you never know how long they'll stay in a confined space together before coming to blows.

"This will just take a minute." He gave a quick glance to his minivan, where Joanne still sat.

"What's up, Stan?"

"My wife had been feeling a little rattled. I hope you understand. She's not a well woman."

"She seemed perfectly in control at the home-owners' association meeting the other night."

"Depends on her meds. I don't know if you know this, but she had a miscarriage. The whole thing led to some sort of chemical imbalance. She's fine when she takes her Prozac, but whenever she forgets, it's trouble with a capital 'T'."

"Oh, the poor dear," Mom said sadly.

"I don't want to go to the store," Nathan said. "Greenie's tail is gone and I want to see if he climbs onto the raft."

"Greenie's *mine!* Brownie is yours."

"You gave me —"

"I'll let you each pick out a pack of gum," I said into the rearview mirror. Following the instructions for the frog kit, we had placed a small piece of wood in the punch bowl to allow the frogs to climb out of the water. That led to both children trying to claim ownership of the first official frog. "Yes," I told Stan, "that's too bad. All is forgiven."

"Here she is now. Ixnay on the ozacpray."

Oh, good. Pig latin. That'll fool her.

Joanne stepped up beside Stan to peer into my window. "Molly? I wanted to apologize for my behavior last night. I had some misconceptions, and I overreacted. Please accept my apologies."

Nathan was starting to spit at the window. Any second now, he'd direct it at Karen. "No problem. We've got to run."

"Quite the tragedy with Simon, wasn't it?" Stan said, shaking his head knowingly, but watching us every minute.

"Yes. He was your neighbor for . . . what? Ten years now?"

"Six. Felt like ten, though. No need to speak ill of the dead, but let's face it. He was a mean old geezer."

"Yes, but he meant well."

"Only if you consider spying on your neighbors well-meaning."

"We were on our way out, until you blocked us in. By the way, Mom, do you know a good mechanic? The emergency brake seems to slip. Yesterday, I had the brake on and the car backed all the way down the driveway by itself."

"Well," Stan said, casting a nervous glance at his van. "We'd better get going."

"Again," Joanne said, "I'm dreadfully sorry about my outburst last night. I don't know what got into me."

"Don't mention it. I don't know what gets into me half the time, either."

"You have very strange neighbors," my mother muttered the moment the Abbotts were safely back in their own car.

"You noticed," I said, glancing in my rear-view mirror. As I watched them drive off, I waited an extra minute to make sure they were out of sight, then started off slowly. "We should have known something was up when we saved tens of thousands of dollars on the house."

At the store, Mom grabbed a separate

cart, and she went off to find the items on her carefully written list, while I went off to work on my own mental one. The children, who found shopping with Grandma to be less of an ordeal than with their mom, went off with her.

I have my own method of shopping in which I start at the leftmost aisle and wind up and down each aisle till I reach the far end of the store. That way I combine my exercise regimen with my errands.

I was a couple of aisles in, selecting among the brands and flavors of boxed rice, when I heard a deep "Hello, Mrs. Masters."

I turned and almost screamed. It was the phony newspaper reporter. "Arnold." I was scared out of my wits to see him, and blurted stupidly, "Uh, Hark the Herald. This is a surprise."

"I'll bet. I've gotten pretty good at following people in cars so that they don't spot me."

I looked to either side of the aisle, panicked at the thought that my mother and my children would cross paths with me at any moment. "Are you still looking for a story?"

"Writing my own now." He pulled a small, shiny hand-gun from the pocket of his windbreaker, then stuffed it back in his pocket, the bulging barrel pointing right at me. I glanced up, hoping for a surveillance camera, but the nearest one was far away. "Just come with me."

Though I was scared witless, I managed to mutter, "I'd really rather not."

"Either come with me or I'll do some shooting practice at smaller targets." He pointed behind me with his chin.

I turned around and spotted Mom and the kids at the end of the aisle, heading our way. My eyes filled with tears. I sent up a silent prayer.

"You tell your mom nice and calm that you have to go. Make it convincing if you want everyone to leave this store alive."

"Uh, Mom, this is . . . Tommy's good friend, Arnold."

"Nice to meet you, Arnold."

"We have to go."

"Go? Why? Where?"

Where? Good question! "Um, I . . . forgot that . . . it's Tommy's birthday today. Arnold just reminded me that . . . that they've planned a surprise party for him at his office in fifteen minutes. So he offered to give me a ride." I cleared my throat and said, "Just let me get you the keys, Mom." My hands were shaking like mad as I fumbled through the various compartments in my purse, Arnold staring over my shoulder. I finally got hold of the keys and gave them to her.

The way she pushed Karen behind her left me no doubt that Mom knew I was being kidnapped. What I didn't know, though, was what she would do now. I tried to signal her with my eyes to just play along till we were gone.

She forced a smile. "Have a nice time at the party, dear. Do you want me to come pick you up?"

"No," Arnold said, "I'll give her a ride home this afternoon. It was nice meeting you, ma'am. Let's go, Molly."

I led the way out of the store. On the sidewalk, he grabbed a tight hold of my upper arm and started half dragging me toward a red Chevrolet that was parked illegally in the no parking zone.

"You're lucky I'm a nice guy. Your mother obviously didn't believe that bogus story of yours."

"It was the best I could do under the circumstances," I said through a tight jaw.

He opened the passenger door and gave me a shove. I got in and fastened my seat belt, fully aware of the futility of the gesture. The air inside the car stank with the smell of cigarettes. The ashtray was brimming.

"You don't know my mother," I told him as soon as he got into the driver seat. I was afraid to look back for fear I'd spot Mom chasing after us. "She'll never catch on. She's got Alzheimer's. That's why I had to take her shopping. I should never have left her alone with the children. She'll probably get lost on the way home."

"You're breaking my heart," he growled as he started the engine. We pulled out of the store onto Route 146. Unable to resist, I glanced back. We were not being followed. Mom would be alerting the store management by now, and they would notify the police — but what could she tell them to look for? This was not even the same car he'd been driving before. He must have deliberately switched cars. Would anyone know anything at all about the type of vehicle we were in? Even with an APB, could anyone spot us? We turned north on Route 9. I knew only that this would take us toward Saratoga.

I focused on breathing slowly for several minutes, the smell of cigarette smoke nauseating me. Neither of us spoke. At length, I asked, "Who are you really?"

"Name's Alex Raleigh."

"Raleigh? Some relation to Helen Raleigh?"

"She was my wife. We hadn't even been married two weeks when those butchers killed her."

"You mean Frank Worscheim and his partner?"

The muscles in his undersized jaw flickered. "Jerome Bates. That was the name of Worscheim's partner. I killed that slimebucket almost two years ago back in L.A. Went down as an unsolved homicide. But I couldn't find Worscheim. Last winter, I tracked down that little lawyer lady of his, but Worscheim's disguise fooled me."

"Pardon me for asking, but you already killed Worscheim, so why are you kidnapping me?"

"Cuz I *didn't* kill him. Somebody beat me to it. Like I said. His disguise fooled me."

That still didn't answer why he was kidnapping me, but I didn't want to push any wrong buttons, so I reasoned it was best to try not to push any whatsoever. I sat in a quiet state of terror as he turned off the highway onto some small road. He took another turn, then another and another until I was totally discombobulated, except to notice that we were now on a narrow road, surrounded by cornfields. There were no sounds at all as he pulled over; no passing motorists. For all I knew, this was a tractor path. No one would hear a scream. Or a gunshot.

I tried to swallow. My mouth was so dry it

hurt. I looked at Alex Raleigh. He was staring out the windshield, wild-eyed. He turned his gaze to me. "My life isn't worth jack shit anymore. I wanted to kill Worscheim. I was going to leave a letter saying: This was for the sake of Helen Raleigh. Then I was going to kill myself."

He started to go on, but started crying. "He used my wife's name. He killed her in cold blood, then he soiled her name. My name. He had no right. I wanted to kill him."

The poor man. I tried to force some optimism into my voice. "Now you don't have to. You're a free man. You can start a new life for yourself. Surely that's what Helen would have wanted."

He shook his head and took a stabbing swipe at his cheeks. "Doesn't matter now. I can't. I just want to know." He grabbed my wrist so roughly it hurt, but I managed not to cry out. "Is it over?"

"What do you mean? Is what over?"

"The bastard deserved to die, but I have to know. The article said the stolen goods had been recovered. Did they find everything?"

"I think so. Yes. Why?"

"Everyone responsible has to pay their debt," he said, staring at his handgun as he spoke. "My engagement ring. To my wife. She was getting it appraised for our insurance company when they murdered her. They took that, too."

"Dear God," I murmured. I suddenly felt as though an emotional dam were bursting. I couldn't stop my eyes from filling with tears. "I can't imagine how horrible that must have been for you. To lose your bride that way. I am so sorry."

He let go of my arm. He fisted his hands and took a halting breath. "Just tell me if it's over. Are all the jewels back with their rightful owners? Other than mine?"

I remembered that incredible diamond tennis bracelet of Sheila's, but I pushed the thought from my mind and said, "Yes, it's over. Everything that was stolen had been accounted for."

He nodded. I think he knew I was just telling him what he wanted to hear. But I also think he desperately needed to hear it anyway.

He pulled the gun out of his pocket and pointed it at me. I closed my eyes and held my breath.

"Get out," he said.

I looked at him, confused. He gestured through the rear windshield. "Head back that way. We passed a farmhouse 'bout a mile or two back. You can call there to have someone come get you."

"Where are we?"

He shrugged. "Beats me. You live in this town, not me. Now get out. Quick. Before I change my mind and take you with me."

His last words all but jettisoned me from the car. I ran in the direction he'd indicated. After a minute or two, I stopped and looked back, listening for the sounds of his motor, but heard nothing. I'd gone over a small hill so the car was no longer visible.

I caught my breath and scanned the horizon. Just then, a gunshot resounded from the direction of Alex's car. For an instant, I tried to assure myself that it was just the sound of his engine backfiring. But that wasn't true. I knew now what he meant when he'd threatened to take me with him.

My heart was pounding. I started to stagger back toward Alex's car, knowing I had to get there fast in case he was merely wounded. Somehow I had to prepare myself for the scene I was about to face.

Then I heard the sounds of a car coming. I turned around again and started waving my hands desperately to flag it down even before the car was in full view.

A beat-up old car neared. "Stop! Please! Stop!" I cried, hopping as I waved, dimly aware now that tears were streaming down my face. To my relief, the car slowed.

My relief changed to shock as I recognized the driver and passenger.

Chapter 18

Pick up Grandma This Instant!

Bob Fender brought his beat-up jalopy to a stop. Betsy rapidly rolled down the window. "Molly, are you all right?" she asked, her face pale and drawn, her eyes wide with concern.

For all I knew, the Fenders could be in on this whole plot. But Alex Raleigh, if alive, needed help — fast. "A man just shot himself," I panted. "Up ahead. In his car. On the other side of this hill."

Betsy was already opening her door for me. The front seat was the old-fashioned bench style that held three. She scooted over. Bob drove off while I was still fiddling with my seat belt. I numbly realized we'd arrive before I could even get the thing fastened, and we reached Alex's car a moment later. Bob pulled alongside it. The windows were red splattered. I took a deep breath and fought off a wave of dizziness and nausea. Beside me, I was dimly aware of Betsy gasping and burying her face in her hands.

The three of us sat there, doing nothing,

for what seemed like a long time but was probably only a couple of seconds. I willed myself to move, to stand up and check Alex for vital signs. Another part of my brain forewarned that if I were to open the door and look inside that blood-drenched vehicle just yet, I'd be flat out on the ground in a full faint.

Bob patted his wife's knee. "You stay here, dear. I'll go."

I desperately wanted to stay in the car, too. With my eyes closed and my head between my knees. But I couldn't trust Bob. At any moment, he might announce he was Mr. Helen's killer, grab Alex's gun, and aim it at me. So, I got out on my wobbly legs just as Bob stood up, too. Not that I'd be able to defend myself any better outside, but at least this way Bob would have to exert more effort if he, too, intended to kidnap me.

I steeled myself and managed to look through a clear portion of the driver-side window. Alex was slumped forward against the steering wheel. His right hand still gripped the pistol. I shut my eyes and turned my face away. Over the sound of the Fenders' idling engine, Bob's steps crunched gravel as he rounded his car toward me.

"He's dead," I murmured. "Let's go get the police."

"Shot himself in the head," Bob said calmly, clicking his tongue. He gently guided me aside and opened Alex's door.

Questions whirled through my dazed brain. Was Bob about to grab Alex's gun? What were he and Betsy doing out here in the first place? How could he act so blasé in the face of such a grisly scene?

Perhaps Bob sensed my puzzlement, for he said, "I was in Nam." Then he placed three fingers on the side of Alex's neck and said, "Dead. Probably instantaneous." He shut the door with his foot, then yanked out his shirttail and wiped the door handle. Then he turned and studied my face. Before I could ask why he was removing his fingerprints from Alex's car, Bob asked, "Are you going to throw up? If so, this would be a better place to do it than in my car."

"Bob!" Betsy's voice trilled through her still-open window. "Don't be rude! Molly is perfectly welcome to vomit in our car if she wants to. I've got a bucket she can use."

"Sorry, Molly," Bob muttered while tucking in his shirt. "Let's get you some help."

"Come on, dear," Betsy said, pushing her door open for me from inside and patting the seat. In the meantime, Bob ushered me into their car and shut the door behind me. He didn't wipe away his prints from his own vehicle, I noticed, so he wasn't simply a neat-freak.

My body shivered despite the heat. While Bob got back into the driver seat, Betsy wordlessly wrapped a dusty afghan with purple and blue yarn around me. Then she reached into the backseat once again and plopped a shiny silver bedpan onto my lap. "Just in case," she said gently.

The logic behind their driving around with a bedpan in the backseat was something I truly didn't want to examine too closely.

"I'm not going to need this," I assured Betsy, moving my hands behind me to get as far away from the germy thing on my lap as possible. I eyed my seat belt, but decided auto safety was the least of my concerns.

"You sure about that?" Bob asked, peering over the top of his frames at me. I nodded, and as he started the engine, Betsy swept the pan off my lap and stashed it behind us.

Now what? What were these crazy people doing out here, unless they were somehow involved in the crime? Were they going to take me to the nearest phone? If so, why had Bob wiped away his fingerprints? At the very least, the police would find it suspicious that Alex had managed to get into the car without leaving any prints on the handle. "Thank you for helping me," I said by way of encouragement. My teeth were chattering. I tightened the blanket around me.

"Well, we weren't busy, and it was a nice day for a drive," Bob replied and backed up the car.

As Bob negotiated a K-turn, Betsy asked me, "Aren't you going to ask what we were doing out here in the middle of no place?"

"I was warming up to it."

"We'd just pulled into the parking lot of the store," Betsy explained, her features animated, "when we saw you getting into the car, and it looked like he was forcing you to go with him. Then this tall, elderly woman ran outside with a store employee and was gesturing at the car and shouting something about you being kidnapped, so we took off after you."

Bob drove us up the hill, and I spotted a farmhouse in the distance. I returned my focus to Betsy. "But I didn't see —"

"We got a late start and gambled on which way you went." She smiled and laid her hand on my arm. "You are such a lucky person, Molly. There were three major intersections by the time you get to Route Nine and your odds were only one in eight."

"One in seven," Bob corrected. "We knew the driver hadn't pulled a U-turn." He pointed with his chin at the farmhouse, which was just up ahead and down a long driveway. "There's a couple of vehicles in the garage."

To my great relief, he slowed the car as if to turn into the driveway. Instead, he pulled onto the shoulder of the road and stopped.

In the meantime, Betsy continued, "We picked up the trail on Route Nine, but lost you, momentarily, on that last turn. We doubled back and eventually found you."

"I'm grateful, but we need to —"

Bob interrupted sternly, "You can't tell the police who gave you the ride."

"Why not?"

Bob merely tightened his lips — what little of them showed behind his big, bushy mustache.

Betsy sighed. "We're . . . Bob . . ." She stopped and faced her husband.

"I am withholding my tax payments for ethical reasons," Bob said, holding his chin high.

"Bob hasn't paid taxes for the last ten years. 'Fender' is actually my maiden name. We use pseudonyms for our official dealings. So, you see, we don't want Bob's name on some police report."

The most important thing here, I mentally urged myself, was to Get Out Of This Car. I opened the door and started to rise, still protesting, "But I'm going to have a hard time explaining how —"

"Good-bye. Good luck." Betsy reached out and snatched the afghan from me, then thrust my purse into my arms. "I hope these people are home."

"Um, I should warn you. I already told an officer your name. Yesterday, when the officer came to my door as you were leaving."

The Fenders exchanged alarmed glances. "Sounds like it's time we moved on," Bob muttered through his mustache.

"We were thinking about Florida." Betsy shut the door with a solid thunk and gave me a smile through the open window. "Maybe we'll look you up down there."

They drove off. I watched them in stunned silence, then finally willed my feet to move. At least, whatever happened from here on, the Fenders were out of my life. With the horrendous day I was having, that was truly something to celebrate.

Judging by design and condition, the farmhouse appeared to be a couple of hundred years old and had faded red paint with white trim. As I made my way down the driveway, I wondered whether I was about to face Lassie's family or, with my luck, an ax murderer. The screen door creaked open, and a huge woman with a hawk-shaped nose glared down at me with crossed arms. I gulped. It was the latter.

"If you're sellin' something," she hollered, "the answer's no, so you might as well turn around right there."

"I'm not. There's been a terrible accident." I gestured haphazardly. "A mile down the road. A man is dead. I need to call the police."

In an unexpected and disarming flurry of motion, she charged down the porch steps, grabbed my arm, and hustled me into the house so fast I'm not sure my feet touched the ground. Furious activity continued for the next several minutes. My brain was too sluggish from my state of shock to keep up. On some sort of intercom, she radioed someone — her husband, perhaps — then put a phone in my hand, which she'd already dialed. I told a police dispatcher my story. Then, next thing I knew I was seated at a table with a soup spoon in my hand, a bowl of homemade chicken soup in front of me along with an entire loaf of fresh-baked corn bread, and a pitcher of lemonade.

My stomach was clenched into a tight knot, and though the soup and corn bread smelled delicious, I couldn't eat a bite. I tried to explain, but the woman tsked and shook her head. "Look at you. You're half starved to death. Now you eat something, 'fore you fall over."

"First I need to call my mother and let her know I'm all right."

"You let me make the call." She pointed a chubby finger at me. "Meanwhile, you eat. Now what's the number and your mama's name?"

Resignedly, I started force-feeding myself, all the while wondering whether anyone else on the planet was having as bizarre a day as this. Soon the woman was saying on the phone, "Don't you ever feed your child? She's all skin and bones!"

I pleaded with her to give me the phone. The receiver had one of those snaking, twenty-foot cords that had become obsolete with the advent of portable phones. She finally stretched the cord the length of her kitchen and handed me the receiver.

"Mom?"

"Thank God. The police insisted we wait here in case someone called. Are you all right? Where on earth are you? Did that kidnapper force you to check into an eating-disorders clinic?"

"No, no. I'm in a house, out north of ours in the country. I'm fine. He let me go and —"

Already, I could hear sirens outside. "Here come the police now."

"You tell that woman that you're not skinny, just small-boned! Better yet, tell me where you are and I'll come get you."

There was a knock on the door and some deep-voiced officer began to speak to my food Nazi.

"I don't know where I am, Mom, but don't worry. I'll get a ride home from the police."

"When?"

"Ma'am?" the officer said to me. I recognized him from the day before. He'd been one of the officers with the tape measure.

I held up a finger to indicate to the officer I'd be off in a moment and said to my mother, "I don't know. Tell the kids I —"

The woman snatched the phone away from me. "She needs to speak to the police now," she told my mother. "You feed her a good meal when she gets home." She crossed the room and slammed the receiver into its cradle.

"Can you tell me what happened?" the policeman asked me gently.

At this point, I yearned for a nice, safe, padded room all to myself. "Couldn't I come with you to the police station and tell you there?"

Mercifully, the officer smiled at me, said, "Sure," and helped me to my feet. I collected my purse from where it hung on the back of my chair.

I murmured thanks to the woman and shoved out the door with the officer. As I got into the backseat of the patrol car, the woman hollered, "Wait," from the porch, and soon puffed her way down the stairs with a grocery bag clutched against her enormous bosom. She shoved the bag into the seat next to me, wagged her finger through the window at me, and said, "It's your leftovers. You eat every bite of this."

I nodded and smiled wanly at the woman. If she had owned Lassie, the collie would have been dragging her tummy on the ground en route to rescuing Timmy.

After what seemed like many hours — though, according to my watch, it was just over two — I had reunited with my children, mother, and husband, who had come to the police station to meet me. Upon my urging, they'd returned to Mom's house so that I could finish giving my statement. During the process, Tommy had shown me a picture of Alex Raleigh, which the LAPD had faxed upon request. Alex had told me the truth about his identity. I felt certain that, eventually, authorities would trace the death of Frank Worscheim's accomplice back to Alex.

Now, I was alone in Tommy's office, awaiting his return. He had told me he had something important to discuss with me before I could leave.

He was smiling as he opened the door and took a seat behind his cluttered desk. "Got great news for you, Moll. It's all over. We got a search warrant and seized that diamond bracelet from Sheila Lillydale. Sure enough, it was hot. Got her in custody even as we speak."

"Did she confess to murdering Mr. Helen and Simon Smith?"

"Not yet. She will, though." He leaned back in his chair and bore an expression of utter satisfaction. "She blew it. Asked how we'd gotten hold of her letters. We played along, and it turns out she's got a stack of Worscheim's love letters in her office, datin' back five years now. Already got hold of her phone records. She had a batch of calls between her office and the apartment Worscheim rented after sellin' you your house."

"So you think he dumped her, and she killed him?"

Tommy nodded. "The coward did it in a

letter. Wrote to her and said it was over — that she was too possessive, and he'd decided to move on."

Something was wrong with the theory, but my brain was too scrambled at the moment to figure out what. "And you think she'll confess eventually?"

Again, Tommy nodded. "She's all shook up. She's not used to bein' on the other side of the law, and she keeps insisting she's gonna act as her own attorney."

"What about her husband, Roger? Have you talked to him yet?"

"Yep. Said he knew 'bout her affair all along. He's willing to testify against her, so it's gonna be pretty cut-'n'-dried."

"And you're sure he wasn't involved, too?"

"Yep." He rose, the self-satisfied grin never leaving his face. "Rock solid alibi. We placed him in Boston at the time of the shooting."

"What about Simon Smith's death? Do you still think that was an accident?"

"If not, we'll get the scoop from Ms. Lillydale. She may fancy herself as a savvy lawyer, but believe me, Molly, she's actin' like a scared little girl now."

"And what about Bob and Betsy Fender?"

"Put out an APB, but they're prob'ly

halfway out of the state by now." His smile faded as he eyed me. "Sure would've helped if you'd gotten their license plate."

That had been a foolish oversight on my part, which already didn't sit well with me. Automatically, I launched into an offensive. "What is it with you policemen and license plates? Does it relate back to that guy thing you've got with cars? Don't you have *any* means of catching crooks, other than by their license plates?"

The muscles in Tommy's jaw tightened. Then he rubbed his palms together. "What say we get you home?"

Tommy drove me in his squad car. We made the short drive to my parents' house in silence. I was impatient with the niggling worry that seemed to creep along my spine. The case was solved. Sheila had murdered her spurned lover and her handpicked spy for exactly the reasons that I'd already surmised. There was no justification whatsoever for the feeling that tugged at me — the feeling that I was still in danger.

Karen and Nathan gave me big hugs when I arrived, and I felt overjoyed to be home safe with them. My mother gave me a hug as well, and Jim kissed me and held me in his arms for a long embrace. Then he shook Tommy's hand, and they moved off to the corner. I could hear Tommy explaining how they had Sheila in custody and that everything was over.

"Guess what, Mom?" Karen said. "Greenie, Brownie, and Biggie are all frogs now! They hopped out of the bowl! Nathan had to catch them."

"Biggie got into Grandma's room," Nathan said.

"That's cuz Nathan took him there and let him loose," Karen interjected.

"I did not! It was an accident!"

Their argument continued as we thanked Tommy and he left. I looked at my mother and asked the question I'd asked myself a thousand times in the last couple of months. "Why frogs, Mom?"

She straightened and said, "It is one of my great pleasures in life to give my grandchildren gifts that I would never give to my own children. After all my years as a parent, I've earned that privilege." I had no ready response, but Mom quickly continued, "Jim and I were talking. I convinced him that you two should celebrate. Have a romantic dinner out."

Jim grinned. "I already made our reservations. At Bixby's."

"But what about —"

"The kids will be fine with me for a few

hours," my mother interrupted. "You can have a nice, relaxing dinner for two, and I'll take the kids out for pizza."

That *did* sound like a good idea. I looked at the children, who had finally grown quiet so as to eavesdrop on our conversation. "Is that okay with you guys?"

"Sure," Karen said. "But, Mom, Nathan wants to keep Brownie in *his* room! And that's not —"

"We're not going to take those frogs back home if you two keep arguing about them," Jim said firmly.

Nathan and Karen locked eyes. "I think Littley, Biggie, Greenie, and Brownie, Freckles, and George like it here," Nathan said.

Mom winced.

"Maybe they should stay here for good," I suggested, giving my mother a vengeful grin. "You and Karen can come visit and feed them every day."

"Your grandpa is coming home the day after tomorrow. He's not going to like having all these frogs in the house," she countered to the children.

"But they think of this as their home," I quickly asserted. "And besides, we're leaving for summer vacation soon, and we'll need you to watch them then anyway."

Mom met my eyes, pursed her lips momentarily, then bent down to face Karen and Nathan. "Tell you what. Let's go set the frogs free in the pond, and I'll give each of you a crisp five-dollar bill as a reward."

Nathan pondered this for about a half second, then said happily, "Okay."

Karen stomped her foot. "That's not fair! They were my frogs to begin with, so why should Nathan get money for setting *my* birthday present free?"

Mom tousled Karen's hair and said, "I'll get you another gift to even things out. What do you say?"

"Well," Karen said slowly, "all right."

Mom straightened and winked at me.

Another gift from Grandma? What now? A Remco Turn-Your-Den-into-a-Butterfly-Pavilion Kit? I fought an involuntary shudder, and Jim and I exchanged worried glances.

While Mom took kids and frogs to the pond, Jim and I packed. We decided to load up my car so we could just drop it off at home and take Jim's to the restaurant. Our escape was somewhat slowed when I discovered Jim had packed up my fax machine, and I had to convince him to put it back until I'd had a chance to talk to the phone company and switch its phone number again. However, we were all set to go by the time the rest of the family returned frogless. I gave the kids hugs and big kisses and told them to enjoy their pizza. Jim gave them hugs and told them to "be good for Grandma."

As we were getting into our cars, Jim announced that he was going to fill the tank, and he'd meet me at the house. This was one of Jim's quirks that I tolerate, but don't understand. I've asked him on several occasions, "Doesn't it make more sense to get gas while you're driving past the station than to make a special trip?" He always has some answer about how he likes to wash up immediately afterward so his hands won't smell like gasoline. And he wonders where our son gets his eccentricities.

I pulled into our garage, grabbed an armload of clothes, and went inside. The house needed to be aired out. I kept the front door locked, but opened a couple of windows. I zipped through the house, opening all of the doors, checking the condition of each room. Everything was exactly as we'd left it.

I still felt on edge. Would I ever feel safe alone in this house again? I wanted to take a shower and change my clothes, but couldn't as much as bring myself to undress for visions of undetected hidden cameras.

To help myself relax, I headed back downstairs, sat down at the kitchen table, and flipped though my drawing pad. I returned to a sketch a couple of weeks old that I'd left unfinished. My pencil lines merely needed to be inked, which was all the challenge I was up for at the moment.

Most of the time the humor in my cartoons is conceptual — the humor lies in the gag itself, instead of the drawing. That's because I'm a self-taught artist. My college degree was in journalism, not art. This time, though, the humor was in the artwork. The drawing was seen from the floor, looking up. To get the perspective correct while creating this one, I'd lain on the floor with my pad held over my head.

The foreground shows a pair of elderly women's legs sticking up in the air. In the background, a woman sits on a couch, curlers in her hair, her brow furrowed, her vision focused on her nails as she gives herself a manicure. The woman yells, "Junior! If I told you once, I told you a thousand times! Don't leave your marbles all over the floor! Now get in here and pick up your grandmother this instant!"

I stared at the drawing as my thoughts tumbled. The cartoon reminded me of Tommy's investigation — all the evidence, like the marbles, laid out so clearly.

I heard a noise at the front door that sounded as if someone was rattling the knob. It was odd that Jim was using the front door. He normally came in through the garage.

"It's locked, Jim," I called. "Just a minute."

"Don't bother," came the answer.

Was I just being paranoid, or was that voice nothing like Jim's? Worried, I rose.

I made it only as far as the entrance to the living room before there was a loud bang and the front door flew open, careening on its hinges.

Roger had kicked it in. Before I could even scream, he was through the door.

He aimed a rifle at me and said, "Surprise. You lose."

Chapter 19

Well, There Goes the Neighborhood

My shock at seeing an armed Roger burst into my house was instantly overtaken by feelings of rage rather than fear. In the past eight hours I'd been kidnapped in front of my mother and children, witnessed a suicide, was force-fed by a fat farmer, rescued and re-assured that the culprit was under arrest — only to find myself staring down the barrel of a rifle.

Yet my rational mother side was scream-ing at me: *This is nuts! He's stronger than you and he's got a gun! Stay calm. Keep him talking till Jim arrives.*

"You were in on it, weren't you?" I said through clenched teeth.

"In on it?" He snorted. "Hell. It was my idea." Roger smirked as he managed to shove the door shut behind him despite its damaged hinges. There went my hope of a passerby spotting Roger with his rifle, or even our broken front door. "I knew what my little wifey and her cross-dressing lover were up to."

"You'd hired Simon to spy on them."

"I needed Simon to get me some evidence as leverage." He gestured with the rifle for me to back up. "You —"

"Leverage?" I repeated.

"Yeah. To control Sheila with." Again, he gestured at me with the barrel of the rifle. "Move it. We're going into your attic."

Good Lord! Did he think Mr. Helen had hidden more diamonds there? "My attic? Why? There's nothing up there but my television antenna."

"Let's go!" Roger shouted. "I don't have to explain anything to you. I'm the one with the gun, you moron!"

Point taken. This was a man who'd killed once and would kill again. Oh, dear God. Any moment now, Jim would walk in, unarmed and utterly unaware. Roger would shoot us both.

Stop it! If I let myself panic, it was all over. With two of us, we might be able to gang up on him. I had to hold on to that hope — to battle the urge to fall to my knees and beg Roger to leave me and my family alone.

My legs felt wobbly. My heart was racing. I had to force myself to breathe slowly. I led the way upstairs, choosing not to point out to him that we would need a ladder. "I don't understand what my attic has to do with any of this."

"Sheila told me there's a load of cash up there. It's bad enough I lost out on the diamonds. I'm sure as hell not leaving town without the money."

"She's lying to you," I told him, turning to meet his eyes.

He looked deranged and terrifying. His dark hair was damp with sweat. His body was so tense he seemed ready to strike me if I so much as breathed wrong. No way did I want to be in our grotesque little attic with Roger and a loaded gun when he learned his neurotic wife had sent him on a wild-goose chase.

I could come up with only two reasons why he hadn't already shot me: He either wanted to take me hostage, or he wanted to stash my body in the attic and knew it would be easier for me to climb up there than for him to carry me.

"Roger, I spent a good half hour in the attic when Jim and I installed the antenna. It's empty."

He shook his head. "The money's there, underneath the insulation. I found out about it months ago on one of Simon's tapes."

He gestured with his chin at the small

rectangle of walnut-stained trim in the ceiling. "That's your only access to the attic?"

"Yes." I had to do something. He was still directly in front of the top step. I could knock him down the stairs. After which he'd shoot me. "What about your son? What about Ben? You can't —"

"He'll be fine. He's coming with me."

Coming with him where? Did he hope to uncover vast sums of money and move to Mexico with his son? Roger poked at the attic opening with the barrel of the rifle. "Um, Roger?" I asked in a near whisper. "Frank Worscheim *knew* Simon was spying on him. That's why he put duct tape over the camera lenses when he was trying to dig up the diamonds. Maybe he and Sheila staged the conversation for your benefit, and there's no money."

Roger shook his head. "Worscheim thought Simon was working for some guy back in L.A. who'd shot his partner. Sheila and Worscheim had no idea Simon was working for *me*."

So Frank Worscheim thought Alex Raleigh had located him and had hired Simon to keep an eye on him. That must have been why Worscheim abruptly moved and sold the house. Unfortunately for almost all concerned, the hiding place he'd selected meant the diamonds were trapped until spring thaw — well after we'd purchased our new home.

Roger gestured at the attic entrance. "Don't you have one of those pull-down stairs?"

I ignored the question and asked, "What makes you think he wouldn't take the money out of the attic before selling the house?"

He glared at me. "Where's your ladder?"

"In the garage."

There had to be a weapon of some sort lying around our messy garage. Nothing that could match Roger's firepower, though. Where was Jim? How much longer could I stall?

I moved past Roger onto the stairs, then grabbed the banister and turned back toward him. "Could you please explain one thing to me? How did you shoot Frank Worscheim when the police were sure you were in Boston?"

"I didn't. Sheila shot him." He patted the rifle. "Hell, this is her gun. She's a sharpshooter." He chuckled. "It's a shame, really. I'm never gonna get to tell anyone about how I pulled off the perfect murder. Now, let's go."

By my way of thinking, the only "perfect

murder" was one you didn't actually commit. Since *Sheila* shot Mr. Helen, that meant Roger had *convinced* her to do it. She was an insanely jealous woman . . . so Roger must have used that against her. "You forged a Dear John letter from Frank Worscheim to Sheila," I said.

He froze and gaped at me.

"How did you know that?"

"You convinced her that Frank was dumping her for someone else, and that the two of you would split the proceeds when she . . . got rid of him."

He grinned. A trickle of sweat was dripping down the side of his face. His eyes looked wild. "All it took was a few doctored tape recordings and the one letter. You're very bright, Molly." Again, he lifted his gun. "Too bad you're too smart for your own good."

He was aiming the rifle right at my heart. Maybe Roger wasn't the sort of person who could pull a trigger himself. Maybe that was why he was keeping me alive. The concept gave me a glimmer of hope.

"Oh, believe me," I said in as obsequious tones as I could muster while petrified with fear, "I'm not as smart as you are. I can't figure out how you did it. How you managed to be in Boston and get Sheila to shoot him right as he was digging up the diamonds."

"*I'd* bugged Simon's phone and had Sheila keep watch. Worscheim had told Sheila precisely how he was going to lure Simon out of the house. Meanwhile, I stayed in Boston until it was over."

He paused and grimaced. "But she screwed up. She was supposed to wait till he actually dug up the diamonds. Then we were going to divide the spoils and go our separate ways. She shot him too early. Says she got overanxious."

"But how did you know that she wasn't just going to confront Frank with the letter and —"

"I know my wife, okay? Now let's go get that ladder and get this over with."

My mind worked feverishly, trying to put the pieces together in hope that some item of knowledge could help me. That was Roger I'd seen on the surveillance tape, digging up my yard. Maybe Tommy was scanning those tapes right at this moment, would recognize Roger, and charge over here. Grasping at straws was better than nothing.

I walked down the stairs as slowly as I could. All the while, a desperate urge to bolt threatened to overwhelm me. The prospect of my getting shot in the back was far too likely. "What do you hope to gain by taking me as a hostage?"

"A hostage?" He snorted. "You wish. If the police catch me, I'm in no more trouble for committing two murders than one. It's only a matter of time till Sheila blabs. She knows I pushed Simon's ladder into the power lines. So I'm hiding your car and stashing your body in the attic. By the time anyone thinks to look there, I'll be safe in South America."

Now I was scared. If I climbed into the attic, I was dead. I had to escape now — or never.

My stomach was in knots as I led the way into the garage. Where the hell was Jim! This was so like him. Right about now he was probably helping the gas station attendant fix his cash register.

I'd left the garage door wide open when I drove in. Maybe I could scream for help. But that would likely be my last act.

The hinge squeaked as I entered the garage through the heavy wooden door. Roger again aimed the rifle at me, staying inside the house himself. "Keep your mouth shut and close the outer door. You know how nosy everyone around here is."

I was trembling and ready to faint.

Weapons. Dear God, let there be a weapon. I scanned the immediate area as I pressed the button to shut the door. The coffee can. It had turpentine in it for cleaning my paint brushes. It was right next to my foot. All I would need was a momentary distraction, long enough for me to pop the plastic lid.

As the door slowly lowered, Roger stepped into the garage beside me. "Okay. You get the ladder off the hooks and —"

The garage door started to open. Jim was coming home.

Roger looked at the door. "What the —"

In a flash, I grabbed the can, flung the lid off, and splashed it in his face. He screamed and covered his eyes.

The rifle fired, shattering a window of my Toyota. The noise was deafening. I couldn't hear my own scream. Planning to dive under the door as it shut behind me, I stabbed at the button for the door, then snatched the rifle with both hands.

Even with one hand, Roger's hold was too tight. He wrenched it away from me as if I were a child grabbing at a candy bar.

"My eyes!" Blindly, Roger cocked the rifle. "I'm gonna —"

The half-open door began to rise again. Jim was still trying to get in. I kicked Roger as hard as I could and took off toward the driveway.

I ducked under the door and yelled, "Roger's got a gun!"

Jim's expression changed from surprise to rage in an instant. He floored the accelerator. I whirled and watched in horror as the Jeep zoomed into the garage, right where Roger had stood. Almost simultaneously, there was a squeal of brakes and a sickening thud.

Roger was moaning as I raced inside. The rifle had careened off the hood of the Jeep and skidded under my Toyota. I snatched the rifle as Jim got out and dashed to the front of his Jeep.

"Help me," Roger groaned. "I think my legs are broken."

"Good," Jim said. "Stay put."

I aimed the rifle at Roger to reinforce Jim's instructions. Roger's once-handsome face, now contorted with anger and pain, turned to me, his eyes bloodred slits. "I'll get you for this!"

"Shut up!" Jim snarled at him.

Just then, I heard a gasp and turned to see Joanne Abbott gaping from my driveway.

"Oh, my God!" she cried. "Sheila was right about you!" She turned and started to run, as if she thought I were a killer.

"Call nine-one-one," I called after her.

Minutes later, my ears were still ringing as I sat on the couch beside Jim and gave my statement. My thoughts were in such turmoil, I probably spoke pure gibberish, but Tommy dutifully took notes.

"These criminals had better learn not to mess with you all," he said afterward.

I said nothing, merely watched my hands tremble. No matter how many times I mentally assured myself everything finally was over — that the house was safe and we would soon get our lives back in order — my hands weren't getting the message.

I sighed and turned my vision to the bouquet of roses that Jim had brought me. Those roses, unbeknownst to either of us, had nearly cost me my life while he picked them out instead of rushing straight home from the gas station. This was one of those rare times when it really *could* have killed someone to be a little romantic.

"Roger was right about one thing," Tommy said. "Sheila was startin' to talk about him. Told us she'd bought that poodle as a gift to Frank. Poor thing only lasted a day, till someone ran 'im over. She said all along she'd blamed Frank for lettin' the dog run around, but then she snarled, 'Bet it was Roger.' "

"She thought her husband deliberately ran over Frank's pet?"

Tommy shrugged. "She clammed up afterward."

Roger had told me the dog belonged to Frank Worscheim's brother, and that *Frank* had run over it. Now that it was clear Roger had surreptitiously known all along about Sheila's relationship with Mr. Helen, I suspected Sheila's version was the truth — though Frank *had* used the poodle's body as a subterfuge.

"What's going to happen to Roger's son, Ben?" I asked.

Tommy frowned. "He's with social services for the time bein'. Roger has a big family, and we're tryin' to locate the boy's biological mother." I sighed, and Jim gave my shoulders a squeeze as Tommy continued, "Look at it this way. The sooner the boy's away from his dad and stepmom, the better."

The baby-faced officer came through the front door. He glanced at the three of us and announced, "The EMTs said both of Mr. Lillydale's legs were broken, but that was it."

"Lucky for him," Jim murmured.

I nodded. It would have been fine with me if every bone in Roger's body had been broken. He got off easier than that poor, defenseless poodle.

Another officer, soaked with sweat, came down the stairs, lowering the white mask that covered his mouth and nose. He was covered with gray dust and cobwebs and pink puffs of fiberglass. A cloud of debris seemed to follow him. "Whew. Hot up there." He waggled his thumb over his shoulder and looked at Jim and me. "I just tore up the last of your insulation. There's nothing there."

"Drat," I said. "And here I was hoping to play finders-keepers."

Lauren flung open our screen door and rushed into the room, her cheeks flushed. "I just now heard about the arrest over the police scanner. Is everything all right?"

"Yep," Tommy said, rising and slipping his cap into the permanent dent in his hair. "Where's Rachel?"

"Jasper and Joey are watching her." She turned her attention to me. "Are you all right, Molly?"

Lauren's eyes were full of concern, but mine were drawn to her left hand. "I'm fine, thanks. What was that blinding flash of light I saw?"

Lauren giggled. "I wanted to tell you later, when things were calmer." She held out her left hand. Her ring finger sported a large round-cut diamond. "I'm hoping you'll be my matron of honor."

"It's beautiful," I told her. "And I'd be delighted to be in your wedding. Congratulations, Tommy."

Jim congratulated him, too, pumping Tommy's hand vigorously. Then he gave Lauren a quick hug and kiss.

Tommy left, explaining he had to head back to his office and get going on the paperwork. Though still numb with shock, we decided to walk Lauren home and stay at Mom's with the children until the police were completely done spreading dust and bits of insulation through our house.

Tommy's sons and Rachel were playing monkey-in-the-middle with a volleyball. We said hasty good-byes to Lauren, anxious to spend time with our own children. Karen was running toward us as we stepped inside. I knelt, assuming she wanted to give us hugs, but she raced right by me.

"Rachel's outside. Can I go play with her?"

"Sure," I called as the screen door was already swinging shut behind her. Her nonchalance was my fault, I reminded myself, for not having told my children or Mom what I'd just been through.

Nathan slumped down the stairs. He was frowning and looked to be on the verge of tears. "My ears are too big. And they're pointy."

"Let me see," Jim said, his voice full of feigned concern. He leaned over and looked at each of Nathan's ears, clowning as if this were a doctor's exam. "Nope. No points and no big ears here."

"They're too big! I look like a jerk!"

Already on my knees, I pulled Nathan into an unreciprocated hug. "They're just the right size to hear your daddy and me tell you how handsome you are. And that we love you exactly the way you are."

"I'm an elf! I have the biggest ears in the whole world!" Nathan pulled away and stomped up the stairs.

I looked up at Jim, who patted my shoulder as I rose. "Even our best child psychology is falling on deaf, though perfectly proportioned, ears. If only our children would at least *pretend* to listen to us."

"Hear, hear," my mother murmured as she entered the room. "Aren't you two supposed to be sharing a nice dinner right about now?" Without awaiting my reply, she handed me a sheet of paper. "This came out of your fax machine a minute ago. It's from Tommy, but I don't know what he's talking about."

I read Tommy's message and chuckled. He'd written:

Molly — Just wanted to let you know, in case you had any doubts, I *bought* that diamond.

A few minutes later, I faxed him a reply. On the top, I handwrote:

Of course you did, Tommy. I guess this means you're moving into Sherwood Forest for good.

Beneath my words, I'd drawn a cartoon. A couple is standing in a desolated area. A tornado in the distance is full of houses. The woman says to the man, "Well, there goes the neighborhood."

The employees of Thorndike Press hope you have enjoyed this Large Print book. All our Large Print titles are designed for easy reading, and all our books are made to last. Other Thorndike Press Large Print books are available at your library, through selected bookstores, or directly from us.

For information about titles, please call:

(800) 223-1244
(800) 223-6121

To share your comments, please write:

Publisher
Thorndike Press
P.O. Box 159
Thorndike, Maine 04986

H